ONLY THE POSITIVE

(ONLY YOU SERIES, #1)

ELLE THORPE

DRAMA LLAMA ROMANCE

For Jira, who believed I could do this long before I did.

REESE

The low, barely audible rolling of an approaching storm reached me first. Then the thunder came as the horses rounded the bend, their hooves churning up the track, chunks of dirt and grass flying in their wake.

I stood frozen, mesmerised. Their bodies were sleek with sweat. The flash of the jockeys' silks, the crack of their whips, the shouts of the surrounding crowd—it all added to the roar. That noise alone, so like the booming of thunder when a storm is right upon you, sent shivers through my body. Goosebumps rose on my arms, and my adrenaline kicked in as my heart raced.

My smile morphed into a grin as I waited for it. That magical moment. The pack of thoroughbreds thundered into the final straight and it happened, just like I knew it would. The sound became muffled. The crowd disappeared. Everything around me ceased to exist and it was me and the horses in my happy place. That one place where my problems and what I'd done didn't matter.

They flashed by the winner's post in a blur of colours, and the spell broke as quickly as it had begun. I had no idea who'd won. It made no difference. I didn't have money on the race. Unlike the rest of the crowd, that wasn't the appeal for me. My connection went bone-deep and dragged me back to a different time, one before everything had gone to shit.

Hand hovering over the phone in my pocket, heart still thumping from the rush of the race, an idea pounded through my head. It had started small but grown in intensity with every passing moment until it was as loud as a siren. I pulled the phone out before I could overthink it and brought up the call function. With trembling fingers, I typed the number my parents had made me memorise when I was five years old.

Hang up. Hang up right now. This will only end in tears.

My brain knew it, but being here, in this spot, so like *our* spot hundreds of kilometres away, I wanted to hear his voice.

My stomach swirled as the ringtone sounded in my ear. My breath came in gasps, but something stopped me from hanging up.

Even if it's like the last time? Even if he yells every obscenity he knows at you again? My brain wouldn't stop, but I stubbornly refused to listen.

"Hello?"

I froze. My breath stuck in my throat, turning into a huge lump.

"Hello? Is anyone there?"

The crowd around me had settled in the aftermath of the race, but they were still loud enough to be distracting. I pressed the phone closer to my ear, savouring every word.

He paused on the other end of the line and tears pricked at my eyes. I wanted him to say something else. I wanted his familiar voice to soothe my pain.

"Reese? Is that you?"

My fingers loosened in surprise and the phone tumbled to the ground. I crouched, grabbing the phone and pressed the red cancel button over and over until I was sure the call had ended.

A hand touched my shoulder, and I yelped as I spun around.

"Whoa, sorry."

I tried to calm my breathing as I straightened and took in the owner of the hand and voice. My mouth dried. Holy hotness batman. He looked a little older than me, maybe twenty-four or twenty-five. He was tall, but not too tall. Around six feet, I guessed. His dark hair was just long enough to look messy. Images of messing it up further when I ran my hands through it taunted me.

He stood with his hands in mock surrender, as if I were a wild animal he might need to back away from, and for the first time I noticed he was wearing a Lavender Fields Racecourse uniform.

"Are you Reese Lawson?"

I nodded, still trying to get my bearings. Between the race, the phone call, and now him, orienting myself was proving difficult. He dropped his hands, apparently satisfied I wasn't about to attack him.

"Thought you might be. I'm Low. I'm the bar manager here."

Shit. Of course he was. His blue eyes sparkled and the corners of his mouth turned up, revealing straight, white teeth, set off by the layer of dark stubble that covered his jaw. His gaze dropped and travelled over my body for a moment, before returning to my face. My blood heated under his amused scrutiny.

"Your uniform gave you away."

Right. My uniform. I was supposed to be starting work here today.

"Listen, I'm on a break, and you don't start work for another seven minutes, so you can finish your call to your boyfriend or whoever—"

"It wasn't my boyfriend," I cut in.

He raised an eyebrow as he leant on the fence. "Good to know."

I laughed. Oh boy. He was smooth. But I respected confidence. Taking a deep breath, I let the cool spring air fill my lungs and calm me. I just needed a moment to recollect myself and I'd be better equipped to deal with him.

Letting my eyes roam over his body, as he'd done a moment earlier, I allowed my expression to convey I liked what I saw. His lavender shirt was hideous on a man that beautiful, but the way it pulled across his shoulders left no question as to the muscled chest that lay underneath. His sleeves were rolled up to his elbows, exposing tanned forearms. My gaze wandered up his chest to his face and I noted the smirk there. He knew I was checking him out, but I didn't care. It was obvious he was no stranger to admiration. His eyes and the hint of mischief there held my interest longer than they should have. He was hot. And he knew it.

A flicker of excitement lit within me. This was what I needed. A new job. A new beginning. A new guy to lose myself in. The past year had been one mess after another. I'd barely kept my head above water, but it was time for a turning point.

"Well, Low," I rolled the name around on my tongue. What kind of name was Low anyway? I guessed I wasn't the only one who went by a nickname. "Since I don't start for another seven minutes, I'm going to leave you to your break. I'll see you at the bar. My orientation starts at noon, right?"

I didn't wait for his reply. With my heart still thumping, I swivelled on my heel and walked away, knowing his eyes followed me.

BY THE TIME Low sauntered up to the bar ten minutes later, I'd composed myself and pushed the phone call to the back of my mind. It had been a stupid idea to call. To call from such a public place, minutes before I started a new job was taking stupid to new heights. I was done thinking about it. I was ready to focus on the job. And maybe my new boss.

The bar was the longest I'd ever seen, stretching almost the full width of the large indoor area of the racetrack. I knew from times I'd come here as a spectator, there were several other bars on the racetrack, but this was the main one. Low held the little swinging door open and motioned me inside. I caught a whiff of his aftershave as I passed; my nose filling with the unfamiliar scent. Something spicy and dark. I liked it.

"So, new girl, do you know how to pull a beer?"

I almost rolled my eyes, but instead I nodded. He might have been hot and flirty, but he was still my boss. "I worked at a pub back at home."

"Where's home?"

"Erraville. It's about twelve hours from Sydney."

He nodded, studying me. "Well, this isn't some dinky little country pub. We have races here every weekend and almost every day of the week during the spring racing season. The Lavender Bar is the busiest on the course. Pretty sure you can handle that, though. Right?"

"Bring it on."

"You'll need to hand your paperwork in at the office, but I'll show you where that is later. I'm also obliged to tell you there's a non-fraternization policy…" He paused so long, I felt like I needed to fill the silence.

"I sense a but coming."

"But it's not enforced." He gave me a little smile and jerked his head in the direction of one of the guys, milling at the other end of the bar. "You know, just in case you find Riley over there so incredibly attractive you can't keep your hands off him."

The corners of my mouth twitched. "Got it."

He chuckled. "All right then."

He motioned for me to follow him and I trailed him to where the two men and a woman worked in their identical Lavender Fields shirts. "Guys, this is Reese. Reese, that's Riley, Bianca and Jamison." He pointed to each person as he said their names before he turned back to me. "The five of us together are the main crew that man this bar. We rotate through positions as we feel like it, but for now, you're up front with Jamison and me, while Riley and B take care of the tables and clean up."

Jamison waved. He was taller than Low, with neat, short blondish hair and a boy next door look about him. The other guy, Riley, was shorter, dark-haired with a ring piercing his bottom lip. He wiped his palms on a dish towel and came over to shake hands. Bianca looked up from un-loading a dishwasher, her fair hair escaping her bun and sticking to her face with the steam. She gave me a huge grin which I returned enthusiastically.

"Try not to sleep with this one, please, Low. She looks nice, and it'd be good if we had another woman stick around longer than Abi did."

I coughed and wondered what had happened between Low and Abi, the ex-bartender, to make her want to leave. Did he ghost her? Probably. He looked the type.

"That won't be a problem," I said at the same time Low said, "Can't make any promises."

Low quirked an eyebrow at me, and I mirrored his facial gesture. I wanted to laugh. Did he assume that by 'not a problem' I meant I wouldn't be sleeping with him? On the contrary, I was already interested. All I meant was I wouldn't care when he didn't call me the next day. I stared him down, delight filling me when he was the first to look away.

Bianca laughed. "I like you already."

Low brushed behind me on his way to the till and I stilled. There was plenty of room, but he was all in my personal space. He brought his lips close to my ear. "So do I. Welcome to the team, Reese." His breath, warm on my neck, spread goosebumps across my shoulder. His mouth just centimetres from my skin, I fought the urge to close my eyes and lean my head to the side to give him better access.

Yep, this was what I needed. This was how I could forget for a little while. But there was a time and place, and it wasn't right here with an audience of hundreds.

I focused on the line of customers. All bars were much the same. We could do the orientation later. Right now, I needed to forget Low's grin and those sparkling blue eyes and be professional.

"What can I get you?" I asked the closest person. Then I picked up a glass and got busy. I stuck close to Low, though not so close that his presence became distracting again. He took my customer's money, and I watched over his shoulder as he entered it into the till. By the time we had a lull, I had it pretty much sussed out. It wasn't rocket science.

Grabbing my bag, I riffled through it until I found my stack of rainbow Post-it notes and a pen. I scribbled words across one, sticking them to the bar near the cash register when I was done with each one.

"What are you doing?" Low arrived at my side as I made a neat little row of coloured paper.

I gave him an apologetic smile. "You don't mind, do you? I watched you at the till and wanted to write notes, just so I don't forget anything."

Low shook his head and picked up my note stack. "Do you always carry the world's largest stack of Post-it notes in your bag, or is it because you started a new job today?"

I snatched them back from his hand with a good-natured grin. Our fingers touched, and I enjoyed the spark. "You act like carrying around sticky notes isn't a normal thing to do."

"It's not."

"Says who?"

Low raised an eyebrow at me and called to Riley and Bianca, who were working behind us. "Riley, B, do either of you carry a mini mountain of Post-it notes with you?"

"I don't even carry my phone or wallet half the time, so no," Riley replied.

Bianca shook her head with an apologetic shrug of her shoulders. "I don't either. Sorry, Reese."

Low regarded me with a knowing look on his face.

I sighed. "Shut up. I like stationery, okay?"

Low laughed and held his hands up in surrender. He went back to his customers as I finished up my note taking. I grabbed a cloth and wiped down the bar top, watching him while I waited for the next rush.

I'd begun to notice a pattern throughout the afternoon. Low's line of customers was always the longest. Even I was able to get through twice the number of customers in the same time Low took. And it was easy to see why. Every eligible woman in the room wanted the chance to talk to him. Men too. And Low seemed happy to oblige them all. Young or old, attractive or not, he flirted up a storm. Making jokes, laughing, letting his hands brush theirs as he passed them their drinks. And his tip jar reflected it.

A cute blond guy reached the head of Low's line, and they chatted as Low poured drinks. The blond's order was large and included cocktails that were time-consuming to make. I wondered if that had been on purpose, so he'd have more time to talk to Low. It seemed to be working out well for him. There was an obvious attraction between them as Low leant over the bar, pushing across the tray of drinks. The blond dropped a twenty-dollar note and his business card into Low's tip jar. Low grinned at him. A tiny flicker of jealousy lit up within me.

"He's something else, huh?" Bianca leant on the bar next to me.

"Hey?"

"Low. I wish I could pick up guys as easy as that." Bianca flicked her head to where Low was now laughing with a pretty redhead in a low-cut green dress. His eyes flicked to the retreating form of the blond guy as the man left with his tray of cocktails and beer.

"He's smart. He'll make twice the amount of tips the rest of us will."

Bianca shook her head. "He doesn't do it for the money. He always splits his tips between us at the end of the shift, anyway. He's just a flirt by nature."

"Yeah, I can see that." I played with the edge of the cloth. "So, he doesn't have a girlfriend then? Boyfriend?" I tried to keep my voice even, not wanting to sound too interested. I'd assumed he was straight after the discussion about Abi the ex-bartender, but now after watching him with the blond I wasn't so sure. He wasn't going to be the distraction I wanted if he was taken or gay.

Bianca frowned as she adjusted the silver bracelets covering her wrists. "He's bi, but there's no boyfriend or girlfriend. He's more the love 'em and leave 'em type."

That worked for me. I hadn't wanted anyone for longer than a night in a long time now either. "Do they know that?" I nodded my head towards the woman Low was chatting with.

She laughed. "Probably. He has quite the reputation. But if they don't know it beforehand, he'll tell them. He's good like that. He's always upfront and honest. They know it's just a one-time thing, and he'll be on to someone new next shift."

"I bet that doesn't always go down well."

"It doesn't. There's always someone trying to tame him. But I've known him awhile now, and I've yet to see him date anyone." She paused. "He doesn't show much of what's beneath the man-whore exterior, but he's worth knowing if he'll let you in."

I went back to serving customers, Bianca's words ringing in my ears. I couldn't help noticing the similarities between Low and myself. The random partners and aversion to commitment. I didn't let people in either. I wondered if it was a something or a someone that had broken Low, the same way I was.

2

LOW

"Two Moscatos, please," the woman ordered. Her hair fell in curls around her shoulders, and her fancy black dress was cut deep enough for me to enjoy her perky cleavage.

I grinned at her. "You got it." I threw in a wink for good measure, because I knew it would make her blush. I was right. She giggled, stuffing a ten-dollar note into my tip jar. I handed her the wine, letting my fingers brush hers. "Enjoy those."

She nodded, turning away, and handed a glass to her waiting friend. They whispered to each other, the woman glancing back at me over her shoulder. I'd already lost interest, though, and moved on to the next woman in line. Fuck, I loved my job. It was a revolving door of opportunities.

Reese appeared next to me and opened one of the beer taps, letting the amber liquid run into her waiting glass. "You're extra popular today," she said with a glance down my line. She was right. We'd only opened ten minutes ago, and I had at least a dozen people waiting already. "Got your sights on anyone yet?"

You. I almost said it out loud, but I was trying to behave. Reese had only started at the bar a few days ago, and I'd promised myself I'd be on my best behaviour. Except her long dark hair, deep brown eyes, and curves in all the right places didn't make it easy. But still, I shouldn't go there. I'd slept with the last bartender right before she quit, leaving all of us to work extra shifts until we could find a replacement. I owed it to the team to keep Reese around. Next week was one of the busiest on the calendar with the official kick off of the Spring Carnival, so I needed to hang onto her. The others would kill me if they were run off their feet because we were a bartender down again. They all seemed to like her. She fit in well and worked hard.

I shrugged at Reese. "Not yet, but it's still early."

She nodded, setting another beer down on a tray. "How'd you go the other night, anyway? Anything happen with that blond guy hanging around after shift?"

I laughed. "Are you asking as a mate? Or because you're a tiny bit jealous?" I hoped it was the latter.

She rolled her eyes as she pushed a tray of beers across the bar top. "One—we aren't mates. We've worked together for three whole days. And two—come on now, we both know I could have you if I wanted. What do I have to be jealous of?"

I grinned. Well, damn if she couldn't read me like a book. My interest had been hovering around a seven, but with the way she kept giving it back to me, it had jumped to an eleven. I enjoyed our little back and forths, and I loved how she wasn't afraid to put me in my place.

"So? How'd you go? You spent all shift flirting with that guy. I'm just wondering if you managed to seal the deal."

I wriggled my eyebrows at her.

"Good for you." A smile tugged at the corners of her lips. "Did you tell him you'd be back here next shift flirting it up with someone new?"

I nodded. "I told him upfront how it is. Always do. You learn to recognise who's up for it and who isn't. But I make it worth their while."

That earned me another eye roll, which I deserved.

"Yeah, I bet you do."

"You could always find out personally, you know. Offer's on the table any time you want it."

Her hand stilled on the beer tap.

I looked over at her, surprised. My pulse picked up. Was she considering it? I'd been joking, but if she was interested, I sure as hell wouldn't knock her back. I'd quit flirting with every man and woman in the room right now.

"I'll let you know if I'm ever that desperate." She flashed me that smile I was beginning to obsess over.

"Harsh, Reese. Harsh."

"I'm sure you'll live," Reese dead-panned. She grabbed a bottle of wine from the fridge and made her way to the other side of the bar to serve a group of guys who'd been trying to get her attention for a while now. As she walked away, I watched the gentle sway of her ass longer than I should have.

We'd been flirting like this ever since her first shift. But pretty new bartenders had gotten me in trouble before, and there were plenty of other prospects here. Working at the racetrack had to be the easiest way to get laid. I had hot guys and sexy women to flirt with all day, as they drank and had a good time watching the horse races. It was like shooting fish in a barrel. I needed to leave Reese alone.

Turning to my next customer, I stifled a groan as I recognised his handsome face. I'd woken up next to that face just a few days ago. My good mood vanished. "Are you here to see me?" I dropped my voice, so I wouldn't draw attention to us. He nodded, giving me a tight smile.

Annoyance rose within me, but I tried to tamp it down. "Why? Didn't you hear what I said the other night?"

"I'm just here to talk." He bit his lip as he drummed his fingers on the bar top. "We *need* to talk."

I sighed. I hadn't picked him as a cling-on. Great. This was the exact scene I tried so hard to avoid. "No, we don't. We had fun, Mason, but that's it."

He shook his head, thrusting his fingers through his short blond hair. "It's not like that. Low, listen, I need to talk to you; it's important."

I leant in closer. "You knew how it was before we went back to your place. I'm sorry if you're having one-night-stand regret now, but I'm at work. I can't do this right now."

Mason's mouth dropped open a little, and guilt flooded me, settling uncomfortably in my stomach. I knew I was being harsh, but I'd learnt from past mistakes it was better to cut the clingy ones off before they could begin. It was awkward for everyone involved otherwise.

Anger distorted Mason's handsome, boy-next-door features into someone different. He shook his head. "You're an asshole, Low."

He stalked to the door of the racecourse, yanking it open and letting it swing behind him. I watched him go for a second before turning back to my next customer. He was right. I was.

3

REESE

"*B*ianca, you're staring at them." I kept my voice low as I nudged her with my elbow.

She snapped her head back around and took a step closer, lowering her voice. "What do you think that was all about? It looked seriously heated."

I shook my head. "I don't know, but it isn't our business and it's bad enough all the customers are staring. Don't make it worse."

She pouted but went back to serving anyway. Taking my own advice, I turned away. It was hard to stop myself from shooting little glances at Low from the corner of my eye, though.

I'd recognised the guy Low was arguing with. He'd been the one Low had gone home with after my first shift. Part of me was amused that Low had had to face his one-night stand in the cold hard light of day. It wouldn't kill him to be a little less cavalier about his conquests. But I did feel an ounce of pity for him too. It hadn't happened yet, thank God, but it very easily could have been me, standing in his shoes. Low seemed to recover well, though, and had gone straight back to his next customer in line.

My phone buzzed in the pocket of my apron. I fought the

urge to pull it out and cancel the call. It would stop in a minute if I ignored it. I just had to wait. After a moment it went still, as the call rang out. I had no voicemail for them to leave a message and I breathed a little sigh of relief.

The buzzing started up again and my heart sank. My phone had been doing this for three days now. Ringing every hour or two, the same familiar, landline number flashing up on the screen. I should have turned it off instead of just ignoring it, but something always stopped me from hitting the power button.

I knew who was on the other end and a big part of me longed to answer it. Every time it rang, a rush of memories cascaded over me. And every time I pushed them down, burying them where they couldn't hurt me. I'd cancel his call before the fear and shame overtook me.

I'd been an idiot to ring him. I'd never thought for a second he might try to return my call. I'd assumed he'd think it was a wrong number and leave it at that. I'd been so in the moment of the race, I hadn't even thought to turn off my caller ID. But now it was all I could think about. A whole different time and years of memories. A different life. Happiness and love and family. But in the next instant, the last time I'd seen him replayed in my head. The tears. The yelling. The hospital and the doctors. I'd spent a year blocking out those memories, turning to alcohol and sex when they became too much. Work and flirting with Low had been my only distraction for the past three days. But it wasn't enough. I wasn't sleeping, spending every night staring at the ceiling, half of me hoping the phone would ring, the other half praying it wouldn't. I was tired. So damn tired, both mentally and physically. I needed something more than a mild distraction. I needed to just switch off completely.

It'd been weeks since I'd been with anyone, which was a long drought for me these days. I needed a drink, and I needed to get laid. I needed someone else's hands to focus on. A night to lose myself in someone else's touch, so I could forget my own problems. From experience, I knew going out for a few drinks and finding someone to take home for the night was about as much relief from my memories as I'd ever get.

I glanced at Low again. I could spend the rest of this shift taking a leaf out of his book, flirting, and maybe finding someone who'd want to go out for a drink afterwards. Or I could save both Low and myself the hassle. We wanted the same thing after all.

"Now who's staring at him?" Bianca said behind me, startling me out of my thoughts.

"Was I?" I cringed. Of course I'd been staring.

Heat rose in my cheeks as Bianca smiled, looking like the cat that got the cream.

"You two have been mentally undressing each other all week."

"What? We have not."

"Fine, maybe not, but there's something between you for sure. I'm getting burnt from the residual heat coming off the two of you. I think you're crushing on him."

"Who has a crush on me?" Low called from his side of the bar. He'd cleared his back log of gushing fans. I groaned. This wasn't the way I'd envisioned this going.

"I can't take you home, remember, Reese. Gotta respect the policy. So if it's you, I'm sorry, but I'm unavailable." His smirk was blatant, and I knew he didn't mean a word he said.

"Lucky for you," I quipped straight back, "because it'd be awful to see you crying at work when I didn't call you the next day." Despite my desire to get laid tonight, I couldn't let his cocky attitude go unchecked. But it was a half-hearted rebuke.

Bianca choked on a laugh, busying herself at the till as a slow, almost predatory smile spread across Low's face. The tension between us took on a subtle change. I knew he'd heard my conversation with Bianca, when his gaze became heated. He'd never been even close to professional with me, but it seemed now some invisible barrier between us had disintegrated.

He took three long steps, stopping just a few inches from me.

His finger ran down the side of my face and circled beneath my chin, tilting it up so our gazes collided again. That tangible tension between us came to life like it had been electrified.

"That sounds like a challenge, pretty girl." His eyes raked over my face and dropped to my lips. I ran my tongue over them. Deliberately. I needed this. I needed to make tonight happen.

The heat in his eyes intensified, and it was satisfying to see. I smiled as I leant towards him, my hand gentle on his bicep. "No challenge." I wasn't interested in playing hard to get anymore. I wanted him to know I was up for it as much as he was.

He moved closer and when he whispered, "Good to know" in my ear, I knew he'd understood my meaning. I ducked my head, a little smile playing at the corners of my mouth. Yeah, we were on the same page.

Riley dumped a load of clean glasses onto the bar behind me, and they clinked together in protest. "If you two are going to eye fuck, can you at least do it away from where I need to load the glasses? They're heavy, you know."

Low winked and moved back to his side of the bar where more than one woman was giving me a death look. I smiled sweetly at them.

There were a couple of men who flirted with me throughout the rest of the afternoon, and I smiled back but kept it professional. Low shot me looks from the corner of his eye when he thought I wasn't looking and a little thrill skittered through me with every glance.

My phone buzzed again in my pocket, and this time, I pulled it out and turned it off. I felt sick as I held down the off button, shutting down my only remaining link to my past. Maybe he'd stop calling now. I wasn't sure whether I wanted that or not.

The last race was at 5:00 p.m., and the crowd dispersed soon after. The women took off their high heels and carried them as they walked barefoot to the parking area. Men loosened their ties and slung suit jackets over their shoulders. Jamison decided I needed to know how to balance the till for the next day's trading, and we left Low to break it to his crowd of women that the bar was closing. We were cutting off their alcohol source, and some of them weren't taking that too well.

Bianca and I restocked the bar while laughing to ourselves over the tipsy whining of Low's harem. There was a lot of "Come on, just one more drink," and "Why don't you come out with us after your shift?" A part of me almost envied those women. At eighteen, I'd been much too innocent and lacking in confidence to be so forward with a random bartender, no matter how gorgeous and charming he was. I wouldn't have been able to speak under Low's intense gaze.

Oh, how times changed. I hadn't been that girl in over a year now. She was so far in my rear-view mirror I could no longer see her.

I missed her sometimes, though. I'd had a family once. And a future. They should have been memories that made me smile. But instead, I did everything in my power not to think about the past. Because every time I did, the gut-wrenching pain and loathing followed, threatening to overwhelm me. I could never go back to being her. I didn't deserve to be her.

"Low, if you want to take off, Reese and I have this covered," Bianca announced, inciting a cheer from the girls trying to convince Low to come out with them. I watched him, eager to hear his response.

Low shot Bianca a dirty look, to which Bianca replied with a shrug. "He's never minded any other time I've told him to take off with a few girls," she mumbled under her breath.

I smirked. I hoped that meant Low was planning to go home with someone else. Like me. I'd already thought about the night of wild sex we'd have. Hours upon hours of not thinking, just using his body as a tonic for mine. I closed my eyes and drew in a shaky breath. Yeah. I needed to lose myself in somebody else tonight.

"Sorry, ladies, but the track is closed, and I have work to do. You're going to have to make your way to the exit now," Low said, using his professional voice for the first time all day. There were a few last-minute whines before they dragged themselves away from the bar. I saw Low breathe a sigh of relief as he watched them stumble towards the exits. "Bloody hell, thank God for that."

"You didn't want to go partying with them, Low?" I asked, feigning sweet innocence.

Low shook his head. "Not tonight. Tonight, I have plans."

"Oh yeah?" God, I hoped those plans involved me. And his tongue.

"Mmmm hmmm," he said, the rumble of his voice deep and low and oh so hot. "But first, we drink."

He grabbed a bottle of tequila from the top shelf of the bar and bellowed, "Riley, Jamison, Bianca. Shots on the bar in one minute."

"Do you regularly steal the booze and get drunk on shift?" I asked as I looked around the empty racetrack.

"It's 6:01 p.m., which means we're off clock. Plus, it's not stealing if you pay for it, and I'm buying." Low lined up five glasses, pouring a shot of tequila into each.

Taking his cue, I grabbed the little container of cut up lemon wedges from the fridge. Then I grabbed a few salt packages from below the countertop. Riley, Bianca, and Jamison all filed over as they finished their tidying.

"Oh Jesus, Low, tequila again?" Bianca groaned. "You know that always ends badly."

I guessed that was a yes to them regularly drinking after shift.

"It's Reese's first Friday night at the Lavender, B! That calls for tequila, don't you think?"

Bianca looked at me. I shrugged and ripped off the top of a salt package. Bianca sighed in defeat as she ripped open her own salt. I ran my tongue along the back of my hand and poured out the grainy white powder, leaving a trail of salt stuck to my skin. When I looked up, Low was staring at me in fascination.

I made out like I was looking at my watch, waiting for him to catch up.

He laughed. "Sassy little thing, aren't you?" His voice was soft, so the others didn't hear. They weren't paying us any attention anyway, too busy laughing at Bianca's hatred for tequila. Low handed out the small glasses of clear liquid, and we formed a circle.

"To Reese's first week!" Low said, raising his glass in salute.

"To finally having a full team and not being run off our feet every shift," Jamison chimed in.

"To having someone around who can put Low in his place."

Low faked offence when we all laughed. Riley winked at me.

"To having another woman around to break up all this testosterone." Bianca reached out and squeezed my arm. I smiled at her.

A warm glow spread along my skin that had nothing to do with the way I was standing close enough to Low to feel the heat radiating from him. The last few days had been good. I was looking forward to getting to know Riley and Jamison more. I already liked Bianca a lot. And Low, well, I figured I'd know him a lot better by morning.

My smile was wide as we clinked our little glasses together. I licked the salt from the back of my hand and swallowed the contents of my glass, feeling the liquid burn down my throat. I shoved my piece of lemon in my mouth, which took the edge off.

Across from me, Bianca's eyes were watering as she sucked on her lemon. "Ugggghhh," she groaned. "It never gets better."

"Not true. The second one is always better," Low said, tilting the tequila bottle in her direction.

She waved her hand at him, shaking her head. "Nope, no way. One is more than enough. I've got to drive." Her gaze darted between Low and me before she turned to Riley and Jamison. "Come on, I'll drive you guys home."

Jamison and Riley looked bewildered as Bianca hustled them out the doors. "See you two tomorrow!" Bianca called, her sing-song voice echoing through the empty room. And just like that, the three of them disappeared, leaving Low and me in an empty racetrack bar.

He watched me, his eyes unashamed as they drifted over my body. "You gotta go too, Reese?"

Damn, his voice could bring a girl to her knees. I let my eyes drop to his crotch as I contemplated that possibility for a minute. Shaking my head, I reached for the tequila bottle. I didn't need Dutch courage for what I knew would happen between us tonight. But it sure wouldn't hurt.

Low took the bottle from me, placing it back on its spot on the shelf. He leant in close and lowered his mouth to my ear. The five o'clock shadow along his jaw scratched pleasantly at my cheek. "I want you sober for tonight. I don't want you forgetting anything I plan to do to you."

His words made me want to throw the whole damn tequila bottle in the bin. Sober or drunk, I didn't care. I wanted him. If he wanted me sober, then so be it. I tilted my head to the side a little, an unspoken invitation for him to kiss me.

To my surprise, he pulled back. His eyes lost the fuzziness of lust I'd seen in them a second earlier. He was crystal clear and straight to the point when he spoke. "You know I go home with a lot of women, right? Men too, on occasion."

He braced both hands on the bar top behind him and leant farther back, giving me even more space. "We're both adults. We both know what this is. I have every intention of sleeping with you, even though I promised the others and myself I wouldn't. But you need to know how it is. I'm not boyfriend material. I'm not interested in a relationship, and I don't do repeats."

He waited as I let his words sink in. He thought I'd run. Expected it even, judging by the wary look on his face.

"I won't want you for more than one night, Low, no matter what you do to me tonight."

That damn eyebrow quirked again. "Not as innocent as you look, are you, sweet girl?"

"I'm not particularly sweet either."

Business side of the deal seemingly over, he nodded. "Fair enough." His crystal blue eyes stared into mine for a long moment. I didn't look away, letting him see the determination in my own eyes. I wondered how long it would take him to realise I was up for this. He didn't need to pussyfoot around me.

I got sick of the stare-off first.

I grabbed my stack of Post-it notes from beside the till where they'd been sitting all week and threw them in my handbag. "Your place or mine?" I walked out the bar door and held it open on the other side, waiting for him to follow.

Low chuckled, and I thought I heard him mutter the word 'impatient' under his breath. He took the heavy wood door from me and pushed it back into place, locking it in. I sauntered off towards the main entrance, but then I felt more than heard his presence behind me. His arm shot out and grabbed my hand, pulling me to a stop. I spun around and found myself chest to chest with him. I had to tilt my head back to look up at his face.

"Not that way," he said, his voice low and gravelly.

My stomach flip flopped as electricity sparked where his skin met mine.

His hand was warm, and I was surprised to find callouses across his palm. He didn't have the skin of someone who worked inside all day, pouring drinks. I wondered what he did outside of work hours to rough his hands up like that.

"Where are we going?" I asked as we pushed through a door marked staff only. The door slammed shut behind me. I'd barely noted the rush of fresh air surrounding us before he spun around and dropped his lips to mine. I stopped breathing. My eyes closed as my lips parted. Blood rushed through my body as sensation exploded within me. My brain began switching off as his touch and his scent chased away my thoughts. Relief flooded me. All I needed to think about right now, all I *wanted* to think about, was him.

He walked us back against the door we'd just come out of and pressed me into it, his lips not once leaving mine. My breath caught up with me as he broke away from my mouth, trailing his lips along the corners, along my jaw, and down to my neck. The scruff on his jaw scratched at my face, adding another sensation to concentrate on.

His thigh moved between my legs and pressed against my already aching core. I bit back a moan. Yes. This was what I wanted. I didn't even care we were in some service alley along the side of the racetrack, and that I could hear cars driving by on the road that couldn't have been more than a hundred metres away. Pulling him closer, I pressed myself into him, as he trailed kisses down my neck.

"I want to take you back to my place, Reese, where I can lay you out and do this right," he mumbled into my neck, his body fitted to mine like a glove. "But I can't wait. I've wanted to do this all week. I want to fuck you right here in this alleyway."

Sparks ignited in my centre at his crude words. He could have recited his grocery list in that voice and I would have been a puddle at his feet. This was too much.

"Do it."

He groaned as he pressed his hips towards my own. He was already hard beneath his pants. I couldn't help grinning. This is what I loved about sex. The ability to feel powerful and in control. To lose yourself in another human being for a while, to think of nothing but hands, and tongues, and pleasure.

"You're impatient, aren't you?"

I shook my head, no longer interested in talking. I just wanted to feel.

His hands cupped my breasts through my shirt, and I ran my hands through his hair, messing it up the same way I'd thought of doing the first day we'd met. His mouth was all over my neck and cleavage as his hands tugged and twisted at my aching nipples. I pressed my pelvis towards him, trying to hook one of my legs around his waist.

"Fuck," I bit out, when my fitted skirt prevented me from doing it.

He ran his hands down my thighs and yanked my skirt up until it gathered around my waist. I glanced at the top of the alley, at the cars driving past, their headlights illuminating the darkness.

My knees buckled a little as I got my leg where I wanted it and felt the thickness of his cock pressed against my centre. My core ached for release as blood thrummed through my body. I brought my hands to his belt and pulled. I grinned. He wasn't wearing any underwear, the tip of his cock already poking up above his waistband.

My eyes met his, and he shrugged. "I've been hard off and on all day, just thinking about this. Didn't want to alarm the customers, so I tucked it away."

"So thoughtful of you." I laughed but cut myself off as his warm fingers grazed my inner thigh. Anticipation swept through me and I started up my fumbling with his button again.

He pulled aside the scrap of lace covering me and ran one finger through my wetness. My mission to undress him came to an abrupt halt as the sensation roared through me. Oh God, I needed more. I needed him in me.

With a new sense of urgency, I renewed my efforts to get his pants undone. I frowned when I noticed they were buzzing and vibrating.

With a sigh, Low removed his hand from my folds and reached back into his pocket, pulling out his phone.

I stumbled back a step, confusion and irritation replacing all the good feelings I'd been experiencing a minute earlier. "Are you seriously going to read your messages right now?" What the actual fuck?

"Hold on a second, baby," he murmured, his eyes still full of lust. "It's been buzzing this whole time we've been out here. I'm just going to make sure it's not an emergency, then turn it off."

I huffed out an impatient sigh, ignoring the fact he'd called me baby, and dropped my hands from his pants. I hated when a one-night stand talked like that. Terms of endearment were for couples who loved each other, not a couple of horny strangers fucking in a back alley. I tried to keep my annoyance from showing too much. But I was standing in the dark, with everything hanging out and on display for anyone to see. And he was checking his phone. What an asshole.

I grabbed the hand he wasn't holding the phone with and pressed it to one of my breasts. He gave me a huge, shit-eating grin and pressed the home button on his phone. His thumb flicked absently over my nipple as he read his text message. I closed my eyes, leaning into the wall behind me again. He had thirty seconds to read that message and there had better be a mind-blowing orgasm at the end of it. I opened an eye when he stopped his fondling. He'd taken a large step back, his pants still half undone, his belt hanging open. He stared at his phone like he no longer knew what it was.

I let out another sigh, and his head snapped up. His face, lit up by the phone screen, looked blank. Not horny like it had a moment earlier. I stood up a little straighter, worry creeping in.

"I...I've got to go," he said, stumbling back a few more steps. He gripped the back of his neck, his eyebrows drawing together in a frown.

"What?" I felt exposed. And frustrated. Every part of me still tingled. My skin was already mourning the loss of his touch, every nerve ending anticipating its return. Disappointment mixed with embarrassment threatened to take over. I needed this tonight. Had he gotten a better offer?

He shook his head, backing away as he tucked in his cock and did up his work pants. Leaving me standing there alone, tugging my skirt down.

"Are you serious right now?" I squeaked out.

He shook his head again, that mussed up hair I'd been running my fingers through moments earlier falling in his eye. He headed toward the top of the alleyway before breaking into a run.

My mouth dropped open. He was leaving. He was actually leaving me here alone in the alleyway. And not just walking away. He was *running* away from me. My face blazed with embarrassment.

"What the fuck, Low?" I yelled at his retreating form. I watched him until he rounded the corner out of the alleyway, but he never turned back. Not once.

4

LOW

*M*y fist slammed into the polished wood door.

"Mason!" I bellowed before I started up with the banging again. Pain vibrated down my arm, but I ignored it. "Mason!"

Every muscle in my body was wound too tight. My thighs burned from running here all the way from work. The muscles in my arms contracted and released as I alternated between flexing my fingers then curling them tight into fists. My chest heaved. I couldn't breathe. I tried sucking in another breath. *Shit.* I really couldn't breathe. The muscles in my chest locked as if trapped in an iron vice. I was twenty-five years old and ran five kilometres a day. I wasn't a prime candidate for a heart attack, but it sure as hell felt like I was having one.

"Mason!"

The door flew open, and I pulled my arm back, just in time to avoid punching Mason in the face. His eyes travelled over my heaving, sweating body.

"I guess you got my message then." It was a statement. Not a question.

"What do you fucking think?" I fished my phone out of my

pocket and held it up, millimetres from Mason's face. "Who sends messages like that?"

Mason said nothing.

I took a deep breath, not wanting to ask, but needing to know. "Is it true?"

Mason looked down at the floor. "I didn't want to tell you in a message, you know. I tried to talk to you today—"

"While I was at work!"

"I know! I know, I'm sorry! That was a mistake. But I had to talk to you."

I couldn't keep still, impatience coursing through me. I bounced on the balls of my feet. "Answer my damn question. Is. It. True?" I spat the words at him, venom lacing every syllable.

Mason sighed and opened the door wider. "Look, you'd better come inside."

"No! Just answer me. Goddammit, Mason. Is it true or not?" I was shouting now, but I was beyond caring who heard.

Mason looked away. Fucking coward couldn't even look me in the eye when he told me. His voice was barely more than a whisper. "I'm sorry, Low."

I stopped breathing. *I'm sorry, Low.* Three tiny words. Three tiny words that would fuck me up for the rest of my life. Rage coursed through me, igniting my blood and re-energising my tired muscles. I drew back my arm and slammed my fist into the doorjamb, missing Mason's face by centimetres. He flinched away from me, his eyes growing wide.

"Bit bloody late for sorry, isn't it?"

5

REESE

"Shut the hell up," I mumbled into my pillow as my alarm went off. I pulled one arm out of my blankets and fumbled around the nightstand, jabbing at my phone until it went silent. Then I buried my face again. The light streaming in my bedroom window was trying to cause me permanent blindness.

I groaned as I took stock of how seedy I felt. How much had I drunk last night? There was the tequila I'd done at the racecourse —that wasn't enough to cause a hangover of this magnitude. My stomach rolled, and I held my breath for a few seconds while I contemplated throwing up. Sweat beaded on my forehead, but the queasiness passed. I threw off the quilt, feeling flushed and needing fresh air. The sudden movement caused my stomach to roll again. Shit. That had been a bad idea. I changed my mind—I was going to be sick after all. I shot out of bed and sprinted for my little bathroom, dodging the moving boxes that threatened to bury me alive if I knocked one too hard.

After emptying the contents of my stomach, I slumped against the cool tiled wall. Once the world stopped spinning, I used the sink as leverage to pull myself up and splashed cold water on my face. Looking in the mirror was a mistake. There was mascara-smeared down my cheeks and my eyes were bloodshot. My long dark hair looked as if birds had taken up residence during the night. "Classy, Reese, classy."

I opened the bathroom cabinet, just so I didn't have to look at myself in the mirror anymore. Rummaging through it, I came up triumphant with a bottle of ibuprofen. My disappointment when it was empty made the pounding in my head worse. Miserable, I shut the door, wincing at my reflection again before staggering out of the bathroom. Everything was still spinning. Last night must have been a doozy.

I traced my way back through the maze of packing boxes, this time noticing the empty wine bottle on my coffee table. And another one, half empty, sitting beside it like twin towers of judgement. That, plus the tequila? No wonder I wasn't feeling so hot.

I crawled onto my bed in slow motion, excruciatingly careful not to move my head or jostle my stomach any more than necessary. God, it felt good to lie down. But shit. More than one full bottle of wine plus shots? That was excessive, even judging by my recent standards. I was lucky I hadn't vomited and choked on it when I'd passed out.

I rolled over and hugged a mascara smeared pillow to my chest. At least there were no random men here I'd have to make awkward small talk with until they got the hint and left.

The memory of Low leaving me hanging in the alley suddenly made me felt like vomiting again. Regret flooded me. I was an idiot. I should have known better than to take on someone I worked with. Nothing good could have come from that, even if he hadn't left me with a raging lady-boner. I'd come home and taken care of my frustrations by myself, but it didn't have the desired effect. I was too pissed off to lose myself in an orgasm, the way I wanted to. So instead, I'd turned to alcohol. A bottle of sauv blanc would never leave me high and dry in an alley, with my goods on display. And by my sixth or seventh glass, I'd found the oblivion I'd been looking for.

After a year of casual sex, I thought I was a good judge of character when it came to picking who'd be up for it. When I set my sights on Low, I never expected he'd leave the way he had. He'd been into it. He'd been the classic one-night-stand sort of guy, just the way I liked them. No strings attached. He'd flirted with me as much as I flirted with him. The way he'd pushed me up against that door, too impatient to even make it back to somewhere private... no, he'd wanted it as much as I had.

Until he hadn't.

I tried giving myself a pep talk. This was his problem. Not mine. But the rejection stung all the same. It was hard not to imagine he'd suddenly found something about me so repulsive he couldn't continue. No, no, no. I would not go down the rabbit hole of self-doubt. Low had left last night because of something in that text message. But had that text been staged? The old, 'call me in an hour with an emergency to get me out of here?' Or had he gotten a better offer? Maybe he had a secret girlfriend or boyfriend Bianca didn't know about?

"Uggggggggggghhhhhhhhh," I groaned. Why was I doing this to myself? Grabbing my Post-it notes from my bedside table, I wrote in capital letters, *DON'T WASTE TIME STRESSING OVER DOUCHEBAG BARTENDERS.* I underlined the word douchebag a few times just to make myself feel better, then peeled it off and added it to the other Post-its stuck on the headboard of my bed. They weren't all mean notes about men. I wrote down motivational quotes that appealed to me as I came across them, or song lyrics I was into. A few were covered in doodles I'd done one day while I was on hold to the electricity company. I don't know why I'd kept those.

Glancing at my phone again, I realised how late it was getting. I had another shift at eleven, so I needed to get a move on. A shower made me feel marginally better, and the room had stopped spinning by the time I'd thrown on a clean uniform and applied makeup, concentrating on the bags under my eyes. Shame there wasn't much I could do for the redness of them.

I made my way out to my tiny kitchen bench, surveying the mess while I waited for the world's slowest kettle to boil. There were boxes everywhere. I'd moved to this tiny apartment months ago, and I'd unpacked nothing more than the bare essentials. And by essentials, that meant a corkscrew, the kettle, and my vibrator. I nudged a box by my foot, and it twisted around to reveal a hot pink Post-it labelled 'Veterinary text books.' Sighing, I nudged it back around, so I couldn't see it. I didn't even know why I still had that box. This place wasn't big enough to be storing things I no longer had use for.

The kettle finally boiled, and I made my coffee in a travel mug. A big one, adding extra sugar because it was that sort of morning. Taking my coffee with me, I headed for the sliding glass door that led to the balcony.

My apartment sat opposite the sprawling Lavender Fields properties, so I had a great view from my vantage point on the third floor. The racetrack itself was situated farthest away from me, with a large stable area, warm-up tracks, and the buildings I now worked in lined up beside it. Closer to my apartment was their breeding and training property. Green grass paddocks, white fences, and an array of buildings occupied the space; a tall fence running the perimeter of the whole thing.

I checked my watch and smiled. I had time to see Mabel. Grabbing my shoes from where I'd kicked them off last night, I locked my apartment door behind me. Increasing my pace, I emerged onto the street, then slipped through a gap in the tall fencing I'd found on my first day living here. I'd been sneaking through the gap almost every day since.

They kept the valuable horses, the ones that would race later that day or next week, close to the track. Out here on the edge of the property, it was quiet, the paddocks home to a handful of older horses.

I clicked my tongue and smiled as I watched Mabel's velvety grey ears prick up. Her name wasn't actually Mabel. I had no idea what her name was; it's not like they'd etched it into the wood of her paddock fence. But I thought she looked like a Mabel. She was an ex racehorse for sure; she was the perfect shape for it. They'd likely put her out here to breed, though I had yet to see her belly swell with a foal. She tossed her head, her silky black mane flowing in the air like a shampoo ad model, and trotted over.

"Hey, Mabel," I mumbled, reaching up to stroke the side of her face. She nuzzled her nose into my hand and snorted. I laughed. "Yeah, yeah, you know I brought you a treat." I produced a few bits of cut up carrot I'd grabbed when I made my coffee, and she snatched them from my palm with a speedy flick of tongue and teeth. I rarely made myself food at home, but I always had fresh carrots to feed to Mabel.

"Greedy this morning, aren't you?" I took a deep breath in. The familiar smell of horse, grass, and fresh air was better than any hangover remedy. Mabel stood there patiently, letting me stroke her. Letting me just be. That was the best thing about animals. They knew when to just be there, their presence alone comforting.

"I really blew it last night, Mabel." I looked up into the deep brown depths of her eyes. "I need this job. I want it." I smiled as she sniffed at my hair. "You think he's going to stuff it up for me, girl?" She tossed her head from side to side, trying to escape the early spring flies that were already hanging around. I took it as a positive sign, though. "Yeah, maybe he'll be cool. If I can be cool after being humiliated like that, then there's no reason he shouldn't be, huh?"

Mabel just blinked at me before walking off to chew at some

grass. I watched her for a moment longer before making my way back through the gap.

I tried to shake my melancholy mood. I both loved and hated how much Lavender Fields reminded me of home. I was so drawn to the place—had rented this apartment for the sole reason I'd be able to see horses every day. And when this job had come up, I hadn't been able to stop myself from applying. But the reminders of everything I'd lost were like a collection of cuts on my skin. Some shallow, some so deep I could see the bone.

I finished my now-cold coffee as I made my way around the fence. The paddocks disappeared behind the buildings, and the racetrack entrance came into view. Nodding at entry security, I pushed through the turnstiles and made my way over to the bar. A hand grabbed my arm and spun me around before I'd even made it the whole way through the bar door. I jumped.

"Oh my God, I'm sorry," Bianca said in a rush as I threw a glance over my shoulder, while I tried to calm my thumping heart. For a second, I'd thought she was Low.

"I didn't mean to scare you, but I'm so glad you're here before the boys!"

I scanned the room. She was right, we were alone.

"So, how was it? Tell me everything!" she squealed and clapped her hands together.

"Excuse me?" I was having trouble following her, she spoke so fast.

"You and Low! Was it amazing? I've always thought he'd be amazing in bed."

Ohhhh. I'd forgotten we hadn't been discreet in our flirting. The entire bar crew probably knew what we'd intended to do last night. I wasn't shy about telling people about my sex life, but I wasn't sure I wanted to tell Bianca about how Low had ditched me. That was embarrassing. So, I stalled. "Does that mean you haven't slept with him?"

Bianca flicked her hand, dismissing my question. "Nope. I had a boyfriend when I first started working here, and by the time we broke up, Low and I were firmly in the friend zone. But that doesn't mean I haven't wondered if he's any good in the sack. And he only ever hooks up with randoms at the bar that we never end up seeing again. It's not like I've ever been able to ask one of them." She looked me up and down. "So, come on, let me live vicariously through you because I haven't had sex in months." She pulled a face, and I couldn't help but laugh. She was bouncing on the balls of her feet, looking at me like an eager puppy. "Quick, tell me before the boys get here."

I shook my head. "There's nothing to tell. Honest. Nothing happened."

She tilted her head and stared at me with disbelief. "Yeah, right, I saw the way you two were eyeing each other. I figured I'd better leave before he started making out with you on the bar top."

Heat rose to my cheeks. Was I blushing? For God's sake, Reese, stop. Just stop. "I swear, we didn't have sex. He had…uh… Something came up and he had to leave."

She frowned. Maybe she believed me this time. We both looked over at the door when it opened, and Riley and Jamison appeared. I breathed a sigh of relief as Riley began an animated retelling of last night's football game, complete with a tackling demonstration on Jamison. Bianca turned her attention to him, and I scampered away to find my apron before she could ask any more questions I didn't want to think about.

Low didn't show up for work that day. Or the next.

I'd been self-conscious when he hadn't shown up the first day, but that had quickly turned to relief. We'd been so busy with the weekend rush of customers, I hadn't had time to consider his absence as much. But as we moved into the new week, the races weren't as popular, and that left me with more time to think.

Jamison had told us he'd left a message on his voice mail, saying he was sick. The others all seemed to buy it, but I wasn't so sure. A whole week off because of an awkward sexual encounter was a bit excessive, though. Maybe he was just sick. Maybe his absence had nothing to do with me. As the week went on and he continued to not show up, I thought about it less and less. I was having a great time working with Jamison, Riley, and Bianca, and not having Low there to complicate things was actually kind of a relief.

So, it was a kick to the stomach when I showed up for work on Saturday and he was the first person I saw.

6

REESE

"*Hi.*"

His voice was so quiet I barely heard him. I wasn't sure how to react. Should I still be angry about the way he left? Should I ask him if he was feeling better? Should I give him the cold shoulder? My anger had had time to dissipate over the week, and although I wanted to ask him what had happened, I was also desperate to just forget about the whole thing. So, I settled for echoing his greeting with my own lacklustre, "hi."

He shut the door behind me. I went out the back to the kitchen area, and he went to the front to serve. I leant back against the stainless-steel bench and took a deep breath, trying to steady the nerves that had exploded in my belly. Bianca glanced over at me. "Do you want me to serve today?"

I shook my head, pasting on a fake smile and trying to look cheerful. "No, I'm fine. I'll go."

She shrugged at me. "If you're sure..."

I nodded and dawdled my way out to the serving area. I didn't want to be out here. It would have been much easier to hide out the back, clean tables and wash dishes, but I couldn't let him think his presence bothered me. And it didn't. I just wasn't sure how to act around him. I'd never been dumped in the middle of a one-night stand before. I wasn't sure what the protocol was for such a situation.

The front gates hadn't opened yet, but they would any minute now, and we'd be inundated with customers. I found myself a place on the bar between Jamison and Low, and waited.

"Reese?" The deep gravel of Low's voice coursed through me.

I sighed. "Yeah?"

He looked tired. There were dark circles under his eyes, and gone was the deliberate two-day stubble from last week. He looked like he hadn't shaved at all while he was off. I guessed maybe he had been sick.

He paused, his eyes flicking over my shoulder. "The gates are open." He went quiet as we watched the wave of customers, flowing in a steady stream.

"Looks like it's going to be busy."

"Yeah."

Wow. We were awesome at the whole conversation thing this morning, weren't we? God, we'd made this awkward.

The crowds had been big this week, with the Spring Carnival officially kicking off. It had sucked to be down a team member; we'd all been run off our feet without Low. But weekday crowds had nothing on the weekend racegoers. My line was long. Low's was too. Not because of his flirting today; it just seemed that neither of us was moving very quickly. Jamison was the only one keeping us afloat.

I tried to refocus and lose myself in the repetitive work. But I was acutely aware of Low's every move. His gaze was a laser beam, burning me every time our eyes accidentally met. We should have talked before shift. Our personal problems were making us distracted. I'd already spilt three drinks and dropped a glass, smashing it into shards. And I'd heard Low get more than one order wrong. People were getting impatient with us.

"Three beers and a bourbon on the rocks, please," a cute young guy at the head of my line said.

"No problem." I reached down to grab a beer glass, finding the rack empty. I smiled at him. "Just gotta grab more glasses. Hang tight for a second, okay?"

"Fine."

I winced. He'd already waited ten minutes at least.

I jogged to the kitchen area and grabbed a tray of glasses fresh out of the dishwasher.

"What's up with Low today?" Riley asked as I passed by.

"Um, nothing?" I stopped, the tray in my arms shaking a little. "He's quiet."

"Is he?" I didn't know what to say. "I hadn't noticed."

"Very quiet," Bianca chimed in, her brow wrinkling with concern. "I've never seen him so subdued."

"Well, I don't know. You both know him better than I do." The words came out sharper than I'd intended. "Why don't you just ask him?" I grabbed my glasses and made my way back to my customer.

"What's up with her today?" Riley asked Bianca, but I didn't hear her reply.

Guilt washed over me. I'd need to apologise to Bianca and Riley later. And I needed to be more professional. I poured my beers, trying to be friendly to my irritated customer, without being flirty.

Now that they'd pointed it out, I realised Riley and Bianca were right. Something was definitely wrong with Low. I could have put it down to the drama between the two of us, but it wasn't just me he was awkward with. The Low from last week, and the guy in front of me now were like two different people. This Low was quiet—taking orders and pouring drinks, but gone was the flirty chit chat, the confidence, and the constant banter.

The afternoon passed in much the same way. Low regained none of the spark he'd had a week before, and I caught the concerned glances Jamison threw his way. At one point, Jamison had a break in his line, and he went over to help Low. I watched them talking, their heads leaning in close, but I couldn't catch what they were saying. Anyway, it wasn't my business. It's not like Low and I were friends.

Low had just finished balancing the till, and Jamison and I were restocking for the next day, when Riley came out from the kitchen and slung an arm around Low's shoulders.

"We're going out," he announced. "All of us."

I looked over and accidentally caught Low's eye. I snapped my head away, looking at Riley before I could register Low's expression. "Sure." I tried to muster as much enthusiasm as possible. Going out with them would be better than sitting home alone drinking by myself on a Saturday night. Even if it meant spending the evening in Low's subdued company.

"I'm in," Jamison said. "I'll call Bree and get her to meet us there."

Riley cheered and gave us both high-fives. Bianca pulled a face when Jamison turned away and I raised an eyebrow at her.

"What's the face about?"

Bianca lowered her voice so only I would hear. "Jam's girlfriend, Bree, is..."

"You don't like her."

Bianca shook her head. "None of us do. She's shallow and phony and catty as hell. But Jam doesn't see any of that, so we're just waiting until he comes to his senses."

"Right."

"What about you, Low?" Riley asked, ignoring the whispered conversation between Bianca and me. My ears pricked up, as I waited for Low to answer.

"Not tonight," Low mumbled. He was already taking off his apron and loosening his ugly purple tie.

"Yes, tonight," Riley said, voice firm. "You're the whole reason we're going out. B and I decided we're getting you out of your funk."

Low shook his head and grabbed his wallet from his locker. My stomach clenched. I wasn't sure if it was because I really wanted him to come out, or because I was relieved he wasn't.

Low made to move for the door, but Riley blocked his path. Riley wasn't quite as muscular and filled out as Low was, nor was he as tall, but he had a gleam of determination in his eye.

"Come on, Low, you look like shit, and I've never seen you so down. We're worried about you. You're gonna come, get some drinks, get your dance on, and we'll get you laid. You look like you need it."

Low sighed, his shoulders slumping in defeat. "I'm fine. Really. If I come for one drink, will that be enough to make you happy?"

Riley nodded and clapped Low on the back. "We're all in! Let's go!"

Bianca grinned. "I knew you'd convince him." Bianca and Riley high-fived as they headed out the door, with Jamison right behind them.

"I'm just grabbing my bag. I'll meet you guys out front." I didn't want to be left alone at the back of the pack with Low.

I scuttled off to the back-kitchen area, grabbed my bag from my locker, and wasted a minute or two, giving Low time to leave. I fumbled with my keys, looking for the one that locked the bar door.

"Don't worry, I have my key."

My head snapped up and the butterflies in my belly started up again.

"Sorry," Low said. "I wasn't sure if you had a key yet, so I waited for you."

"Oh, yeah. Jamison gave me one while you were away..." I found my key and held it up for him to see.

He nodded but made no move to leave. I didn't want to be alone with him. The embarrassment I'd buried over last week was rapidly rising now that we were alone. I could feel it heating my cheeks.

I took an extra-long time locking the door, double-checking it, doing whatever I could to avoid looking at him. But he wasn't going anywhere.

"Listen," he said, when I'd run out of things to pretend to do. "About the other night…"

I wanted to groan. Did we really have to do this? Couldn't we just move on without all the awkward?

"It's fine. Don't worry about it." I tried to sound breezy and carefree. I gave a little laugh, then abruptly shut my mouth. What the hell was that? It didn't sound breezy or carefree at all. More like panicky and a little hysterical.

"No, I want to explain—"

"Low." I lifted my head to look him in the eye. "The last thing I want to hear is your explanations. I want to forget it ever happened. So can we do that? You can go back to flirting with your bar groupies and I'll just do my job. I'm not the type to get all psycho about it, okay?" And that was true. Normally I wouldn't have given a one-night stand a second thought, but I'd never been dumped mid make-out session either, so this was kind of new territory.

"Let's just go out and have a good time, okay?" I turned away from him, not giving him the chance to reply. I hustled to where the other three were waiting for us outside.

"So where are we off to?" I asked in a strangled, high-pitched voice. Bianca gave me a quizzical look that clearly said I was being weird, but I already knew that.

Jamison slung his arm around my shoulder as Low caught up with our group. "Marx Club. We haven't taken you there yet, but it's our local. You'll love it."

7

REESE

*I*t was wall-to-wall bodies at the Marx Nightclub. Bianca grabbed my hand and led me through the crowd of people dancing and drinking to a booth in the back. Sliding in next to her, I tensed for a moment, waiting to see who'd squeeze in next to me. I relaxed when it was Jamison. I turned forward again, my eyes meeting Low's as he settled into the booth across from me. Crap, I hadn't thought this through very well, had I? Now I'd have to look over the table into Low's eyes all night. Awkward.

"So how did we score this table?" I yelled in Bianca's direction, over the thumping bass pouring through the speakers.

"Riley's brother Mark owns the club," she yelled back. She pointed across the room to a guy serving behind the bar, who was as adorable as Riley was. Even from this distance and in the dim light, I could see how alike they were. "They're twins," she yelled again, and I nodded.

"I'm the good-looking twin," Riley piped up with a laugh. They had different haircuts, and Mark wasn't sporting a lip ring, but I could definitely tell they were brothers.

"So how come you work at the racecourse bar instead of here?"

Riley shook his head. "Ever heard of the saying never work with family? Well, it's even more true if you're twins, and if your twin is your boss."

"I can understand that." My words sounded flat, even to my own ears. I'd learnt the hard way just how true it was. I swallowed the lump in my throat and forced a smile, as Riley continued with his conversation, not realising the effect his words had had on me. Low was looking at me, though, and I avoided the curiosity in his gaze. Damn this booth. Why couldn't we have sat at the bar where I wouldn't have to look at his icy blue eyes? Drinks. I needed drinks.

I went to stand up but stopped when Low stood and offered to go to the bar. Relief coursed through me once I was out from under his gaze, but I couldn't help watching his broad shoulders as he moved through the crowd of people on the dance floor.

"What's up with you tonight?" Jamison asked me.

Riley and Bianca were deep in conversation about something, paying no attention to the rest of us.

"Me? Nothing. Just looking forward to that drink. Was a busy shift, yeah? Where's your girlfriend? I'm looking forward to meeting her."

Jamison ignored my obvious attempt at changing the subject. "He's not normally like this, you know. I don't know what's wrong with him. But I'm worried. I've never seen him look this down. Or subdued."

"Who?" I asked, feigning ignorance. I was glad the music was loud because my voice was coming out all high and unnatural. Jamison gave me a look that clearly said he knew I was being dumb. He didn't even bother answering my stupid question. I didn't blame him.

"I don't know what happened with you guys. But if that's why he's being weird, you two need to sort it out. We've all worked together for a long time, and we need you to stick around too. You saw this week how much it sucks to be a team member down."

"Nothing happened with us," I blurted out. Low was on his way back towards our table. "I don't know what his problem is, but it isn't me."

Low placed the drinks down in front of us, and I gave him an overenthusiastic smile. He tilted his head to the side slightly, confusion warring on his features before he tentatively smiled back at me.

I gave Jamison a, 'see? We're fine' look. He didn't look convinced. Oh well. I had a buzz to get on, and this club was full of eligible men.

I sipped at my glass of wine, letting Bianca and Riley monopolise the conversation. It wasn't long before I was grabbing the wine bottle and pouring myself another.

By the bottom of my second glass, I could feel myself loosening up and my shoulders beginning to move to the beat of the music. We'd been so busy at work, I'd skipped my lunch break, just grabbing a few bites of a sandwich in the kitchen hours ago. My head had just an edge of fog from drinking my two glasses of wine too quickly, and I was feeling the songs the DJ was playing. Old school '90s RNB and hip hop vibrated through the room, and the dance floor was jumping with bodies. Most had come straight from the racecourse so were already tanked enough to be cutting ridiculous dance moves. But who cared? I was ready to dance. Plus, there was only so much avoiding of Low I could do when I was sitting right across from him.

"Let's dance," I yelled to Bianca, pulling her away from Riley, who gave me a look of annoyance. I raised an eyebrow at him as I grabbed her hand and pulled her up.

"Is something going on with you and Riley?"

"What? I can't hear you," she yelled.

I shook my head, indicating that it didn't matter, but when I looked back over my shoulder at the booth, Riley wasn't the only one watching us walk away.

My hips swayed in time to the beat as we reached the dance floor. Let him look.

Them.

I meant let *them* look. Not just Low. Ugh, whatever.

Bianca moved in time to the beat, a huge grin on her face, singing along to the song. I did my best to keep up with her, suddenly realising that maybe I wasn't quite drunk enough for dancing. She was having such a great time, though, and her enthusiasm was infectious. The song changed, and she held up a finger in my face. "Wait here a minute. I'm going to get us some shots!"

I nodded and tried not to feel self-conscious that I was now dancing alone.

I spun around, still moving in time with the music, and searched out our booth. Riley and Jamison were deep in conversation; a leggy blonde I'd never seen before, but I assumed was the girlfriend, draping herself over Jamison's side. But Low had his eyes trained on me. So much for just staying for one drink. He'd had at least three that I'd noticed. Sprawled across the booth like he owned it, he looked much more like the overconfident Low from last week. One muscled arm rested along the back of the seat, his long legs spread underneath the table. I ran my tongue over my lips. The pained look he'd worn all day was gone, his features relaxed, probably thanks to the alcohol he'd consumed. My heart sped up when he didn't look away.

I wished I wasn't wearing my work uniform. It wasn't sexy in any way, shape, or form, and the skirt was hard to dance in. I hiked it up a little, so the hem settled at mid-thigh instead of around my knees. That was better. I could move my legs enough now to dance the way I wanted to. Every beat thrummed through me, along with the alcohol. Low's eyes on me made my heart thump unevenly. I undid my top button. It was the best I could do with what I had.

Judging from the look on Low's face, he didn't mind the view. His gaze burnt through me, and though I tried to look away, my eyes kept finding his. That same tension from a week ago was back, stronger than ever.

I couldn't deny I wanted him. Still. Even though he'd ditched me. Maybe it was that I hadn't gotten what I'd wanted last week. Maybe it was that everything about him intrigued me. I didn't know, but there was something between us that crackled like tangible energy. The way I was dancing; staring at him and only him was an open invitation. One he looked like he wanted to accept. I could see his leg bouncing underneath the table, and he gripped his drink with an iron fist. He was holding himself back, and I didn't understand why.

Without warning, Low's face darkened, and I felt a set of hands on my hips. I dragged my eyes away from him and turned to find a tall blond man dancing behind me. Dancing wasn't really the right word. He was grinding on my backside.

"Hey, sweet thing, want to dance?"

I sighed. I should tell this guy to back off. But this was what I did, wasn't it? I went out. I drank. I danced. I took men home, and then for a few blissful minutes or hours, depending on the man and how drunk I was, I got to forget about my life, my past and the one mistake I'd made that I'd never forgive myself for. I'd already given Low one chance, and he hadn't taken me up on it. Who cared how hot he was or about the tension between us that was so thick I could almost see it? I'd get my fix somewhere else if he didn't want it.

I turned my body to face the groper, and his hands slid to my ass. He wasn't wasting any time, was he? He was good-looking in a slick, smooth sort of way. His features a little too sharp for my taste but not unpleasant. He had nothing on Low, though. Groper grinned at me, looking like he'd just won a prize, and I forced myself to smile back. Any other night, I would have been flirting up a storm with this guy, and I'd have him out of here and back in my bed in less than half an hour. But tonight, I wasn't feeling it.

Without warning, he lurched forward and pressed his lips against mine. I opened my mouth and let his tongue in, but it was an automatic reaction. There was no passion in the kiss for me. It was sloppy and drunk, and I felt none of the heat or excitement I'd felt in the past when I let a man kiss me. When Low had kissed me.

God. Why was I doing this? I pulled back, pushing on his chest to create a little room between us, when suddenly there was a *mile* of room between us. The groper stumbled back onto the dance floor like I'd electrocuted him. It took a second to realise that Low was behind him, pulling him off me. My mouth dropped open.

"Get your hands off her. Can't you see she isn't interested?" Low bellowed, his voice deep with just a hint of dangerous. He was completely in control of himself, though, his tone calm despite the volume. I was anything but. My pulse spiked, my heart thumping in my chest.

The groper was looking between the two of us, waiting for me to say something. When I didn't, he held his hands up in surrender and slunk away. Which left Low and me staring at each other with about a foot of dance floor between us, and a handful of onlookers, waiting to see what would happen next.

Low moved towards me until he was so close I had to tilt my head back to look up at him. I wasn't about to take a step back. I told myself it was because I wouldn't back down to him, but the heat pooling within me told me that maybe I just wanted to be closer to him.

"You eye-fuck me all night, then let that tosser kiss you? What kind of game are you playing?"

My blood instantly boiled. "I'm not the one playing games, Low. I might have been"—I raised my hands and forced my fingers into air quotes—"eye-fucking you, but you ignored an open invitation." I pushed his chest, frustration rising when he didn't budge a centimetre. "And while we're laying cards on the table, I'm not the one who left you high and dry in the middle of an alley less than a week ago. So don't talk to me about playing games. You could have had me twice now if you'd wanted. You snooze, you lose, Low."

My eyes burned into him. But right alongside the anger was something else. My traitorous body was turned on, every nerve ending coming alive in his presence. And the way he moved even closer, so close that my breasts brushed his chest, didn't help.

Just kiss me, asshole.

Every fibre of my being wanted to pick up where we left off last week. His chest heaved, and his breathing became rapid. Those ice blue eyes dropped to my lips. A little spark of excitement exploded within me. I leant in farther, my nipples thanking me for the increased friction against his chest. *Kiss me, Low. I'm standing here, putting myself on the line yet again.* He leant down just a little, and I braced myself for the impact of his lips. My eyes were shuttering when I saw him look away and he stepped back.

"I can't give you what you want." The words got lost in the music, but I didn't need to hear the words to understand him. I got the message crystal clear. My spark of excitement fizzled out as surely as if he'd thrown a bucket of cold water over me.

He spun around, no doubt searching for the exit so he could ditch me again. In his hurry to get away from me, he walked right into a bar table, the whole thing coming crashing down to the floor. Empty glasses shattered into pieces at his feet.

My hand flew to my mouth. Well, fuck. If we hadn't already made a scene, we sure as hell had now.

Low was already down on his hands and knees, trying to pick up the glass shards. Without thinking, my bar training kicked in and I dashed over and knelt down to help him. It was only when I was next to him that I saw the gash on his palm. Bright red blood spilled from the deep cut, and I saw him wince with pain as he used his other hand to cover it. Blood still dripped between his fingers, splattering on the glass shards and the dirty club floor.

In a heartbeat, I forgot how angry I was with him.

"Low." I reached out. "That looks bad, let me see."

His head snapped up, his face filled with horror. He jerked his hand away from my outstretched fingers. "Don't!" he yelled. I jumped and pulled my hand back as if I'd been burned. "Don't touch me," he said again, quieter this time. Someone in the crowd knelt next to us and moved to help clean up the glass.

"I've got this!" Low growled at the stranger. I stared at him dumbfounded. What the hell had gotten into him? I couldn't even help him with a cut? And he was yelling at complete strangers now as well?

Mark, Riley's brother, appeared and crouched next to Low. Low turned and said something in his ear. I was still kneeling, dumbfounded, so I saw when Mark's head nodded slowly. He clapped Low on the back before telling people to move back and give him some space. Mark looked to me, his face deadly serious. "You, too."

Mark walked off, presumably to get a clean-up bucket. Low didn't look up. He was crouched on the floor, his chin on his chest, clutching his hand and protecting his pile of glass like a mother hen protecting her chicks.

"Gladly," I said, my words as cold as his eyes. My cheeks blazed with embarrassment and I fought to keep hot, angry tears at bay. Confusion and self-doubt tugged at me. I was done. Done with this whole night and more than done with Low and his mixed signals.

I stood up stiffly and made my way to the exit. I didn't even have my bag, but at that moment I didn't care. All I cared about was getting out of that club and as far away from Low as possible.

8

LOW

I couldn't concentrate. My eyes kept straying from my customers, seeking Reese out. Every time she moved, I forgot an order. Every time she spoke I dropped a glass or poured the wrong beer. I couldn't get my head in the game today.

We'd worked two shifts together since the incident at the club, and she still wouldn't talk to me. I hadn't tried speaking to her either. We seemed pretty set on avoiding each other.

Across the room, her eyes met mine for a moment, before she jerked her head around. But it was long enough for me to see the anger still illuminated there. I sighed. My silence was because I didn't understand how I'd managed to fuck things up with her so royally, in such a short space of time.

"You two are the biggest downers," Jamison complained as we cleaned up the bar for the next day's trading. He was right; we were.

"Sorry, I'm just tired, I think," Reese said quietly.

Her voice cut through me, as it had all day. I closed my eyes, tossing my cloth in the sink. It had been a huge mistake to go to the club the other night, when I knew I needed to leave her alone. I'd made things so much worse. When I'd seen that guy grab her

51

hips, I hadn't even thought about it. I'd seen red; the jealousy streaking through me like a lightning bolt. When he'd leant in and kissed her, I'd wanted to kill him, right then and there with my bare hands, in front of three hundred witnesses.

I rubbed at my eyes, a headache beginning to pound behind them. This was the shift that would never end. Her presence engulfed me every minute—the slightest of touches as we both reached for a bottle, her perfume drifting around me, filling my nose. The tension between us was layered so thick, I could almost taste it, and the unnatural silence that descended over us was so awkward, it was the elephant in the room. It was too much, and I couldn't take it a second longer.

I spun around to face Jamison. "I'm going to take off. Do you mind?"

The bar closed in half an hour, and I didn't have to ask his permission; I outranked him. But he was a mate, and it was enough that Reese hated me right now. I didn't need to add anyone else to the list.

My stomach dropped at the thought they might all want nothing to do with me once they found out anyway.

Jamison shook his head. "Go, we're just counting down the clock."

I grabbed my wallet and keys and left without saying goodbye to anyone. I felt Reese's eyes burning holes in my back as I fled through the glass doors that led out to the racetrack.

Outside, the sun splashed oranges and pinks across the horizon. I breathed raggedly, letting the fresh air flood my lungs. Part of me was freed by every step I took away from Reese and the tension between us. But the other half of me craved her presence like a drug I couldn't say no to. I'd never had more than a fleeting interest in anyone, yet something about her made me want more. Maybe it was solely because I couldn't have her, but maybe not. Something deep in my gut told me it was just her. I wanted to find out, but I'd stuffed up any chance of that. There were so many things I'd do differently if I could go back. If I'd never met Mason. If I hadn't been so fucking drunk and stupid.

I wandered down to the racetrack railing and leant on it, the edge cutting into my skin. I welcomed the sting. How had this all gotten so complicated? Her face, full of hurt and anger, burned in my memory. After I'd cut my hand on that damn glass, panic had coursed through me, fear for her making my blood run cold. Keeping her away from it and safe had been my only concern. My fear had come out as anger, though, and I'd yelled at her. Guilt swirled through my stomach. I hated myself for the way I'd acted. She had every right to hate me right now.

A horse galloped past me on a training run, but I barely registered its presence. I wanted to rewind the clock and go back to the day Reese had arrived at the bar. Go back to the fun flirtation we'd had going. The tension between us was tangible from the minute I'd laid eyes on her. I'd wanted her. And the fact she hadn't been shy about pursuing what she wanted? Hot. Everything about her appealed to me. From her silky, almost-black hair to her deep brown eyes, her sassy attitude to her confidence. And there was something vulnerable about her that she tried to hide. She played her cards close to her chest, which only made me more intrigued. Then Mason had dropped his fucking bombshell and everything had gotten messed up.

I needed to leave her alone and get my personal shit together. I knew it, but I didn't want to.

Frustrated, I pushed off the railing and headed for the back area of the racetrack. Holding my staff-swipe key up to a little black scanner, I waited for the light to blink green. The door lock sprang open, and I slipped through, making sure it locked behind me.

People bustled around, leading horses to stalls, loading others onto trailers to make their way back to their home stables. Some would stay a night or longer and leave when they'd completed their races.

"Low!"

I nodded in greeting to the trainer but tucked my head back down and moved past. People were talking. The bar crew's concerns about my abrupt change in behaviour hadn't gone unnoticed by the stable staff. I'd heard their whispered questions about me, asking where I'd been last week and if it had anything to do with 'the new bar girl.'

I couldn't remember ever going a week without flirting or chatting up customers at the bar. I'd stopped participating in conversations, and I don't think I'd laughed since I'd been back from my week off. Normally I would have stopped to chat with almost everyone in the outer areas of the racecourse, asking them about whichever horse they had running. But I'd been on autopilot ever since I'd gotten that text.

I hadn't even told Jamison, who'd been my best friend since I'd come back to Sydney years ago. I'd tried to find the words, tried to find a time to tell him, but something always stopped me. I didn't want to worry him and burden him with problems I'd created for myself. My doctor had encouraged me to tell some-one, to get myself a support team while we waited for news. But how did I even begin, when I could barely wrap my own head around it all? The doctor had been kind and patient, explaining the procedure in simple terms that my shell-shocked brain had still struggled to comprehend. After a while, he'd taken pity on me, handed over a stack of pamphlets, and told me to make an appointment with the specialist in three months.

My grandparents would freak out if they knew. They'd already lived through enough drama with my mother over the years. I couldn't tell them I was just as bad, in my own way. Which only left Jamison to tell. But talking wasn't going to help anything anyway. What was done was done.

I was alone in this.

The stables loomed ahead of me. They homed close to a hundred horses when the big races ran. I let myself into the quiet interior. The only noises, the soft whickering and snorting of the horses as I passed their stalls. The air was cool, and the light dim. No one had bothered to turn on the artificial lights yet, so only the last of the sunlight trickling through the windows lit the cavernous building.

My pace increased as I neared Lijah's stall. She stuck her giant head over the top of the doors as I approached. My shoulders relaxed as I reached to touch her. "Hey, girl." I spoke as if in church. Speaking any louder than quiet conversation was never a good idea around a lot of horses, but something about coming in here felt almost religious. It was a place my soul always felt at ease. My troubles were always a little lighter as I stroked the neck of a horse. I stepped close to the door, unlocking it to let Lijah out. She turned her head to nuzzle at my shirt pocket. The corners of my mouth lifted, and I was surprised to find I remembered how to smile. I pulled out one of the apples I'd swiped on my way in and gave it to her, smiling as she chewed through it with ease.

"You like those, huh, girl?" I smoothed my hand along her coat and leant in against her, resting my head on her mane. My confession tumbled from my lips. "I fucked things up this time, Lijah. And I have no idea how to fix it." I let out a shaky breath. Her apple gone, Lijah stood still, letting me draw comfort from her. The tension across my shoulders eased. I needed comfort today.

The rattle of the lock as someone opened the stable door let me know I wasn't alone. My breath hitched as that ever-present tension flared to life once more.

Reese.

I knew it before I looked up to confirm it. What was she doing out here? My heart raced, excitement coursing through me at her nearness, then dropped just as quick when I realised she'd spotted me and was trying to get back out the door.

I should let her go.

"You don't have to go, Reese." My mouth was clearly not taking commands from my brain today.

How was my voice so calm? On the inside, I was anything but.

I looked around for a brush, a comb, a feed bag—anything so I'd have something to do while she made her decision. She was still hovering in the doorway.

Stay. Just stay, Reese.

The words burned on my tongue, but I bit down to stop myself from voicing them. My brain yelled that I was an idiot, and I should go grab her hand, lace our fingers together, and lead her in from the door. Judging by how long she stood there for, she was as confused as I was.

"It's okay. I didn't realise you were here. I shouldn't be back here anyway." Her gaze darted around as if the horse police were going to jump out at any minute. Or maybe she just didn't want to look at me.

"You can be back here if you're with me. No one will stop you." I went back to brushing Lijah's coat, so my hands had something to do. She tossed her head, whinnying, probably sensing my nerves.

Reese would run, I could tell without even looking at her. Out here, in my quiet place, I felt different than I had for the past two weeks. I felt more like me. The me I wanted her to know.

"Please stay." I forced the words from my lips. "Do you want to come meet Lijah?"

9

REESE

*W*ell, blow me down. Low had manners. And he'd invited me to meet the most beautiful chestnut mare I'd ever seen. Her reddish-brown coat gleamed in the waning afternoon light, her intelligent eyes trained on Low. My anger was still there, simmering away, but he seemed different, and it made me pause.

Everything about Low's posture had changed in the short time he'd been gone from the bar. His shoulders had lost the tight tension that had been plaguing him all day, and with his shirt sleeves rolled up and his tie sticking out of his pocket, he looked casual and relaxed. And hot. So much hotter than Asshole Low. This new, quiet side of him that seemed to love horses intrigued me.

I nodded and walked down the aisle, my footsteps tentative. He hadn't heard me come through the doors at first. I'd watched him as he'd held the horse's head and after a moment, stepped in closer to her. Such a quiet, tender moment between the man and the animal, it was like watching something sacred. Something not meant for me to witness. That quiet peace you got as time seemed to stand still was as familiar to me as breathing. It was the reason I'd sneaked in to see Mabel every day since I'd moved here.

The desire to walk away from Low was still strong. I didn't want to get into yet another argument with him; we'd already had too many of those in the short time we'd known each other. But I wasn't going to try to make up with him either. That was on him.

"She's amazing." I reached up to pat the horse's velvety nose. She sniffed at my hand, quickly losing interest in favour of Low's, which held treats.

"Here. Want to give her some?" He passed me a few chunks of apple. "She loves apple, this one."

I held my hand out flat under Lijah's nose, smiling at the familiar rasp of horse lips over my palm.

Low shifted his weight, his arm brushing against mine. "Listen, I wanted to say this to you tomorrow anyway, but since you're here…I owe you an apology."

I snorted. Yeah, he did. A mighty big one.

When I lifted my head, his eyes sought mine, the honesty in his gaze pure. I crossed my arms over my chest but let the frown slip from my face. "Okay, I'm listening."

"I just… I have stuff going on that I'm not dealing with well. Stuff I'm not dealing with at all if I'm being truthful."

He kept on stroking Lijah's neck, but he didn't look away. He seemed sad, the corners of his eyes downturned. "It's no excuse for the way I've been acting towards you, though. I…well, I guess don't really know how to deal with you either."

My brow wrinkled, and I sighed. It wasn't exactly the greatest apology, but at least he was trying.

He shook his head and squeezed my upper arm. The heat from his hand radiated through my thin work blouse. "I'm stuffing this up. I can tell by the look on your face." He ran a hand through his hair. "I really am sorry. I'm not always such an asshole. The way I yelled at you in the club the other night… that's not me. I don't do things like that."

He sounded tired and resigned. But he sounded sincere. He held my arm in a gentle grip, and I tried not to focus on how much I liked it. I wanted to accept his apology. Maybe he didn't deserve to be let off the hook so easily, but he looked like someone had kicked his puppy, and I didn't want to add to the weight I saw piled on his shoulders. He wasn't the only one who didn't know how to deal with their problems. I could relate to that. Plus, I didn't do grudges well, and I just wanted to go back to being friends. I was sick of the drama.

"Okay."

"Okay? That's it?"

"Would you prefer I don't forgive you?"

"No, of course not."

"Well, accept my okay then. It's the best you'll get for now." I gave him a little grin before Lijah lurched forward, thrusting her head between us.

"Sorry, Lijah, did we stop paying attention to you?" I laughed, as I fed her the last of the apple. I was relieved at the break in the tension. But I needed to say one more thing to him, because I was a prime example of why bottling things up was a shitty idea.

"Listen, Low, I don't know what's eating at you, or what you're dealing with, but I can see your friends are worried about you. They want to help you with whatever is going on, and if you want to spill to them, awesome. But if you need to talk to someone you aren't close with, I'm here."

His eyebrows rose, but I continued before he could cut me off.

"I went through some of my own stuff last year, and I didn't talk to anyone about it. I was too ashamed to talk to my friends. I didn't want their pity or their judgement or whatever else their reaction might have been. I know all about pushing people away.

I wrote the book on it." I looked away from him, his gaze too intense.

"I'm just saying, sometimes it's easier to talk to someone you haven't got a history with. And I'm here. Use me." A blush rose in my cheeks at the memory of the way we'd used each other in the alleyway. That was a bad choice of words. I hoped he didn't think I'd meant it like that.

But all I saw in his expression was an echo of my own old hurt. Something was eating this man alive. I didn't dare move. I'd meant what I'd said. I wanted him to confide in me. Truthfully, part of it was I wanted to know why he'd ditched me in that alleyway, and why he'd reacted so aggressively at the club. Why we'd gone from the beginning of a flirty friendship to these awkward silences, unable to even look at each other. I didn't understand any of it. But a bigger part of me wanted to help him. I wanted to spare him some of the pain I'd felt, if I could. Our problems may not have been the same, but I understood pain and could recognise it in others. The silence hung in the air between us.

"So, you like horses?" He quietly changed the subject. I wasn't disappointed. I wanted to help, but I respected his need to keep it to himself for now.

"Very much so." I nodded. "It's the whole reason I applied for this job. The thought of being around horses all day, even if from the distance of the bar, was too good to pass up. You too, I guess? Lijah here seems to like you."

"Lijah is my buddy. She knows all my secrets."

"Does she? How long have you been sneaking out here to have deep and meaningful conversations with her?" I joked.

"Well, Lijah is only two years old, but I think I was nine the first time I snuck out here."

"You've been coming here since you were nine? How's that?"

"My grandparents own this racetrack."

My mouth dropped open. "They own this whole thing?" Well,

that tidbit of information brought up a lot of questions. And answered a few others.

"Yeah. The whole thing. The track and the breeding farm on the other side. Though they aren't involved in the day to day running like they used to be." He tilted his head. "Do you want to come sit down? I have to clean Lijah's tack and I can't do it standing here."

I nodded and we sat on the hay bales beneath the window, the straw sticking into my calves, its scratch familiar. I couldn't count how many times I'd cleaned my own tack sitting on a bale just like this one. Though the stables I'd been sitting in were a lot less fancy than this.

"So how is it you're the grandson of some obviously wealthy people, but you're cleaning your own tack? And working at the bar? Wouldn't they give you a more glamorous job?" I tucked my hands under my knees and kicked at some straw on the floor. It was difficult to sit this close to him. My fingers itched to reach out and touch him, and just thinking of touching him stirred parts of me that really needed to be kept in line. We obviously didn't work in a sexual way. We'd tried that twice, and both times had ended in me being humiliated. But maybe, if we could keep our attraction in check, we could be friends. God knows I needed a friend.

He smiled. I liked this smile, from this version of Low. It wasn't the arrogant, flirty smile I'd gotten the first day we'd met. And it wasn't the forced smiles I'd seen from him in the last few days. It was natural. Casual. A 'we're friends' smile, the kind you didn't have to think about. I wanted to see more of them from him.

"Somewhere a bit more glamorous would have been nice, but my grandparents are hard-working people. They built all this from nothing. They wanted me to learn every aspect of the business, and I agree. Plus"—he grinned at me, with just a hint of flirty Low shining through—"I like the opportunity to meet pretty girls every day."

I rolled my eyes at him. "I bet you do. Your grandparents have probably been begging you to move on to a new position, but you want to stay for the free perv."

He chuckled. "There might be some truth in that."

I liked his laugh, even better than his smile. "So is Lijah yours then?"

"Yep, sure is. Her dam was a birthday present from my grandparents when I was a kid. Lijah here is her most promising filly, and secretly, she's my favourite. She's running in the races later this week."

I sat up straighter. "Yeah? That's exciting."

Low's expression became animated. "Yeah, I can't wait. Her trainer has been great with her. We think she should do okay, but you're never 100 percent sure until they're out there." He paused, examining a non-existent spot on his saddle. "This is what I'd like to be doing one day, you know?"

"Cleaning saddles? Not hugely ambitious, are you?"

"Smart-ass. I meant working more with the horses. Training them."

"Why one day? What's stopping you from doing it now? Surely the hook-ups from the bar aren't that appealing?" Working in the bar, while knowing you could be out here where the action was didn't compute with me at all.

He shrugged. "I need to earn it. I meant what I said about learning each aspect of the business, but the more I see of it, the more I'm sure my heart is here. In the stables, in the training yards. But I don't have the experience yet. I don't want to be just the grandson of the owners. I want the respect that only comes with paying your dues."

My chest tightened. He was so lucky to have all this. To be around these beautiful animals. To have opportunities and a career with them, one that would fulfil him. One that he wouldn't have to walk away from. I tried to push my surge of jealousy aside. "Haven't you been coming here all your life? That must make you more experienced than most."

He sighed and scrubbed harder at the imaginary spot he seemed determine to remove. I saw him wrestling with his thoughts and didn't push him. He'd tell me what was on his mind if he wanted to. Or he wouldn't. But I'd said he could talk to me about anything and I wanted to prove it.

So I waited. Eventually he looked up, letting out a long breath. "My mother is a junkie. She could never hold down a steady job, when she could even be bothered working, so we moved around a lot. We couch-surfed her junkie friends' places, or slept in her car when things got really bad." He started scrubbing again. "Every now and then, I guess when she got desperate, she'd dump me at my grandparents' place."

He smiled wistfully at me. "I loved when that happened. My grandparents are so kind and generous. It astounds me how someone as messed up as my mother came from them."

His smile quickly fell, though, disgust creeping into his voice as he continued. "So right before I turned ten, my mother dumped me at my grandparents' farm, then disappeared. This wasn't unusual, she did it often enough." He laughed, but it sounded forced and his smile didn't meet his eyes. "Having a kid around is inconvenient when you only live for your next high."

I nodded, not wanting to interrupt him. A lump was forming in my throat, so I doubted I could have found the words anyway.

"By the time my birthday rolled around, she'd been gone six months—the longest time we'd ever not heard from her. My grandparents tried to shelter me from it. But I knew they thought she'd overdosed somewhere. I'd overhear them on the phone to the hospital, and the police came to our house once or twice to talk to them."

Low glanced up at me and I tried to keep my reaction from showing on my face. "You know what, though? I didn't even care.

For the first time I was going to school regularly, and I'd made friends. I loved living with my grandparents. There was always food for dinner, and I had my own bedroom. And they had horses. The day they gave me my first horse was the best day of my life." The happy memory lit him up from the inside. I wondered if that was how I looked when I spoke about horses as well.

"That was Lijah's dam?"

He nodded, but then his face clouded over. "I'd had her for a week, when my mother resurfaced. She came to my school and picked me up early one day. Said we'd go out for ice cream and then she'd take me back to my grandparents. I wasn't excited to see her, but I wanted to leave school early. And I wanted ice cream. I would have gone with anyone who'd promised me an ice cream."

His shoulders slumped. "I should have known she was full of shit. She had no money. She would have just spent it on drugs if she had. I don't know why I believed her. I should have known she'd be too selfish to do anything that might have made someone other than herself happy. But I just kept on believing things would be different and kept on giving her second chances."

He put the saddle down on the hay bale. "She didn't take me back to my grandparents. She took off with me in one of her ratty boyfriend's cars, and we drove for days. I had no idea where we were, and she wouldn't let me contact my grandparents. Years went by before I got to see them again."

"Wow," I whispered, swallowing hard. Nobody deserved a childhood like that. A flicker of anger ignited within me. How could his mother do that to him? He could have had a normal childhood—a wonderful childhood, with his grandparents, but she'd been too selfish to allow it.

He scrubbed his hands over his face. "Yeah."

I didn't know what to say, but I'd listened like I promised. He didn't need my pity. It wasn't like anything I could say would change the past. My fingers itched to reach out and touch him, to give him some comfort, but I didn't know if he'd want that either. Needing to do something with my hands, I picked up a bridle from the stack and cleaned it absent-mindedly.

Low shot me a look of surprise, but we cleaned side by side in silence for a while before he said, "You look like you know what you're doing there."

I nodded. "It's not the first time I've cleaned a bridle."

"You ride?"

"I used to."

"Used to? So not anymore?"

"No, not anymore."

Silence stretched out between us as I shifted around on my hay bale. Where the silence between us had been comfortable moments earlier, I now felt twitchy. He was waiting for me to elaborate, but I couldn't bring myself to. I jumped up, walking back to Lijah, patting her one last time before I forced myself to look at Low.

I bit my lip, needing to leave before I could run my mouth. "I should let you get her ready for the night. But thanks for this." I tilted my head towards the horse. He hadn't moved from his hay bale, still studying me with those ice blue eyes.

"You don't have to go, Reese. I wasn't going to press you to share just because I had. This isn't a tit for tat situation."

The heat rose in my cheeks, and I was glad it was almost dark in the barn. "It's getting late. I should get home."

He stood up. "I'll walk you out."

I shook my head, backing away. I didn't want to walk out with him. That would just give me more time to say things I really didn't want to voice, or for silence to drag out between us and things to get awkward again. I didn't want that. This being friends with him business seemed to be working out better so far, but it was a tremulous link. I didn't want to break it.

"I'm fine. I'll see you tomorrow?" Not giving him time to answer, I jogged down the aisle of the barn and yanked on the heavy door. He didn't move to follow me. I slid the door closed, leaving myself standing on the other side. Alone. Just like I'd been for the past twelve months.

10

REESE

*J*amison slammed the dishwasher door on the last load of the day and switched it on. The display panel lit up and a quiet hum filled the room. "All I have to say is thank God you two sorted your shit out. I don't know what you said, or did"—he paused, looking like he was trying to stifle his own amusement—"but this shift was way more pleasant than yesterday's."

Low looked over at me and smiled, his friend smile. The smile that made his eyes warm and showed off his straight white teeth and the slight dimple in one cheek I hadn't noticed before. He'd attempted to keep things pleasant between us today, starting casual conversations and shooting me that look. Each one dissolved a little more of the lingering tension until I'd begun smiling back at him.

"Shut up, Jam," Low joked, "I'm always a delight."

Jamison snorted, and I raised an eyebrow. Low winked at me. My breath caught a little, and my attempt to muffle it resulted in a coughing fit. Low clapped me on the back, and I smiled weakly at him.

"It's just good to see you both happier today. That's all I'm saying." Jamison looked at the clock on the wall. "I'm out. You guys right to lock up?"

I nodded, rifling through my bag for my keys.

Low moved to stand beside me. "Actually, Reese, can you stay back tonight for a few minutes? We have to count stock at the end of the month and I want to go over a few things with you before then."

I paused. We'd had a slow shift. He could have shown me the stocktake stuff more than once today. "Uh, sure?"

I tried to quiet the hopeful little voice in my head that whispered, *he wants to be alone with you*. The 'just being friends' thing had worked well so far. I wasn't about to ruin it.

After Jamison left, Low pulled up the bar's accounts on his laptop and we spent a professional forty minutes poring over it. He showed me how to run the stock level reports and how to reconcile the results. We went through last quarter's stocktake, and I jotted a few notes on my Post-its as he explained each step we'd need to take. I was trying to memorise the stock locations when he threw his pen down on the table and ran his hand through his hair, pushing it off his face. "Screw this, I'm over it. Do you want to come down and see Lijah with me?"

"I'd love that," I responded quickly. Going to the dentist would have been more fun than looking at stock levels, and I'd never pass up an opportunity to go out to the stables.

Somehow, every evening for the next four days, that's where the two of us ended up after our shifts. We always made some excuse to stay later than the others, and then we'd slip down to the stables to see Lijah. Standing there, in the semi dark with Low by my side, and Lijah eating treats out of the palm of my hand, became my favourite part of the day.

Early on Friday evening, I hung over the fence of a paddock, watching Lijah prance around in the twilight. Low stood next to me, our arms touching, his eyes trained on her. We'd talked about tons of random stuff during the week while we'd been out here.

All of it frivolous. He'd shared something so private, when he'd told me about his mother earlier in the week, but I had yet to let him in, in the same way. I didn't bring his family up again, and he hadn't asked about mine. Instead, we'd talked about TV shows and movies, music, and sports. Discussed if Riley and Bianca were secretly dating behind our backs. Talked about the best bars in town, and how the public transport sucked.

Lijah pranced over to us and nuzzled her nose into my shoulder. Here, with the setting sun, a beautiful animal and fresh air, I was content. Lijah, Low, and the track were all helping to fill the gaping void I'd been carrying around since I'd been forced to leave my home behind. The peace I found here soothed the ragged edges of my soul.

"Why don't you ride anymore?" Low's voice was quiet, his question no more than a ripple in the silence around us as he pulled me from my thoughts. I flicked a glance at him and realised his eyes were no longer trained on Lijah. I drummed my fingers on the rough wood of the fence and debated whether to answer. The old, familiar guilt rose within me.

"I don't want to tell you."

"Why not?"

"You won't like me very much if I do."

He tucked a piece of hair behind my ear and ran his finger along my jaw, tilting it, forcing me to face him.

My breath became uneven. We'd been working on this friend thing all week, and it had been going well. I'd pushed aside the tingles when he touched me accidentally and ignored that simmering heat that always seemed to be present between us. We worked as friends. But that hadn't been a 'friend' sort of gesture.

"You don't have to tell me, but I doubt anything you say could change my opinion of you. I didn't even mean to ask; it just sort of slipped out. It's so obvious how much happiness you get from the horses. I don't understand why you wouldn't want to ride one."

Moving away from his touch, I dropped my chin onto my folded arms. He'd been so honest with me when he'd spoken about his childhood. I hadn't told anyone what I'd done, and the weight of keeping such a huge event in my life a secret was crippling. But it was terrifying even considering voicing the words out loud. Was this what he'd felt before he'd told me about his mother? Had he worried I'd judge him? I sighed. I didn't know where to start.

"I used to ride. All the time. My family owns a stable, and my dad teaches horse riding to local kids. Their place is nothing like this, though." I gestured around me at the vast property, filled with its dozens of paddocks, barns, and million-dollar horses. "Dad still worked a day job, but he taught lessons on the side for extra income. We rode every day before I'd go to school and he'd go to work. It was a special thing we did together. My mother hated riding, so it was always just the two of us.

"They had another baby just after I turned ten. I have a little sister. Her name is Gemma." My voice cracked. I hadn't spoken her name out loud in a year now. My shoulders slumped inwards as I trained my eyes on the dirt.

He moved closer, so our arms were touching again, and his head tilted towards me. "It's okay, we can talk about something else."

I shook my head. "I just don't talk about it often."

Out of the corner of my eye, I saw him nod, then I focused down on the ground again. It would be easier to get the next bit out if I didn't look him directly.

"Last year, my dad got a promotion at work and had to put in longer hours. So I took over most of the riding lessons for him. I was first year at uni, and I needed a part-time job, so it worked out for both of us. I took a group of students out one afternoon, one of them being my little sister…" I trailed off, thinking about that day. My throat tightened.

"I saddled up the horses, like always. The lesson went fine at first, but..." I bit at the corner of my thumbnail and debated making another run for the exit. "I don't want you to hate me," I whispered.

"I won't hate you, Reese, I promise. Trust me." His warm voice had a soothing effect on me. The words were on the tip of my tongue. I wanted to tell him. I really did. It would be a relief for him to know, to be able to talk to someone about it.

"She was the most experienced rider in the group, even though she was only nine, so I'd given the tame old nags to the other kids. She could handle the horse, though. He was a good, solid animal; he didn't spook easily. Except this time, he bucked." Words began tumbling from my lips. Now that I'd started, I needed to finish before the words imploded within me. "She tried so hard to hold on, but he wanted her off. He threw her straight into the fence."

My throat had closed up, I was sure of it. Pressure spread through my chest and behind my eyes. I was suffocating. I sucked in a deep breath, but it wasn't enough to quell the emotions and tears dripping down my cheeks. I wiped them away, not wanting to cry in front of him.

"She landed so awkwardly, and then his hooves came down on top of her. She looked like a broken rag doll, just lying there in the dust." I tried to steady my voice. "I've gone over it in my mind a million times. I must have done the cinch up too tight, or maybe too loose, and it slipped. That's all I can think of. That his saddle hurt, and he wanted it gone. I was distracted by my phone, too busy messaging a friend from uni about some guy she was dating. I don't remember if I checked the saddles the way I normally did." My head ached, full of dark memories. I thought it would feel better if I told someone, but the words stabbed like jabs directly to my heart.

"Jesus." Low blew out a long, deep breath, as if he'd been holding it. He took my hand, and I found I'd clenched it into a fist. Low eased it open and massaged my aching fingers.

"I don't remember the trip to the hospital. I'm not sure if I went in the ambulance or if I drove myself there. All I remember is sitting in the waiting room, waiting for my parents to arrive. And I remember the shaking. I couldn't stop the shaking no matter how much I rubbed at my arms and legs."

I sighed and twisted my neck, trying to relieve the tension. I looked down at our hands. Low had stopped his massage, but he hadn't taken his hand away. He moved his thumb in slow circles over my palm.

"She wasn't okay, was she?"

Tears spilled over again, but it was a losing battle to blink them back. I shook my head.

"Here's the worst bit. I don't even know for sure. The surgeon came out and told us that along with broken ribs and other superficial injuries, he thought she'd damaged her spinal cord." I didn't bother mentioning that even though the doctor hadn't confirmed anything right then and there, his face told us everything we'd needed to know.

Silence fell between us, and Low squeezed my hand. "That wasn't your fault, though, Reese. It was an accident. You know that, right?"

I shook my head again. "Of course it's my fault, Low! I was the one in charge. I was the one who saddled that damn horse. I gave him to my little sister, and now she won't ever be able to ride again. Or walk. She's in a wheelchair for life because I thought my social life was more important than being thorough."

"I don't agree with that at all. Accidents happen. You couldn't have foreseen this."

"Yeah, well, you're the only one who sees it that way. My dad wasn't as forgiving as you." I sniffed, remembering the way I'd stood in the hospital waiting room, while my father screamed every obscenity under the sun at me. My mother hadn't stopped him, too consumed in her own grief over my sister to worry about me.

"Dad blamed me. Said I'd always been irresponsible, and he should've never trusted me to run the riding school. He wouldn't even let me see my sister." I let the tears run down my face freely.

Low reached out and pulled me into his arms. He ran his hand up and down my back, over and over as I cried into his shoulder.

"I'm so sorry," he murmured into my hair.

He pressed his lips to my forehead before he pulled away and cupped my face in his hands, using his thumbs to wipe away my tears. "But your dad is wrong. He would have been in shock and not thinking clearly. How was he when things calmed down?"

His gaze was unwavering, and for a second, I wanted to lean in and kiss him. It would be so easy. Kiss him, take him home. I could forget about all this shit for a few hours if I could lose myself in him.

I pulled back a little. I had to stop thinking of him like that. He wasn't the Band-Aid to my problems.

"I have no idea. He kicked me out. Told me to pack my bags and get out of his sight, because he didn't know how he could look at me again without remembering how I'd destroyed their lives. I left that night." Those had been his exact words. They were burned into my memory as clearly as my name and date of birth.

"How long ago was this?"

"Just over a year."

"A year! And you haven't spoken to them at all?"

"No."

"Jesus…"

We turned back to watch Lijah, but he kept an arm around my shoulders, and I snuggled a little closer to him, enjoying the comfort of his body, even if I didn't deserve it.

"So…what? You moved out and haven't spoken to your family since?"

I shrugged. "Pretty much. I couch-surfed for a few days, then I found a job at a local pub that had rooms above it for rent. But I couldn't stand being so close to home. Driving past the hospital, knowing my family was inside, and not knowing how Gemma was...I kept running into people in town who knew me. They all wanted updates on my sister, and I just wanted to die all over again every time I had no answer for them. I only lasted a few days before I moved out here."

"What happened to uni?"

"Gave it up to work full-time."

I didn't expand any further, but Low still had questions. "That's a shame. What were you studying?"

"Bachelor of Veterinary Sciences."

"You were going to be a vet?"

"Mmmhmm."

"That doesn't surprise me. You'd be an amazing vet, if how you are with Lijah is anything to go by." He paused, his eyebrows drawing together as if he were working something out.

I didn't say anything.

"You gave up riding to punish yourself, didn't you?" His voice was flat.

"I just didn't want to anymore," I whispered. I couldn't bear to peek at him, though I felt his gaze burning into the side of my face.

"What have you been doing for the last year then?"

"Working. Drinking. Having a lot of sex," I admitted with a short laugh.

Low abruptly moved his arm from my shoulders, and I turned to look at him, instantly missing the weight. To my surprise, his eyes were dark, his mouth drawn in a tight line.

What did I say wrong?

He hadn't looked angry when I'd confessed about my sister. Was he jealous I'd been having sex? That was ridiculous. It's not like we were together. We were barely even friends.

"You've been sleeping around?" The cool tone to his voice shocked me even more than his facial expression had.

My gaze narrowed. A chill rolled over me that had nothing to do with the temperature. I didn't like his tone, and the accusation was bloody rich coming from him.

"I have sex. And no, I don't have a steady partner, so if that's your definition of sleeping around, then yeah, I guess that's what I've been doing." Sometimes the only way to forget my own problems was to be oblivious. Alcohol and sex did that for me. I wasn't about to apologise to him for it.

"Tell me you've been using condoms." Urgency replaced the anger as he searched my face, waiting for my reply. His gaze was too intense, so I turned away. But he grabbed the tops of my arms, forcing me to look at him.

"Well? Have you?"

"Who are you, Low? My keeper? How is that any of your business?" I shrugged him off, and he let go of me, stepping backwards. "I don't need you slut shaming me."

"Slut shame—" His eyes widened, and he held his hands up in surrender. "Shit, Reese, I'm not! I swear, I…" He paced back and forth, the dirt of the paddock floating up in clouds around his shoes. He came to a halt, his eyes boring into mine. "You're right, you're right. God, I can't believe I said that. I'm sorry. It really isn't my business."

I folded my arms across my chest. "I'm no worse than you."

"Agreed. If anyone gets an award for sleeping around here, it's me. It's just… I'm just worried about you, that's all. I only wanted to make sure you were safe."

My shoulders relaxed a little. "I'm a big girl, Low. I've been taking care of myself for a long time now. I don't need you or anyone else looking out for me."

He sighed, and I let the subject drop. One minute he was sweet and kind, the next minute he was a standoffish jerk. And yet, no matter how he acted, or how many times I told myself we were just friends, the sexual attraction between us was there, always bubbling below the surface.

Frustration simmered in my blood. Just as we'd been getting close, just as I thought we'd reached some common ground where we could share thoughts that went deeper than what our favourite pizza toppings were, he went cold. And just like that, I was again no longer certain where we stood. The only thing I was certain of was I'd done enough sharing for one afternoon.

11

REESE

*L*ow walked me home after we left the racecourse. We walked in silence, both lost in our own thoughts. He kissed me on the cheek in a brotherly fashion at the door to my building, and I didn't invite him in. I wasn't angry, but I was still annoyed. I needed time alone to process.

I dumped my bag on the nearest packing box, poured myself a glass of wine, and sank into the lounge I'd bought second-hand online. It was old and threadbare but comfortable. I grabbed the stack of Post-it notes on my coffee table and doodled on them, while I let the drone of reality TV repeats calm my thoughts. When the third episode of *Deadliest Catch* finished, I realised I'd been doodling Low's name over and over. Sighing, I ripped the note off, crumpled it into a ball, and pitched it across the room. I was ridiculous.

My phone buzzed from over on the packing box. I eyed it, the message tone pinging. After my dad had kicked me out, I'd left my phone on the nightstand of my childhood bedroom. I hadn't wanted it. I didn't want to deal with people ringing to get the gossip about Gemma. I'd welcomed the clean slate a new number and a new home brought me. But leaving everything and everyone behind and starting over meant for a long time, no one, apart from the occasional telemarketer called me.

Until I'd lost my mind for a minute that first day at the race-track and called my dad. His return calls had tapered off when I'd refused to answer any of them. But he'd never sent a text message. He'd always been old school like that. I wasn't even sure he knew how. But maybe it was my mum? Or my sister? Had he told them he suspected I'd tried to call them? I bit my thumbnail as I berated myself yet again for calling him in the first place. I couldn't bear it if this message was more of the hate he'd spewed at me in the hospital.

Reminding myself it could just as easily be an SMS from the bank or the woman who waxed my eyebrows, I picked up the phone and took it back to the lounge with me. I hit the little green message icon and breathed a sigh of relief when I didn't recognise the number. Not my parents.

I was out of line before. I'm sorry.

I frowned at it. The phone buzzed in my hand again.

It's Low, by the way. I got your number from your staff file.

I rolled my eyes. Of course he did. The heir to the racecourse throne would have access to everyone's personal information, wouldn't he? I wanted to be annoyed about the invasion of privacy, heir or not, but I didn't have it in me. In a display of girly-ness I was too old for, I let a little thrill shoot through me. He'd gone out of his way to get my number.

It's fine, don't worry about it. My thumb hovered over the send button before I pushed it.

It buzzed back within seconds.

It's not. I want to make it up to you. Can I call you?

My stomach flipped, and I ran a hand through my hair. Then I shook my head at my foolishness. It's not like he could see my hair all flat from lying on the lounge for the past three hours. My phone rang before I'd even composed a reply.

"Hello?"

"Hey." His voice was deep and sexy as hell. My heartbeat picked up. I hoped I wasn't breathing heavily into the phone because I was suddenly out of breath.

"Can you go out on your balcony?"

I paused. "Uh, yeah, I guess. Why?"

Standing up, I padded in bare feet over to the glass sliding door. I unlocked it and stepped out onto the cool tiles of the little balcony and grasped the metal rail. My apartment wasn't high, being on the third floor, but there weren't many other high-rises around, so I had a nice view.

I hadn't realised how late it had gotten while I'd been watching trash TV. The streetlights cast little circles of light, and the moon was almost full. The breeze blew around me, the temperature balmy. I loved nights like this, when the coolness of spring gave way, and a hint of summer came through on the breeze. I didn't even need a jacket out here tonight. It was perfect.

"Look over to your left," Low said in my ear.

The racetrack and stables were closed for the night, but there were still lights placed at intervals around the edge of the property. I scanned the track, wondering what I was looking for. Then underneath a light, in the paddock where I sneaked in each morning to see Mabel, something moved. I squinted, as the something waved at me.

"Is that you under the light? What are you doing?"

He moved closer to the centre of the light. He was sitting on Lijah's back, the horse's dark form standing quiet and patient, waiting for an order from him.

"Can you come back down here?" he asked, his tone polite. "Please? There's something I should have told you before, instead of flipping out at you. I want to explain." He went quiet and I could hear him breathing.

His horse whinnied. "Lijah says she misses you."

A grin pulled at the corner of my mouth. "Tell Lijah I only saw her a few hours ago. And that I need ten minutes. I'm still in my uniform."

"We'll wait."

I hung up without saying goodbye, then slipped back into the apartment. I took a deep breath, in an attempt to calm down. Friends. Friends. Friends. I stopped and scrawled it in block letters on a Post-it, ripped it off, and slapped it to the door hard enough to leave my palm stinging. "Friends. Friends. Friends," I chanted as I slipped on a pair of jeans, my boots, and a T-shirt. I flicked my head upside down, fluffing up my hair, then flicked it back, watching it fall over my shoulders.

I was ready and out the door of my apartment in less than nine minutes. My strides were long and quick, and I told myself I was in a rush because the deserted street was dark and kind of creepy. It had nothing to do with wanting to see Low again.

He was waiting where I'd seen him from the balcony. Lijah wore only a bridle around her head, her back bare underneath Low's denim-clad thighs. They stood right outside of Mabel's paddock, and she came trotting over as soon as she saw me. I gave Low an apologetic smile and stopped, rubbing Mabel's soft neck.

"Hey, Mabel, two visits from me in one day, huh? Sorry I didn't bring you a treat this time."

Low chuckled. "Her name is Buttercup. And how did you even get in here? I was going to open the gate for you." He peered into the darkness of the fence.

"There's a gap. And Buttercup? Seriously? That doesn't suit her at all." I snorted.

Low shrugged.

"Well, I'm still going to call her Mabel," I huffed. Buttercup was a stupid cliché of a name. I climbed up on the fence so I'd be closer to Low's height while he was on Lijah's back.

"So you know Buttercup here, do you?" he asked.

I shot him a look, and he held his hands up in mock surrender.

"Sorry, sorry, I mean Mabel."

I couldn't help but laugh a little. He was cute.

"I shouldn't be telling you this, since you'll own this place someday, but yeah, I sneak in on my way to work. She's so beautiful and friendly. I can't help myself."

"Do you want to ride her?"

My smile fell. "I don't ride, remember?"

He sighed and shook his head. "Because you're punishing yourself. Right?"

I looked away, glad it was dark out here. He slid off Lijah and walked her over to the gate that opened into Mabel's paddock. I watched him, trying not to stare at his ass as he walked away. He'd also gotten changed, and we'd ended up wearing similar clothes, though his T-shirt was black, while mine was white.

He unlatched the gate and slipped inside, leading Lijah behind him. Mabel trotted over and greeted them both with enthusiastic horse noises. I smiled. She looked so happy to have company, even at this late hour.

Low came back over to where I sat on the fence and perched beside me, watching the two horses frolic around together in the dark.

"I want to say something. Again. Even though I know you don't want to hear it. What happened wasn't your fault, Reese. No matter what your family thinks. You're punishing yourself unnecessarily."

Easy for him to say. He hadn't been there. He hadn't been the one to watch his baby sister lie in a crumpled, broken heap on the ground. He hadn't been there when that doctor had said she'd probably never walk again.

I shook my head. "I can't," I whispered.

Lijah trotted over to us, and Low climbed on her back from

the height of the fence, making it look effortless, despite the lack of saddle.

"Okay. You don't have to ride, but I'm going to. This night is too beautiful to not be on horseback."

I wanted to melt into a puddle on the ground. Low on horseback, bareback of all things, was like a cowboy fantasy come true. He only needed the hat and spurs.

He let Lijah walk where she pleased, the reins held lightly, his hands resting on his thighs. He sat tall, but his shoulders were relaxed, his features calm as Lijah trotted around the paddock. A tiny smile ghosted his lips.

I envied him. I'd had so little peace or contentment in my life since the accident. I was highly strung all the time; I never got a break. It was why I drank and why I had a lot of sex. They were my only ways to switch off. But maybe he had another way. I hadn't ridden a horse in almost a year now and every part of me ached to get back on. It was only my damn head that told me not to.

Mabel came over and rubbed herself against me. I scratched her behind the ears and ran my hands down her glossy neck, patting her shoulder. God, she was beautiful. It would be so easy to just slide onto her back.

Low was watching me, his gaze intent. "We don't have to go far. We'll just let them walk around the paddock."

I bit my lip and clenched my fingers around the wood beneath my ass to stop them from trembling. My head screamed I didn't deserve this, that I didn't get to do things like this anymore. But my heart wanted it.

I swung my leg and laid myself on Mabel's back, patting her neck and murmuring soothing words in her ear. Her coat was smooth and warm under my palms, and I spent a moment concentrating on the way her bones and muscles moved ever so slightly beneath me. I breathed deeply as I sat up and used her mane and my leg muscles to steady myself.

Low grinned at me like the Cheshire cat. A smile twitched at my mouth.

"Come on, let's go." He let Lijah lead the way, and I nudged Mabel to follow. After a few laps around the large paddock, Lijah broke into a trot.

"I thought we were just walking!" I called as Mabel changed gaits with no encouragement from me. My heart rate doubled as the breeze blew in my face. Trotting bareback wasn't all that comfortable, the movement jarring without the support of a saddle and stirrups, but it was exhilarating. Goosebumps pricked at my arms as we moved along the edges of the fence line and the horses went faster, enjoying the free rein we'd given them. Low's grin spread wide across his face when I looked over at him.

"Are you okay?" he yelled.

"Amazing!" Blood thrummed through my body as the horses broke into a gallop. It was only for a few strides, the paddock not big enough for any more, but it was enough. I held on to Mabel's coarse mane for dear life, but I didn't want it to stop. The rush of the speed, and the power of the animal beneath me...there was nothing else like it. It topped getting drunk and getting off any day. God, I'd missed this.

Low pulled Lijah to a halt, and Mabel pulled up next to them. I was breathless and giddy and I'm sure my hair looked like a windblown mess. But I didn't care. I grinned at him, with adrenaline pumping through my veins. My eyes dropped to his mouth. Damn, I wanted to kiss him so much.

"I don't understand you, Low. You're such an asshole sometimes, but then you do something like this and make me want to..." I bit my lip.

Low's eyes dropped and his gaze grew heated.

"What do I make you want to do?" he asked, his voice husky.

Heat pooled low in my belly. What I wanted to do was decidedly un-friend like. But I didn't care about only being his friend anymore. Had I ever?

He leant towards me and a thrill shot straight through me, my nipples tightening. He wanted this too, and it was now or never. The horses wouldn't stand like this forever. I closed the gap between us and pressed my lips against his. His mouth was soft and warm and yielded to mine. My lips tingled, sending sparks of pleasure through my body. With my fingers woven loosely into Mabel's mane, I leant in farther, desperate to deepen the kiss, to feel his mouth open to mine, to feel my chest pressed against his. But instead, the pressure of his lips vanished, and my eyes flew open as Lijah moved. I swayed into the widening gap between us.

"Shit!" I squeaked out, grasping for Mabel's mane and desperately trying to gain traction with my thighs.

I was going to fall.

Low's arm shot out as he reached for me. He wrapped his fingers around the arm of my shirt as I slid, but it was too little, too late.

I hit the dirt, stumbling before falling on my ass, then laughed as Low's other arm wheeled, my fall putting him off. He tried to regain his balance on the horse's back to no avail and landed in a pile beside me with a thump.

He groaned from his awkward looking position. "You okay?"

I pushed myself to sitting and looked down at him lying next to me, unable to stop the laughs racking my body. "I'm fine. I did tell you I can take care of myself, you know. But thanks for trying to save me. Sorry you went down in the process."

He propped himself up on one elbow. I was fascinated as that tiny hint of dimple appeared in his cheek, and I couldn't help but tease him further.

"Are there security cameras out here? I'd like to see the video replay of that."

"Yeah, I bet you would. A bit of warning next time before you launch yourself at me, huh, Reese?" He was joking, but a blush began to heat my cheeks.

"I didn't launch myself at you," I lied. "I fell." It was a stupid thing to say, but it was embarrassing how badly that had gone.

"I liked it. Maybe next time I'll push you off, if it means we end up kissing again."

He sucked his bottom lip a tiny bit, as if tasting the brief kiss we'd shared. His face changed from joking to intense in a heartbeat and heat rose within me.

I brushed the dirt and grass off my palms. Maybe I needed to be more direct. With words this time, instead of actions.

"I want you to kiss me again."

It wasn't a whisper, but it wasn't much louder. He was staring at me with those deep blue eyes. His gaze dropped to my lips and back again, and he sat up, pushing himself onto his knees so he hovered just above my cross-legged form. His eyes burned, our gazes locked as he reached out a hand, letting it drift across my cheek to the back of my neck, burying it in my hair. My breath hitched. He tugged me forward, and I went willingly. I rocked forward on my legs as he leant down to meet me. His other arm came around my waist, pulling me close against him. My skin tingled in every place he touched me.

Our lips hovered centimetres apart, our breath mingling. It had to come from him this time. I refused to make the first move yet again. His fingers dropped to my hips and squeezed as he let out an agonised groan. "I want to. I want to so bad, but I shouldn't."

I shook my head. "You really should."

"Yeah?"

"Yeah."

He gripped my hips tighter and lifted me until I was straddled across his lap. I scrambled closer, locking my legs around his waist so we were face to face, chest to chest, hip to hip. His hard-on pressed into me.

Restraint forgotten, he closed the gap between us and pressed his lips softly to mine. I responded, opening and allowing him access as my fingers ran through his hair, our mouths exploring each other, taking our time. I tried to keep myself from grinding down on him, the temptation agonising with the ache in my core driving me on.

"We shouldn't be doing this," he murmured against my lips, but he didn't pull away when I ignored him and moved in to kiss him again. I didn't care he was technically my boss. Plus, we'd already done a lot more than this; it was a bit late for *we shouldn't be doing this.*

I pressed my chest to his, unable to get close enough and his cock kicked in his pants beneath me. I moaned as he pressed his hips towards mine. I wanted more. More of his mouth, more of his body, more of the way his hands held me tight to him. The kiss became deeper and more frenzied, and my hormones kicked in, flooding my body. I ran my hands down his sides and found my way back up underneath his shirt, delighting at the smooth skin and hard abdomen under my fingers. His skin prickled everywhere I touched him.

He groaned. "Stop, Reese, I can't." He moved back, panting, both of us trying to catch our breath. Then he pulled my hands away from where I'd been exploring his chest. "Really. Stop. I can't."

His words froze me in place. He was rejecting me again? I was a bloody idiot. I untangled myself from him and slid off his lap, scooting back in the darkness. I scrambled to my feet and turned for the gate.

"Reese, wait." He appeared beside me and grabbed my arm, and I spun around to face him.

"What are we doing? I've made it more than clear I want this. Do you? Because one minute you're hot, the next you're telling me we can't. You're my boss. Is that what it is? Or is it that you only fuck random strangers from the bar?" I couldn't stop the hurt that crept into my voice.

"NO! I like you Reese, a lot. We're friends." He grimaced, as if he knew he'd said the wrong thing and wished he could take it back. Tough luck, he couldn't.

"Friends. Right. Of course. Do you kiss all your friends like that? Do you pull them all onto your lap and grind into them? Do you take them all to meet your horse and tell them all about your family secrets?" My hurt and humiliation was rapidly turning into anger. I fought to dial it back.

He ran his hand through his hair and let out a frustrated groan. "I like you. A lot. Yes, we're friends, but that doesn't mean I don't want you. I do. You don't understand how bad. But I can't."

"Why not?" I spat the words. "Do you have a girlfriend or a wife no one knows about? I know you've been with men. Is that it? Are you gay?"

He shook his head. "Gender doesn't matter to me. I'm attracted to whoever I'm attracted to. I definitely don't have a wife or any sort of steady partner."

"Then what? I've made a fool out of myself, how many times now? I sure as hell don't plan on doing it again." Hot, disappointed tears threatened to spill over. I dug my fingernails into the palm of my hand to distract myself so I wouldn't cry.

"It's not you, it's my problem. I swear it."

"Whatever, Low, I'm done." I twisted out of his grip and ran for the gate.

He let out that frustrated groan again. "Reese, stop! I have HIV."

The words exploded from his lips like a cannon blast, halting me in my tracks. The silence was deafening as I slowly turned around.

"What?" I honestly wasn't sure I'd heard him correctly.

He shook his head, one hand gripping the back of his neck. He took a step towards me. "There's a *chance* I have HIV. A good chance. I've had direct exposure and I'm being tested for it."

My hand flew to my mouth as my heart skipped a beat. HIV? As in AIDS?

He grimaced, his features twisting, his hurt clearly evident on his face. "And that's why I didn't want to tell anyone. I didn't want to see that look of disgust. Especially not from you."

I dropped my hand, shame creeping over me. I wasn't disgusted, but shock rolled through me like a wave, making my movements sluggish. How was I supposed to react?

"Don't worry, you can't catch it from kissing, or from anything else we've done. You're safe." All the heat and passion between us had disappeared, and where moments before his voice had been sweet, he now sounded sharp and sarcastic. He shook his head and jogged over to Lijah.

My feet were rooted to the spot. I wasn't responding the right way. I didn't need his body language to confirm that. But my brain seemed to be disconnected from my body. I had no idea how to make it move, or make it talk. No idea how to make it do anything that would salvage this situation, so we could go back to making out. I touched my fingertips to my lips. Making out was okay, he'd said so, but I already knew that much anyway.

I watched him lead Lijah over to the fence and use it to climb on her back. His face was blank when he turned back to face me.

"You see now why we had to stop? I told you it had nothing to do with you. Do you believe me now? I couldn't stay away from you. So maybe you could do me a favour and stay away from me."

He clicked his tongue and dug his heels into Lijah's belly, urging her into a trot. I stood there for a long time after they disappeared into the dark, with no idea what to say or what to do.

REESE

*T*he kettle was taking forever. I tapped a metal spoon against the bench top and willed the water to boil faster. I needed coffee. The biggest mug I owned sat waiting on the bench top, the words 'Live. Love. Ride.' printed in bold letters on the smooth white ceramic. I sighed. Even my coffee mug made me think of Low.

I'd lain in bed last night, tossing and turning, while I replayed the moment of Low's confession in my mind. I had so many questions, but by morning, I had no answers and no sleep.

I liked him. I knew that much. He was smart and funny, and so hot I could cry. But beyond that, I could talk to him in a way I'd never been able to talk to anyone else. He made me want to open up to him. He'd listened as I'd confessed my sins and he'd shared some of his own demons. Low and his friendship were the best things in my life right now.

But HIV? God, that was huge. Every question I'd lain awake thinking about rushed back. Could we even have any sort of romantic relationship? How would people react when they found out? How long would it be before he got sick? I was terrified of Low lying frail and in pain in some hospital bed, like my sister had. And then there was one overwhelming thought that over-rode all the rest, one that made me feel like shit, but I couldn't block out, no matter how hard I tried. Did I still want him?

Stomach churning with guilt, I added milk to my coffee and took a sip. It scalded my tongue but warmed my chest, calming my nerves. Jesus Christ. I was a horrible person. Was I really that shallow, that I'd call things off between us before we'd even really begun? More than anything else, right now he needed a friend. Hadn't he been there for me when I'd needed one? We might not have known each other long, but there was something between us. Something I wanted the chance to explore.

Shame heating my cheeks, I dialled Bianca's number and told her I had a cold. Low would be hurt when I didn't show up for work, and I felt bad for lying to Bianca, but I couldn't face him. Not yet. I needed time to make a game plan.

I put my phone down and dragged my laptop across the kitchen bench, knowing I couldn't stick my head in the sand forever. I hit the power button, watching as the screen flickered to life. My leg twitched under me, nervous energy expending itself. I'd avoided Google all night, terrified that the basics I knew from high school health class were only the tip of the iceberg. But it was time to get answers.

Grabbing my stack of Post-its and a pen, I got ready to become a HIV guru. My fingers hovered over the keys while I waited for the Google home page to load. When it appeared, I took a deep breath to settle the churning in my belly, typed in HIV, and clicked on the first website the search brought up.

Hours later, I sat back in my chair and smiled. I had a whole kitchen bench worth of Post-it notes with HIV facts scrawled across them. I had notes on transmission, testing, and the End HIV campaign. But only one had the words I'd most wanted to read. *With daily medication, a person with HIV has a similar life expectancy to non-HIV sufferers.* Relief flooded me as soon as I'd realised he wasn't facing a death sentence any more than I was.

The tension in my muscles eased one by one the more I read. He'd need a lifestyle change if his tests were positive, but he could still live a full life no matter what.

I clicked my pen a few times and eyed the last tab on the website—HIV and Sex. I'd avoided it so far, but now that I knew he'd be okay, all I could think of was the two of us as a couple. Or whatever the hell we were. Low had said everything we'd done was safe, and I believed him, but I couldn't just rely on him to learn this stuff. We had to be a team. Every time we were together, the physical attraction between us was electric. It would be impossible to ignore forever. If we kept going the way we'd been, at some point, we were going to get carried away. I needed to know what was safe and what wasn't. It wasn't just about protecting myself, but protecting him. He was already so worried about hurting me, I wanted to take some of that pressure from him.

I carefully read through the Dos and Don'ts of a sexual relationship with an HIV-positive partner, each line more encouraging than the line before. My warring emotions came to an abrupt halt, as my fears evaporated, one by one. We could have a sexual relationship. With medication and a few precautions, there would be no risk to me. There were HIV-positive patients with husbands, wives, and kids. My knee-jerk reaction to Low's confession was ignorant, and my stomach rolled when I thought of the way I'd let him leave. I'd royally fucked this whole thing up.

Pushing away my now cold coffee, I shut the lid of my laptop, folded my arms, and laid my head down on top. My mind whirled with a new set of questions that no one but Low could answer. How long ago had he been exposed? Where was he in the testing procedure? There was so much I wanted to know, but overriding my curiosity was a desire to apologise. My lack of knowledge on the situation had led me to jump to conclusions. Conclusions based on a Hollywood movie made twenty years ago and a few paragraphs of text in an out-of-date, high school biology textbook. My reaction had hurt him, and when I thought about it, that was what had really kept me up all night. I'd hurt him, and I hated myself for it.

My stomach rumbled, and I glanced over at the clock on my oven. Already 1:00 p.m. I'd been sitting here researching for hours, and Low was about to go on his lunch break. I picked up my phone and tapped it on the bench, debating whether to call him. It seemed more like a conversation that had to happen in person, though. I decided to text him instead.

Can you come over tonight? After your shift?

I pottered around the kitchen, wiping down the already crumb-free bench tops while I waited for him to reply. When he hadn't replied after ten minutes I looked at the clock again. He was definitely on his lunch break. I shot off a second message.

Please, Low. I want to talk about this.

This time he messaged back almost immediately.

Okay.

I sighed. It wasn't an encouraging response, but I'd take it. I just needed him to come. I could worry about getting him talking once he got here.

REESE

*K*nowing Low's shift didn't finish until six, I sat cross-legged on my lounge and tried to distract myself with a book. I'd been hooked by the story last week, but tonight, after reading the same line five times and still having no idea what it said, I gave up. Instead, I nibbled on a thumbnail and stared at the door with unseeing eyes. When a knock echoed through the apartment, I was up and out of my chair, flinging the door open before he could even lower his hand. Or change his mind.

"Hey," I said tightly, trying to rein in my nervous energy and keep myself from word-vomiting everything I wanted to say.

"Hey."

When he didn't move to come inside, I realised I was blocking the doorway.

"I'm sorry, come in." I moved aside, while scanning his body and face for a sign of how he was feeling or what he was thinking. My stomach was a mess of butterflies, and I clamped my teeth together, reminding myself to be patient and not make things worse by speaking before thinking. That hadn't worked out so well for me yesterday.

He nodded and strode past me into the apartment, still refusing to make eye contact. I closed the door and took a deep, steadying breath before I faced him. My hands trembled, so I tucked them inside the pockets of my jeans.

Low hovered around the maze of Post-it covered boxes, looking unsure of himself.

"I made us dinner," I announced, trying to fill the silence. But my enthusiastic, too loud voice seemed out of place, and I snapped my mouth shut.

His gaze travelled around the apartment, before coming to rest on my face. "I can't stay long."

My heart sank.

"Oh, okay, that's fine too." God, this was so awkward. I didn't know where to look and I was fighting the urge to fidget. Motioning to the lounge I'd vacated a minute earlier, I asked, "Do you want to sit down? The lounge looks ugly, but I swear it's comfy."

He nodded and sat down on the edge of a seat cushion, resting his forearms on his thighs, his eyes trained on the wall in front of him. My apartment was so small, I had few seating options. Either sit on the coffee table, facing him, or on the lounge, next to him. Neither seemed like a great choice. I went with sitting next to him, perching on the other end of the lounge, giving him as much space as possible. The silence dragged out between us, uncomfortable as hell. I didn't know how to begin.

"Look, I'm—"

"Low, I—" We said at the same time. He shifted his body to face me. The sadness in his eyes tore at my heart.

"You go first," he said.

"I'm so sorry," I blurted out. "I reacted without thinking. I just didn't expect you to say anything even close to...that. I knew I'd said the wrong thing, but I couldn't help it, and then you were gone and...and I made you feel like shit and there's no excuse, and I suck." I bit my bottom lip. It wasn't an elegant apology, and it wasn't at all how I'd practised it, but it was an apology, none-theless.

Low shook his head. "No, you don't need to apologise. I would have reacted the same, if not worse, if our roles were reversed. Storming off like that was childish—I didn't even give you a chance to take in what I'd said. You needed time to process it all."

I sat back, sagging against the cushions of the lounge. "So you don't hate me?"

He smiled a little. "No, Reese, I don't hate you…I'm angry at myself, not you."

"Okay." I nodded, though I didn't like that he was beating himself up. The silence drew out between us.

"Can we talk about it now?" I held my breath, hoping I wasn't pushing him too much.

"What's to talk about? I'm an idiot, and I might have HIV. There's not much else to it." He scrubbed at his face with his hands, then looked away.

My fingers itched to reach out and touch him, but I held back. I didn't think he'd welcome it at the moment. "You're not an idiot."

"I am, though. I did this to myself. I was the idiot who slept with someone I didn't know and didn't use a condom. We were drunk and got carried away in the moment. It didn't even cross my mind until we were already in the middle of it."

"It takes two to tango, though, and if this girl…or guy…?"

"Guy," Low supplied.

"Well, if this guy knew he had HIV, then he had a responsibility to take care of you, one-night stand or not."

He shook his head. "I'm as at fault as he is. I confronted him…" He shrugged. "I'm sure his neighbours now know all our business. But in the end, what's done is done. Nothing he says or does is going to change what happened."

I studied him for a moment, impressed with his maturity. If I were in his shoes, I didn't think I would have been as forgiving. "Is this why you flipped out on me about having one-night stands?"

He shrugged. "Mostly. But if I'm being honest, it was also because I didn't like hearing about the other men you've been with. I'm male, and I'm into you, and sometimes I'd rather just pretend there was no one else before me." He gave me a wry smile. "It's a dumb guy thing, I know. Sorry."

The tension between us eased and I smacked him on the arm with the back of my hand. "You're an idiot."

"I know."

He looked boyish and happy, and the knowledge I had some part in that made me warm all over. I liked seeing him like this. Was it time to lay everything on the table? There'd already been far too much confusion and too many misunderstandings between us. Now seemed the ideal opportunity to let my mouth run free. I swallowed back the fear of rejection and rested my hand above his knee, testing to see if he'd push it away. He didn't. "Low?"

"Yeah?"

I let the words tumble.

"I don't want to just be your friend anymore. There's something more here. We both know that...don't we?"

His smile faltered, his eyes dropping to stare at my hand on his knee before he pushed to his feet. I snatched my hand back as he paced the small area in front of the coffee table.

"What's the point, Reese? I probably have HIV, so it doesn't matter if I like you. We can't be together. I can't be with *anyone* right now." The muscles in his shoulders bunched and tensed.

"Why? I did so much research today, there's no reason we can't still date and—"

"I won't put you at risk," he interrupted. "And I won't ask you to wait for me. It'll be months before I get a final diagnosis. That's not fair to you."

I stood up and put myself in his path, trying to stop the situation from spiralling. "Stop. Please. You're getting way ahead of yourself. Talk to me. Tell me what's going on. Start at the beginning." I placed my hands on his shoulders and gave him a little push towards the lounge.

He sank back into it with a sigh of defeat, and I sat next to him, a lot closer this time. Our legs brushed as he moved around restlessly.

"You remember the night we hooked up?" he asked.

I cringed, wishing I didn't. I tried to stop the flow of memories—some made me hot, some made me angry, and I didn't want to be either right now.

"Yes."

"You remember I got a text message when we were…well, you remember?"

I was hardly about to forget the most humiliating moment of my life so far, but I wasn't going to tell him that. "Yes."

"It was from him. His name is Mason. I met him at the track, the day you started." His gaze lowered, a blush creeping up his cheeks.

I waved my hand around, implying it didn't matter and that he should continue. I remembered Mason, the cute blond from my first day. The chemistry between him and Low had been tangible, and Bianca and I had gossiped about the argument the two men had had when Mason had reappeared at the track a few days later.

"The text said he had HIV and that I needed to get myself checked."

My mouth dropped open. "You're joking?" My blood boiled in my veins, heat flushing through me. "That callous bastard. He told you in a text message?"

Low didn't answer.

I eyed him. "How are you so calm about this? I'm pissed off just hearing about it." So much for staying cool and collected.

Low sighed. "Trust me, I've already gone through the anger stage. We were drunk, Reese. So drunk. I don't think I've ever been that wasted in my life. Neither of us was in a state to be making good decisions."

He shifted to the edge of the wooden coffee table in front of me. We were so close, he blocked my view of the rest of the room. There was nowhere to look but into his eyes and their bottomless blue depths. Neither of us said anything, his eyebrows pulling together as his gaze searched my face. I didn't dare move while he wrestled with his thoughts, but I saw the exact moment something changed—his brow smoothed, and his shoulders relaxed. I started breathing again.

"I'm really sorry, Reese."

I blinked. "Why are you apologising?"

"For leaving you like that in the alley." His hand broached the gap between us, coming to rest on my knee in the same way I'd done to him a minute ago. "God, I'm sorry for trying to fuck you in the alley in the first place. That was poor form. I was a jerk."

I squirmed in my seat. "I liked it, though." I averted my eyes so I didn't have to look at him. "Well, until you left."

His big hand inched up my leg and squeezed my thigh. "I'm sorry anyway."

I nodded. My gaze dropped to watch his thumb tracing circles on my skin, the warmth radiating from that tiny spot more distracting than getting lost in his eyes. I tried to steer the conversation away from topics that were messing with my hormones.

"So, what's the process now? You said you've already had your first test? I read up on it today. I thought if your first test came back negative you were in the clear?"

He shook his head. "The first test is pretty reliable, but only if you were exposed weeks or months ago. I was tested only a week after exposure, so they said there hadn't been time for the disease to make itself present in my blood."

"So, you have to go back again?"

"They always do a second test, but yeah, I get tested again in three months. Two and a bit now, I guess. I have a specialist appointment before then, though. My local doctor thought I should go see them as soon as I could get in because his HIV knowledge is limited. Plus, they offer counselling and other stuff he wants me to do. But he said by three months I'd be able to get a definitive diagnosis."

I nodded. "That one will be negative too. I'm sure of it."

He looked away. "I wish I had half your positivity. I'm not feeling confident about it at all. Maybe it's my punishment for being such a man-whore for the last few years."

"You don't get punished for having a sex life." I let my fingers drift over his hand that was still drawing absent-minded pictures on my leg. He didn't object when I wove my fingers through his.

"I don't feel like there's much to be positive about right now, though. All I can think about is the negatives."

I squeezed his hand before I disentangled my fingers and stood up.

"Where are you going?" Low asked, his eyes following me.

I smiled at him as I walked backwards towards my bedroom and held up one finger, motioning for him to wait. Turning, I trotted down the hall to my bedroom and crawled across my mattress. I searched the headboard full of Post-it notes, many so old they had been taped back on after their adhesive had worn away. I skimmed each note, not remembering where the one I wanted was. But I knew it was here somewhere. After a few moments, my eyes settled on a neon blue note that had faded from the sunlight. It was an old note, but one of my favourites. Simple and straight to the point.

I went back to the lounge room, waving the little blue square through the air in triumph.

Low's eyebrows drew together. "You have some sort of obsession, you know that, right? There are Post-it notes all over this damn apartment."

He was right. They labelled my moving boxes, and there were still all my HIV research notes on the kitchen bench. I had motivational quotes randomly on the wall and grocery lists stuck to the fridge.

Flopping back down next to him, I reached over, sticking the Post-it to Low's ugly lavender work shirt. I gave it a pat for good measure, trying to ignore the firmness of Low's pec muscles and how much I would have liked to be touching them without his shirt on. Despite my efforts, the note didn't stick for longer than a few seconds, and Low picked it up as it fluttered to his lap.

"What's this?"

"You said you only had negatives. I want to give you a positive," I said with a smile.

He read the note out loud. "Life is tough, my darling, but so are you." When he lifted his head, he was smiling. "Thanks. I think? Since when am I your darling?"

I rolled my eyes. "It's an old quote, dumbass. I didn't make it up." I leant around him, picking up a pen and a pad of Post-it's from beside him on the coffee table. I wrote another note, holding it as close to my chest as possible to prevent his curious eyes from seeing it. When I was done, I passed it over to him.

"And you have a bitable ass," he read out loud, his laugh reaching his eyes this time, the corners of them crinkling.

I grinned, happy my lame attempt at distracting him had worked. "It's true."

He winked. "Good to know."

We grinned at each other for a few moments, relief coursing through me.

"What are you smiling about?" he asked, shifting closer. This had all gone better than I'd hoped and being back on the same page with Low was a good feeling. It might have only been a few hours that we'd been at odds, but it was a few hours too many.

I shrugged, not willing to divulge my true thoughts. "I don't know, just—oh my God!"

I jumped up and sprinted to the kitchen, banging my hip on the kitchen bench in the process. "Ow!" The frozen pizza I'd put in the oven was barely visible through the dark tint of the oven door, but I had a sinking feeling it had been in there way too long. My fears were realised when I opened the oven door and black smoke poured into the tiny room. Coughing and wincing in pain from the hit to the hip, I dumped the charcoal onto the stove top and opened the kitchen window. *Shit.*

"So much for dinner," Low said, coming up behind me and surveying the mess I'd made.

"You weren't staying anyway." The smoke alarm went off, piercing the air with a shrill beeping.

"I'm just cooking! The place isn't on fire!" I yelled at the ceiling in frustration. This was what I got for trying to be a good hostess.

Low grabbed a tea towel and went over to the smoke detector, waving the smoke away until the deafening alarm quieted.

My stomach grumbled, matching the grumbling I was doing under my breath.

"What's that you're muttering over there?" Low asked, barely concealing his laughter.

"Nothing. I'm just starving and cursing my lack of cooking skills. I could have sworn I turned the timer on."

Low pulled open my fridge door and rummaged around.

I sat myself up on the kitchen bench, watching him. "What are you doing?"

"Making you dinner."

"I thought you weren't staying."

"Changed my mind." He glanced over his shoulder at me. "That okay with you?"

I nodded, my stomach doing a little flip of happiness. It was more than okay with me. "We should just order take-out. You won't find much in that fridge. I'm not much of a cook, as you can see." I motioned around the still hazy room.

Low shut the fridge door with his hip, bringing over eggs, bacon, milk, some cheese he'd probably have to cut the mould off, and an onion I didn't remember buying. But it still looked okay.

"Omelette good?" he asked. He didn't wait for me to respond, just started opening cupboard doors.

"Yep. What are you looking for?"

"A bowl? Chopping board? Frypan? Seriously, is all your stuff still in boxes? Didn't you get this apartment last year after everything happened with your parents?"

I shrugged. I'd made no effort to make this place a home. It was merely somewhere I slept. "Yeah, I did. I don't know why I haven't unpacked."

He stopped his rummaging and looked at me. "Maybe because you thought you wouldn't be here long?"

Maybe because I thought my parents would ring me and say they wanted me to come home. Which made no sense because they didn't even know my new phone number. Well, they didn't officially know my number, even if my dad might have guessed it was me who'd called and hung up on him a few weeks ago. "Maybe."

I slid off the bench and knelt down by a box with a bright orange Post-it note labelled 'kitchen stuff.' "I didn't have much when I left home, but someone on the bottom floor moved overseas not long after I moved in, so I scored a lot of the stuff she didn't take with her. I helped her pack it up, but I don't remember what's in here. There might be something you could use."

Low looked over my shoulder and pounced on a frypan with glee. "Well, at least we can cook this thing."

I poured us both a glass of wine and took mine over to the

breakfast bar. He hadn't been able to find a chopping board, so he was chopping the capsicum on a dinner plate.

I sipped at my wine while I watched. "So you cook?"

He looked up at me through long lashes. "I do. But nothing fancy."

"An omelette is fancy in my world. Much better than the frozen pizza I was going to serve you."

"Nothing wrong with frozen pizza." He glanced at the blackened hunks of unidentifiable food on the sink. "As long as you don't do that to it."

I'd bet good money the tips of my ears were turning red.

He cracked four eggs into a cereal bowl and threw the shells into the bin by his feet. "So, there's an awful lot of boxes over there labelled *vet stuff*..."

I looked over at the three boxes wistfully. "I know. I think that's part of why I haven't unpacked. I don't want to deal with those."

"Why not?" He poured milk into his eggs and began beating them with a fork.

The heat from the tips of my ears spread into a blush across my cheeks. I guess he hadn't been able to find a whisk either. My apartment really was pathetic. I'd never found it embarrassing when I'd had random men here, but with Low, I wished I'd made more of an effort.

I took another sip of my drink, stalling instead of answering his question. "The vet thing is the past. I don't like thinking about it."

"You could go back to it, though?"

I shook my head quickly. "No, I can't."

He stopped beating the eggs, his gaze intent. "Because you don't want to? Or you think you don't deserve to?"

"Both."

He frowned. "I saw your face when you were riding the other night. You looked...I don't know, free or something. If that's how you feel about becoming a vet, then you need to start taking classes again."

I sighed. "Can we talk about something else, please?"

"Sure." He looked disappointed, though, that crinkle between his eyebrows deepening.

Low poured his omelette batter into the fry pan and it let out a satisfying sizzle. Standing over it, he prodded the edges with a spatula. I finished my glass of wine and poured myself another. He'd barely touched his.

"That smells amazing." My stomach grumbled again.

He dug the flip under the bubbling egg and turned it. Half the egg stuck to the old, no longer non-stick pan, and the perfect looking omelette became a mess of scrambled eggs.

"Every. Bloody. Time," he cursed, trying to fix the mess he'd made.

I pressed my teeth together to keep from laughing.

He passed me a knife and fork and placed the omelette-turned-scrambled-egg in front of me. Standing on the other side of the bench, he watched me cut myself a bite and taste it. It was fluffy egg heaven. Damn him. I was just starting to feel better about my charcoaled pizza disaster.

"Oh my God, it's amazing." I shoved another bite into my mouth, moaning as the warm deliciousness hit my tongue. It was the first home-cooked thing I'd eaten in I couldn't remember how long. "If you don't start eating, I'll eat the lot. I'm not even joking." I waved my fork around in his direction.

He smirked and cut himself a bite. We ate in silence for a while, my appreciative moans the only noise in the quiet kitchen. Why did food always taste so much better when someone else cooked it?

When there were only crumbs left, I put my fork down and sighed in contentment. "That was way better than frozen pizza."

"Mmm hmm." He was still smirking, his eyes fixed on my mouth.

"What?" I swiped at my face, making sure I didn't have egg stuck to my lip.

"Nothing."

"You're staring at me."

"You sound like you're having an orgasm when you eat."

I choked a little, but he had a point. Damn him and his home cooking. "Yeah, well, it's been a while since I had a home-cooked meal. Or an orgasm."

I clapped my hand over my mouth, my eyes widening. I hadn't meant to say that out loud. My hand drifted to my wine and hovered over the glass. How many drinks had I had? Obviously too many if I was blurting out things like my current lack of sex life.

Low was chuckling to himself and I didn't know where to look. Needing an escape, I pushed my stool out and shuffled past him to the refrigerator. I didn't know why I was all of a sudden embarrassed to be talking about orgasms with him. Maybe because it really had been a long time and it was hard to think of anything else when he looked this good.

"We need dessert. I'm sure I had a block of chocolate in here somewhere." I let the cold air wash over my face for a few moments longer than necessary, trying to cool the heat that had risen in my cheeks.

One by one, every muscle in my body froze as I registered Low's presence behind me. His fingertips grazed the skin of my hip where my T-shirt had ridden up, stroking the tiny patch of skin as he moved closer. His chest pressed against my back.

"Why haven't you had an orgasm for a while?" His voice was deep, his breath tickling across my neck.

I didn't know how to answer that. "I just…I just haven't."

"You haven't gone home with anyone?"

I shook my head, fighting the urge to turn into his arms. The fridge beeped, signalling we'd had the door open too long. He reached out, covering my hand with his, and closed the door. I didn't dare turn around, though, not trusting myself to be this close to him and not want more. Blood pounded in my ears, as he leant in farther, whispering into my ear.

"How long has it been?"

I knew how long it had been, but I paused for a moment to steady myself, debating whether to lie. But I was so tired of holding back with him. The truth was easier. "Not since the night you and I…"

"So no one has had you since me?"

I didn't reply.

"No?" His lips brushed my earlobe.

My brain wanted to short-circuit with the maddening sensation of him being so close, but still so unreachable.

"No," I whispered.

"I like that."

Unable to resist any longer, I turned around and leant back on the refrigerator door, my eyes searching out his. The heat burning there shocked me. I hadn't seen that look since the night in the alley. My grocery list Post-it came unstuck on the fridge behind me and flitted to the floor. Neither of us bothered to pick it up. His arms lifted to rest on either side of me, pinning me in.

I bit my bottom lip, not sure what he was doing. He'd been the one to say we couldn't do this, but now here he was, doing it. He leant in, and my eyes fluttered closed, as I stopped breathing. His lips brushed mine once before returning, and he pressed his mouth to mine. My heart raced as he increased the pressure and ran his tongue along the seam of my lips, urging me to open for him. I did. His tongue swept in and met mine, tingles spreading from my mouth to every other erogenous zone on my body. Excitement mixed with relief flooded my system. He still wanted me, and for now at least, he wasn't letting anything stand in our way. I fisted the bottom of his shirt, pulling him closer, so his chest was firm against mine, pushing me into the refrigerator at my back. Our mouths moved in unison, deepening the kiss, until he groaned and dragged himself away.

"I'm sorry, I shouldn't have done that."

No! How many times were we going to have this conversation? So much for nothing standing in our way. I forced myself to try to be patient. This was a lot for him and I knew I needed to tread carefully. "We've been through this. It's only you standing in our way."

He stepped farther away until he hit the kitchen bench. He gripped it so tightly his knuckles turned white.

"We don't have to do anything you don't want, not until your results come back. I can wait." Every inch of me wanted to scream at the thought of waiting for three months to touch him again, but I pushed those ideas away and took a step closer.

"And if I have HIV? What then? You'll have waited for nothing."

"Remember, only positives."

He reached out a hand and ran it down my arm until his fingers traced mine. He joined his pinky finger with my own.

Lifting my hand to his mouth, he kissed my palm. "I don't deserve for you to be this understanding. I haven't even told Jamison. I don't know how."

Boy, did I know how that felt. "Then tell me. I'm a pretty good listener if you just give me a chance."

His warm hand came up and caressed the side of my face. "I know."

"So say it, whatever you're thinking. Whatever you're afraid of. I'll listen."

He pulled back, a smile making his sombre features softer. "You really want to know what I'm thinking, Reese?"

I nodded. "I really do."

He leant in, his eyes glinting with a sudden mischief. "What I really want to do is kiss you. Not just your mouth, but every inch of you. Then get you naked and do it all over again before I get inside you. And the fact I can't makes me want to do it all the more."

My underwear dampened at his words, need pulsing through me as I moved closer, tilting my head up to him. "There are other things we can do while we wait, you know."

I reached around him and grabbed a Post-it note from where I'd shoved them when he'd been cooking earlier. "See?" I asked, holding the note in his face. "We can kiss, touching is fine, and there are other...more intimate things that are safe too..." I tried not to sound too hopeful.

He shook his head as he wrapped an arm around me. I leant my head on his chest, feeling like a two-year-old whose balloon had just floated away.

"This is enough for now. Enough for tonight. If I kiss you the way I want to kiss you right now, I won't be able to stop."

I could relate. At least I knew I wouldn't be the only one left hanging tonight.

"Are you coming to work tomorrow?" he asked as he rested his chin on the top of my head.

I nodded. "Why?"

"Just checking you weren't planning on throwing another sickie. Lijah is in the third race."

"Yeah?"

I felt his chin moving on my head and assumed he'd nodded. I tried to lean back to look at him, but he wouldn't let me. He kept me pressed to him, his hands running up and down my back. I relaxed into him, letting my eyes drift closed, warm and comfortable in his embrace. The ache between my legs was tangible, but my brain knew better than to push him, and I hugged him tighter. If this was all he could give tonight, then I was okay with that.

14

REESE

*T*he next morning, I swung the bar door open, letting it bounce back into the wall with a crack. I raised an eyebrow as Riley and Bianca jumped apart like they'd been electrocuted.

"Did I interrupt something?"

Bianca shook her head, and I tried not to laugh at the guilty expression on Riley's face. Neither one said anything, but the look they shared told me everything I needed to know.

Throwing my bag and cardigan into my locker, I folded my arms across my chest. "You two have had something going on for weeks. Spill."

Bianca's huge eyes and messed-up clothes were enough to make me think they'd been doing more than just talking before I'd appeared.

An over-the-top grin replaced Riley's guilt-ridden features, as he crossed the space between us and slung an arm around my shoulders. "It's nothing interesting, just back-of-house stuff that need not concern you."

I elbowed him in the ribs. "Yeah, sure it is." I shrugged Riley's arm off my shoulders, moving out of the way so he could get by me.

Bianca leant one hip on the bench, a smile spreading across her face as her eyes followed Riley out of the room.

"So that's going well then?" I asked with a laugh.

She shrugged but then took a few quick steps so we were only a few inches apart. She clutched my arm, her eyes sparkling.

"It's great. He's great." She cringed. "Sorry I didn't tell you, though. Riley's weird about it."

"That's okay. I'm just happy you're happy."

"Do Low and Jamison know?" she asked, tilting her head to the side.

I shook my head. "I don't think Jamison does. But Low and I have had suspicions for weeks."

"Shit, really?"

"You weren't exactly discreet that night at the club."

"Does he care, though? I know we aren't supposed to date..."

I gave her an incredulous look. "You're kidding, right? You guys are his best friends. He definitely doesn't care. He'll be stoked." Not to mention he'd be a complete hypocrite if he did have a problem with it, considering what he'd been doing with me. We might not have been dating, but I'm sure the non-fraternisation clause in our contracts covered getting semi-naked with each other.

Her body sagged with relief. "Good, good. That's good."

"So will you two go public now? Or are you enjoying the sneaking around too much?" I wriggled my eyebrows at her.

She shook her head. "It's not just the no dating rule...it's—"

We both looked up as the racecourse door swung open, revealing Low and Jamison laughing together over something. My stomach gave a delicious little flip as a slow smile spread across Low's face when he saw me. My eyes followed him as he made his way towards us.

"Riley used to be married," Bianca hissed between gritted teeth. "And they have a kid he's only just found out about."

My head snapped back to her. "What!!!"

"Sssshhh!" Bianca dug her fingernails into my arm, her eyes seeking mine, and I registered the pleading look there before she dropped my arm. "We'll talk about it later, but don't say anything to anyone."

She flashed Low and Jamison a tight smile and disappeared into the kitchen.

"What was that about?" Low asked, turning his head to follow Bianca's hasty exit.

I wracked my brain, trying to come up with some excuse for why she'd been whispering and I'd been yelling. "Nothing. Bianca was just saying that *The Notebook* is on TV tonight." It was a lame explanation, but not untrue—I'd seen the ad for it this morning before I'd left for work.

"So?" Jamison asked.

I wasn't the type to get excited over a chick flick, but now I was committed to the lie. And as far as chick flicks went, *The Notebook* was a pretty damn good one. "What do you mean so? Haven't you ever seen that movie?"

Low and Jamison both shook their heads.

I huffed. "Well, you should. It's amazing. And I, for one, am excited about it."

"Alright then," Jamison said under his breath as he moved away from us and took his spot at the bar.

I could practically hear his eyes rolling. He glanced back over his shoulder, looking at me like I'd grown a second head. Oh well. Better he think me strange than for me to be the one to spill Riley and Bianca's secrets. Because boy, did those two have some secrets.

"Ryan Gosling does it for you, huh, babe?" Low said, quiet enough for only me to hear.

I flashed him a flirty grin. "Maybe he does."

Low winked. "Noted."

A swarm of excited race-goers in their fancy hats and smart suits cut our flirting short. Low, Jamison, and I served through the first two races, too busy to do more than yell the occasional work-related comment to each other. But that didn't stop my mind from whirling. After last night and this morning, Low and I seemed to be on the same page. We were in a good place, and I was desperate to keep it that way. I needed his sunshine to keep away my storms. I wanted my light to brighten his dark. We had a little of our original flirtation going, but with a deeper, more emotional undercurrent of connection. The slowly-slowly approach seemed to work best with him, and that was understandable. He had so many fears of his own to deal with, I didn't want to be one of them. I could be patient and take this at his speed and give him the time he needed.

A crackled voice over the loudspeaker called the third race, and a thrill of excitement replaced my Low daydreams. On the TV monitors above the bar, handlers loaded the horses into the starting gate for the main event of the day.

"Look! There's Lijah," I called to the others.

The bar emptied as the crowd, betting tickets in one hand, glasses of wine or beer in the other, spilled out through the glass doors. Some pushed closer to the track to get the best vantage points for the race, others hanging towards the back, content to watch the big screen.

"Come on, let's go watch." Low grabbed his sunglasses from his locker and reached out a hand as he passed by me. I linked my fingers through his, pleased by the chance to touch him.

"All of us, or just your girlfriend?" Jamison asked with a wry grin.

My grip loosened in Low's hand, expecting him to pull away, but he tightened his fingers instead, then shrugged.

"Sure, why not. Flip up the closed sign. There's no one in here anyway."

Riley whooped from the kitchen and pushed past me, dragging Bianca behind him. He stopped and planted a loud kiss on Low's cheek. "Best boss ever. Should we take beers with us?"

Low shoved him away. "Don't push your luck."

The high-spirited crowd surrounded us as we filed out of the bar and formed a single line, following Riley down to the track barrier. The crowd was thick, but most people saw our uniforms and moved out of the way. We let them assume we were on official business. Low squeezed in next to me, as the last horse loaded into the barrier on the far side of the track.

My fingers found his and I squeezed his hand. "You nervous?"

"Nah." He shook his head, then laughed. "That's a lie. I'm surprised you can't see my heart pounding in my chest."

I grinned. Between the push of the crowd and the party vibe around us, not to mention Low's presence, his hand warm in mine, I was hyped up as well. "She's got this."

He nodded, but then the gates flew open and eighteen thoroughbred horses exploded onto the track. I didn't hear his reply over the yells of the crowd.

My throat tightened as the storm of horses thundered down the first straight.

"What colour is Lijah's jockey again?" Riley yelled.

"Gold and blue," Low and I both yelled back at the same time. He squeezed my hand.

Bianca, shielding her eyes from the bright sun, squinted at the horses still on the far side of the large track. "I can't see her. Can you guys?"

"Not yet. They're still too far away. There are too many of them with blue in their silks," I replied. I glanced up at the big screen across the field. "Look!" I yelped as Lijah and her gold and blue striped jockey flashed onto screen. "She's in third!"

Low stiffened beside me, leaning farther over the chest-high railing. "Go, go, go," he muttered under his breath, as they rounded the back corner. "If she turns well, we could have this."

Tension and excitement radiated from him. The horses were moving quickly, approaching the final turn, the noise around us increasing in decibels as the pack moved even closer to where we stood on the finish line.

"Go, Lijah!" Bianca screamed in my ear.

Adrenaline coursed through me as Lijah's jockey got her in prime position to turn. I bounced on the balls of my feet and turned away to take in Low's reaction.

"She's got this; she's good on the straight," he gritted out. His teeth clenched, but his eyes sparkled with hope.

An agonised scream ripped from Bianca's throat, cutting through me and raising goosebumps on my arms. I spun back, my gaze flicking over Bianca, who was staring at the pack of horses, a hand covering her mouth. The horse in first had gone down, I couldn't tell why, and the horse in second, Yesterday's Princess, had gotten caught up and was stumbling towards the rail. She tried to regain her footing while her jockey grasped at her mane, narrowly avoiding being thrown as the horse's head dropped. Then, to my horror, Lijah, with nowhere else to go, careened straight into them and both horses went down in a tumble of limbs and jockey silks.

"No!" I sucked in a sharp breath, my fingers digging into Low's palm. The rest of the horses thundered by the finishing post, but no one in the crowd cheered. They were eerily silent, all eyes on the three downed horses.

I held my breath as Yesterday's Princess and the first horse to go down both staggered to their feet and skittered away, jockeys limping after them. But Lijah was still on the ground, thrashing around like a fish out of water. Bile rose in my throat.

Before I could even register what I was doing, I dug the toe of my shoe into the railing in front of me and hoisted myself up. Swinging my leg over, I dimly registered Low beside me, doing the same.

"Reese! What are you doing?" Bianca grabbed my arm, but I

shook her off, landing my jump in a crouch on the other side.

"Let them go, B." Riley's words hung limp in the air as Low and I took off running for the track.

We hurdled another low barrier and I pushed myself to keep up with Low's longer stride. *She'll be okay. She's going to get up.* I chanted the words in my head as my heart thumped in my chest and my breath came in gasps.

"Hey, stop! You can't be down here!" A tall, broad man in a Lavender Fields security uniform ran in front of us, but Low sidestepped him. I pulled up short, knowing I wouldn't get around the mammoth man without an explanation.

"Please, I'm a vet, and he's the owner. I can help, just let me through." The lie slipped from my lips without thought. I just needed to get past him, to get to Lijah and Low. The security guard's eyes slid down my body, taking in my uniform, and he nodded, stepping aside. I took off running again. Ahead of me, Low slid down to his knees as he reached Lijah's head and I crouched down next to him a moment later.

Lijah was clearly distressed. Her eyes wide, she made several attempts to stand, but each time fell back to the ground. My eyes ran over her heaving body, focusing on her legs. The unnatural angle of one made me wince. My stomach rolled as she moved, and the tip of the bone showed through her dark coat.

"Shh, Lijah, it's okay." Low's voice wavered as he tried to calm her.

"It's her front leg," her jockey said unnecessarily. We could all see what the problem was. "Maybe one of the back ones too. I'm so sorry, Low. I don't know what happened. She came down so awkwardly."

"Where's the damn vet?" Low snapped at him. He ran his palm down her neck and spoke to her in hushed tones whenever she lay still enough to let him. She threw her head and tried to stand again, and I watched Low's heart break right there in front of me as he used his body weight to hold her down.

I touched his shoulder. "Low..."

He shook his head. "I know, I know. Why isn't the vet here yet?"

I crouched beside him, letting my hand rest on his back. His breath shuddered in and out, as he tried to keep control of himself.

"He's coming."

Low nodded.

Four men dragged a large, folding green screen over to us and opened it up, shielding us from the stares of the crowd. My eyes filled with tears. Watching Lijah suffer like this was unimaginable. The guttural noises she was making made my stomach roll and bile rise in my throat. I would have given anything for a euthanasia syringe in that moment. Because that was the only way this would end. There was no coming back from an injury this severe. But instead, there was nothing I could do but stand there, offering nothing better than useless sympathy.

A man carrying a small black doctor's bag rushed around the screens. His eyes scanned Lijah's writhing body, taking in her injuries and her panicked noises before shaking his head, dropping to his knee beside Low, and rifling through his bag. He came up with a syringe.

"Don't look," I said in Low's ear, but he shook his head.

"I need to."

With sorrowful eyes, the vet looked at Low for permission. When Low nodded, he plunged the needle into Lijah's neck, and within moments, the life faded from her big brown eyes, her body settling back to the ground for the last time.

A sob full of pain mixed with relief ripped from my chest. I'd grown up on a farm. This wasn't the first time I'd seen an animal I loved put down, but it was heartbreaking nonetheless. Low's hand stroked Lijah's glossy, sweat drenched neck long after she stopped moving.

"Goddammit," he swore under his breath. His eyes, full of

unshed tears, met mine, and the depth of pain there made me wince. Whatever I was feeling, it had to be a hundred times worse for him.

"Low, we have to move her. I'm so sorry," the vet spoke up.

Low nodded and we both stood. I wrapped my arm around his waist and after a moment felt his settle over the back of my shoulders. I was sick to my stomach as we watched Lijah's body being loaded onto a tractor trailer and wrapped in a tarp. The crowd was quiet as the tractor rumbled off the track, and the green screens came down.

Suddenly conscious of a thousand sets of eyes on us, I ushered Low off the track, and we made our way back to the bar. The whispers and comments of the crowd followed us.

"Oh my God, Low," Bianca cried when we got back to the bar. She threw herself at him, and I stepped out of the way to let her hug him. "I'm so sorry. So, so sorry."

"Me too, man." Riley's normal exuberance was missing, his eyes downturned.

Low gave them both a stiff smile as Jamison pulled him in for a hug. Low's shoulders slumped in Jamison's embrace, the fight to keep himself together visibly going out of him, and the rest of us went quiet, averting our eyes to let the two friends have a moment alone.

Low pulled back and wiped at his eyes. "I need to go home. I can't be here right now."

"Of course. We've got this," Jamison answered.

Low pulled his wallet and keys from his locker. "Thanks. I'll see you guys tomorrow." He paused in front of where I was hovering.

"Do you want me to come with you?"

He shook his head. "Stay. I just want to be alone."

Ignoring the pang of hurt his words created, I nodded. "Okay." I reached up and kissed him quickly on the cheek.

The incident was all anyone spoke about for the rest of the

afternoon, and the rest of the day's races had a subdued feeling about them. I had trouble focusing on my customer's orders, and I was snappy with the morbid curiosity of a handful of people who questioned me about being on the track when they'd put Lijah down.

God, Low had to be in a world of pain right now. My heart hurt that he hadn't wanted me around, when all I wanted was to make things better for him. In that moment of hesitation before he'd put his arm around me down on the track, I thought I'd felt a little piece of him slip away. Felt him shutting me out again. Just as I'd thought we'd found some stable ground, the earth had dropped out from under us.

Beneath all my worries over how this would affect Low, there was also a spark of anger. But I wasn't angry with him. I was angry at myself. I knew I couldn't have done anything more than the vet had, but the fact I hadn't been able to put Lijah out of her misery ate at me. Frustration coursed through my veins every time a whispered comment had me reliving the moment where I'd had to sit by and do nothing, like a useless lump. I didn't have the necessary piece of paper to do a job that mattered. To have a career with purpose. More than anything, I wanted to be out there, helping those beautiful animals, not be stuck behind a bar or watching from the sidelines.

It wasn't the first time I'd had these thoughts since quitting uni, but the anger was always replaced by guilt. My father's words rang in my ears—I didn't deserve to walk or ride, didn't deserve to live my life without paying the consequences of what I'd done. Not when my baby sister would forever pay those consequences for me.

But this time, the guilt didn't consume me. Maybe it was that my anger burned hotter than normal, consuming me as easily as wildfire. Watching that beautiful horse suffer and die just metres from me would do that.

15

REESE

*M*y phone rang as I was getting into my pyjamas. Fumbling around on my bed, I snatched it up, relief spreading through me when Low's name flashed on the screen. I'd hoped he would be at my place when I got home from work and was disappointed when he hadn't been waiting for me. I'd wanted to be the one to comfort him—to touch him and kiss him until we'd both forgotten about the things we'd seen that afternoon. When I didn't hear from him all afternoon, I'd started conjuring up worst-case scenarios—most involved him driving off into the sunset and never looking back.

"Hey," I said quietly.

"Hey yourself."

"You okay?" I sat on the edge of my bed, curling my feet up underneath me. I rubbed at my chest. I couldn't shake the pain there. Lijah thrashing in agony was something I wouldn't be able to forget any time soon.

"I don't know. I'm...sad, I guess." His gravelled voice gave me the impression he'd been crying. Or trying hard not to. "It didn't hit me until I went to her stall tonight, and she wasn't there." His voice cracked, and my heart broke a little bit more.

"I wish you'd told me you were going. I would have met you. You shouldn't have had to do that alone."

There was a muffled noise I couldn't identify and then I heard him sniff. "I feel so guilty."

A sharpness stabbed through my chest and my hand fisted the blankets on the bed. The pain in his voice broke my heart. Why hadn't he come here so I could hold him? Words seemed so insignificant. "It was an accident, Low. There's no blame to be placed. No one did anything to feel guilty about."

"But if I hadn't entered her in the race—"

"Stop. You did nothing wrong. Don't let yourself go there." If it hadn't been Lijah, then it would have been another horse. No one could have predicted this. Lijah had been one hundred percent healthy this morning. The track was in good condition, and injuries as severe as Lijah's were rare in flat racing. There was no reason not to enter her. But he already knew all that, in his head. It was just his broken heart talking.

Silence hung between us.

"Yeah, I guess." There was more shuffling on Low's end and the low drone of his TV in the background. "So, what are you doing anyway? I can't keep talking about Lijah. It's too depressing. Distract me."

What would distract him? I glanced around my bedroom, looking for inspiration. The lilac walls, painted by the landlord, had seemed hideous when I'd first moved in. But now I thought they were fitting, seeing as lilac seemed to be my theme colour these days. I'd pulled the gauzy white curtains open, letting the night-time breeze in, sounds from the street below filtering up. Like the rest of my apartment, it was undecorated and sparsely furnished. My eyes landed on a wet towel in a pile on the floor where I'd dropped it after I'd spent an hour soaking in the bath.

"I just got out of the bath. I smell like strawberries now."

"Damn, I should have called earlier." There was another muffled sound from Low's end.

"What was that?"

"That was me, trying not to imagine you naked."

I laughed. "Did you succeed?"

"Not even a little bit."

I snorted.

"Reese?"

"Yeah?"

"Tell me more about your strawberry-scented bath."

I cracked up laughing. "You're such a guy."

"Okay, okay, just talk to me about anything then." A combination of sweetness and heat edged his voice, and a little of the weight on my heart lifted. I shifted back onto the bed, so I could lean against the headboard, settling in amongst the mountain of pillows.

"Sure." I grabbed my makeup remover from my bedside table and wiped beneath my eyes, knowing I had to have smeared mascara there during my bath. My head had been so preoccupied by thoughts of Low, I hadn't thought to scrub my face while I'd been in there. "So what are you doing?"

"Watching *The Notebook*."

My fingers froze, and I sat up straight. "Bullshit."

"No bulls or shit from where I'm sitting. There are some geese on a lake by the look of it, though?"

"You're seriously watching it!" I laughed as I finished cleaning my face and threw the wipe in the little bin next to my bed.

"That's what I said. I thought we could watch it together. Well, over the phone, together. You are watching it, right?"

"Sure I am," I lied. I scanned the bed for the TV remote, finding it on the floor and half falling out of bed trying to grab it. When I came back up, I pointed it at the little TV in the corner of my bedroom, flicking through the stations until I found the movie. Noah and Allie were out on a rowboat in the middle of a lake.

"I didn't take you for a chick flick kinda guy." Trying to get comfortable, I plumped my pillows and settled back, nestling the phone between my chin and my shoulder.

"I'm not normally. But Rachel McAdams..."

"Yeah, she's hot, I get it."

"You think?"

"You sound surprised. She's gorgeous. I'm straight, not blind."

Low's voice went husky. "Just give me a minute."

I rolled my eyes. "You're picturing me and her together, aren't you?"

"No. I was picturing you, me, and her in a threesome actually," he admitted. He sounded a touch guilty, like he'd been busted with his hand in the cookie jar.

"You can't see it, but I'm rolling my eyes at you right now." It was a half-hearted rebuke. The idea was pretty hot after all.

"I deserve that—oh look, it's raining on poor Noah and Allie. How surprising." His sarcasm wasn't lost on me.

"Ssssshhhh! This is the best bit!" I hissed, watching Noah and Allie climb out of their little rowboat in the pouring rain.

"It wasn't over! It still isn't over!" Low said into the phone, at exactly the same time Noah said it on my screen.

"You liar!" I yelled. "You have seen this!"

He chuckled. "Of course I have, Reese, everyone on this earth has seen this movie."

I sighed.

"What?" Low asked.

"I love this part. That kiss is so hot."

We were both silent, watching as Noah drew Allie roughly to his chest and kissed the ever-loving fuck out of her. My heart flickered a little. Movie or not, they had so much chemistry, it sizzled. It was impossible not to get caught up in their lust and love for each other.

"I want to kiss you like that," Low said, voice deep, as Noah picked Allie up and walked her back through his door and pressed her up against the wall.

Heat rose in me. "You already did. Once."

"I know. But I was interrupted. And it kills me to think about that. I want to do those things, and so much more to you, every damn day. Not being able to is torture." He paused. "Being on the end of this phone right now is torture."

I sucked in a breath, my orgasm drought suddenly all I could think of. I hadn't felt the need to get as lost lately, not since Low had told me about his possible diagnosis. Those treasured moments of escape from my problems hadn't been necessary, when my thoughts were so focussed on his dramas. But with things slowly heating up between us these last few days, I was beginning to think of sex and orgasms for more reasons than as a mind eraser.

"I know. Come over." It stopped short of being a demand, but not by much.

Low groaned. "Don't say things like that, babe. I'm already struggling for self-control around you."

There was another ruffling from his end as I squeezed my legs together, trying to find relief for the ache building in my core.

"Where are you right now?" he asked.

"Bed."

"Wearing PJs? What kind?"

I thought about lying for a second and saying I had on slinky black lingerie. But that wasn't me and the PJs I'd put on weren't all that bad. "A camisole and boxer shorts."

I regretted the words as soon as I heard them. He probably didn't even know what a camisole was, and wearing men's style underwear, even if they did have a delicate flower print and lace trim, didn't sound all that attractive.

"Take them off."

My eyes widened, until they had nothing on dinner plates. My lips parted and my voice stuttered. "Wh-why?"

Oh God, what a dumb thing to say. I knew why. My heart

thumped triple time and butterflies erupted in my belly. I wished I'd had a glass of wine before he called.

"I want to tell you all the things I want to do to you."

"You enjoy torturing us both, don't you?"

"Maybe. Are you naked yet?"

"I need to be naked to hear what you want to do with me?" Curse my tendency to babble when I was nervous.

"Not with you. To you. And yes, you need to be naked. In a minute, you'll want to be. Trust me." His voice exuded confidence, like there wasn't a doubt in his mind I might say no to this. He was right, I wasn't going to, but two could play at that game.

"I'll take them off, if you take off what you're wearing."

"I'm already naked, babe."

Touché. Of course he was. He was better at this game than I was.

"Lift your top over your head."

The spaghetti straps of my silky camisole were already falling off one shoulder as if they were totally down for this. "Okay," I whispered.

I put the phone on the bed for a second and reached down, lifting the lace and silk top over my head. I wasn't wearing anything underneath, and the warm spring air from the open window caressed my skin. My nipples hardened as I picked up the phone again.

"Did you do it? Are you topless?" Low asked.

I nodded. "Yes."

I thought I heard Low swallow. "I remember what your breasts look like, Reese. They're amazing. Are you touching them?"

"No," I said truthfully, although I wanted to. My nipples ached, the sensitive tips standing to attention, waiting to be touched.

"Run your hands over them, the same way I did that night in the alley."

Feeling a bit ridiculous, but also wanting, I put the phone on speaker and did as he said. Darts of pleasure shot from my breasts downwards, and I let out a little moan.

"Make more of those noises, Reese. I want to hear them all."

I pinched my nipple, and another involuntary gasp left my mouth.

"Close your eyes and imagine my hands on you. My tongue in your mouth and my fingers squeezing those pink nipples of yours..."

I squirmed and sank lower beneath the covers of my bed.

"Now take your shorts off, Reese. You need to be naked."

I didn't hesitate this time. My nipples mourned the loss of my hands as I ran my fingers down my stomach and slipped them beneath the waistband of my boxers. I slid them down my legs and used my toes to push them off. They got lost somewhere in the blankets, leaving me bare, damp, and aching. My hands returned to my breasts without instruction from him. "I'm naked."

"Good," he breathed. "Use one hand to reach down. But do it slow."

I did as he asked. One hand ran over my nipple while the other palmed its way down my body and over the short line of hair on my pubic bone. I rested my hand there for a moment, wanting him to give me further instructions before continuing, but I ached so bad. It had been so long since I'd last come, and the built-up frustration of not having Low here was killing me. I dipped one finger through the wetness of my folds.

"I'm wet." My cheeks heated as the words burnt my tongue; my breaths grew quick, my clit throbbing in earnest.

Low groaned and I heard the ruffling noise come from his end again. "Damn. I want to be there, Reese. I want to be the one touching you," he said desperately.

"Me too." My finger moved along my slit again, and I moaned into the phone. "I need more."

"Use your fingers, baby. Rub yourself." His breaths were as short and sharp as mine were.

I ran my fingers over the little nub, eager for the friction they created.

"Use your other hand as well."

Two fingers dipped inside and I groaned at the sensation. I'd had plenty of practice at making myself come, but having Low's voice in my ear heightened my excitement. My clit pulsed while I pumped my fingers in and out, grazing my G-spot each time. I knew my own body well. It wouldn't take long to get off. We breathed in unison for a long moment. "I'm close, Low. But you..."

"Me too. Just listening to you is more than enough for me."

I imagined him stroking himself, his cock slipping back and forth in his hand as he stretched out naked on his bed. It was enough to set me over the edge. My pussy clenched and I moaned like a porn star into the phone. It was over the top, but since he wasn't there to see me come, I thought he deserved to at least hear the audio.

My fingers slid from my body as the aftershocks reverberated through me. Rolling over, I buried my face in the pillow, enjoying the way every muscle in my body contracted, then relaxed.

"Fuck." Low groaned into the phone as he no doubt found his own climax. My core gave an extra, excited little clench at the sound of him getting off.

His breath went ragged as I lay there, coming down from my high. The blankets had slipped down around my thighs and I pulled them back up. Then I leant over to the bedside table and grabbed a stack of Post-it notes.

"What are you doing?" Low sounded lazy. I'd bet good money my visual of him lounging on his bed was spot-on.

"I'm writing you another positive."

"Oh yeah?" His voice was so chilled out he was practically drawling. "What is it?"

"It says you have the sexiest voice I've ever heard."

"Yeah? Anything else?"

"That you can turn me on without even being in the room."

"You'd better stop talking like that or I'll write you a Post-it note of your own. Hearing you come like that, knowing you're touching yourself…"

I stared up at the ceiling, happiness sweeping over me. "It was thinking of you touching yourself that got me over the line."

Low just groaned. "Stop, you're killing me."

"Okay, okay," I said playfully, as I turned the speaker off my phone and tucked it between my ear and the pillow. I tried to clamp down my excitement. This was how I wanted things to be with him. Light and fun and sexy. We could have had this all along, if only he'd stopped holding back. But maybe now that we'd crossed one of his self-imposed borders…maybe now he was ready.

I snuggled back down into my bed, my skin still singing every place the sheets touched me. "Let's just watch the movie then."

"Good plan. And, Reese?"

"Yeah?"

"Remind me to thank Ryan Gosling for his visual assistance tonight."

16

LOW

*R*eese was the first thing on my mind when I woke. The raging morning wood I sported was the second. The two thoughts melded together and resulted in my hand finding its way to my cock. I gave it a quick stroke, letting the memories of last night's phone call wash over me.

At some point, Reese and I had fallen into a companionable silence while we watched the rest of the movie, her soft breaths in my ear becoming slow and even when she fell asleep.

Damn, if that hadn't been the best phone call of my life. I hadn't meant for it to happen. I'd told myself I was only calling her to find a distraction from the Lijah-shaped hole in my heart and the worry over my doctor's appointment at the end of the week. But then she'd started talking about baths and strawberries and somehow we'd both ended up naked. And the worst part was, I wanted to do it again.

I looked down, realising the problem wouldn't go away, not while all I could think of was Reese. I dragged myself off the edge of the bed and tucked the erection away behind a pair of boxer briefs before pulling on my running shorts. After lacing up my joggers, I threw my keys and wallet into my running bag and let the front door slam behind me. Breaking into a slow jog, I moved down the short driveway and onto the street.

Dew still sat in beads on the grass, the sun just peeking over the horizon and not yet warm enough to burn it off. The muscles in my thighs and calves flexed as they warmed, and I increased my pace, settling into a steady rhythm.

By the time I pulled up at the staff entrance to the racecourse and fumbled through my bag for my key, I was sweating but nowhere close to tired. Thoughts of Reese, her voice sultry as she called my name right before she came, played through my mind on repeat. My cock threatened to get excited all over again, proving I needed more running time unless I wanted to be walking around with a hard-on all day.

I moved through the corridors, waving at the cleaners—the only other two people here at this time of the morning—before emerging onto the racecourse. Running around the track was something I did regularly, and had for years, even before I worked here. Back then, I was still trying to process my messed-up childhood and my mother's role in it. I'd only just gotten up the courage to leave and make my way back to my grandparents —the only place that had ever felt like home. The only place I'd ever felt safe or wanted. Running had been a way of channelling those feelings into something constructive. Anything else that might have taken the edge off those feelings could have landed me in jail. I'd seen more than one of my mother's boyfriends land themselves there, with a drug habit to boot, and it wasn't some-thing I was interested in doing. As time passed and I'd come to accept my past, I found I just liked running. I liked the peace I found in the repetitive movement and the time it gave me to think. It was running around these tracks I'd realised following in my grandparents' footsteps wouldn't be such a bad thing.

I ran laps for the next forty minutes, pushing myself hard enough that breathing and moving my legs became all I could think about. When my heart rate was through the roof and every muscle begged to stop, I staggered to the bar to grab a clean uniform from my locker. It was still early and none of the crew had arrived yet, so I took my gear to the staff bathrooms where there was a single shower.

Standing under the hot spray, my thoughts turned to Reese. Her wide smile, her eyes, all that long dark hair that flew behind her when she rode. She was the most beautiful woman I'd ever been with, hands down. I still had to pinch myself that she wanted me. Even after she knew how much of man-whore I'd been, and how I'd never committed to anyone in my life—she still wanted me. Even after I'd told her about the HIV tests, she hadn't gone running for the hills. She was still here, wanting to be part of my life, even after I let her see the real me. And that made me the luckiest asshole on earth, but it also terrified me.

She was so good, and sweet, and quick-witted. I loved her feisty attitude and the way she gave me a hard time. She could have had any guy she wanted, yet she seemed to want to hang around, waiting for me. But I couldn't do this. I desperately hoped she'd gotten as much out of last night as I had, but doubt sat heavy on my chest. Had I used her? I couldn't give her any sort of commitment. But damn, it would be so easy to get lost in her. To let her in, to let her take some of the weight and the fear that pressed in on me. But great phone sex didn't change things between us. I couldn't put my burdens on her. Nobody wanted the baggage I was carrying around these days.

I towelled off and dressed, running my hands through my wet hair as I paced back through the corridors. It was almost 8:00 a.m. and staff bustled around, doing their various jobs, getting the course ready for business. When I reached the bar, the light on the ice machine was blinking red. I dumped my bag on the floor, happy for an excuse to do some manual labour and work out a little of the agitation that knotted the muscles in my back still. It was just a build-up of ice blocking the chute, so I grabbed a metal scoop and shovelled. I'd been hoping for something a bit more complicated to keep my mind busy, but it'd do.

I sensed more than heard Reese come out from the kitchen, the grating noise of metal on ice covering her footsteps. Over the weeks, I'd become hyper aware of her. I wasn't sure if it was my imagination, but I was convinced I could smell her damn strawberry-scented shampoo in the air. I looked over my shoulder, letting my gaze drift over her as my heart picked up speed. "You fell asleep on me last night. You snore, you know?" I gave her a lazy grin, even though just the sight of her had me wanting to stride across the room and take her in my arms. I gripped the edge of the ice dispenser tighter.

Her mouth dropped open, as if that had been the last thing she'd expected me to say. "What? You're joking, right?"

I laughed, noticing that the tips of her ears had turned pink. She was adorable when she was embarrassed. It was the whole reason I loved to tease her. Unable to resist getting closer to her, I left the ice to its own devices and crossed the space between us. She met me in the middle, and although I knew I shouldn't, I stood close enough that she had to tilt her head to look up at me. I glanced over her shoulder, checking we were alone before giving in to the temptation to touch her. I let one finger run down her arm, trailing a pattern along her skin, pleased to see goosebumps rise in my wake. A flame of heat kindled at the knowledge I could have such an effect on her with only the very tips of my fingers. I tried not to imagine what I could do with the rest of my hands, not to mention my tongue.

"I'm joking. You don't snore, but you were talking in your sleep. You were saying how awesome you thought I was and how you'd never had phone sex as hot as that in your life…"

She punched me in the arm, a grin spreading across her face. "Well, I know that's not true." Her voice dropped to a whisper. "I've had much hotter phone sex than that." Her posture relaxed, and I wondered if she'd been nervous about seeing me this morning. I'd been a little worried about things being awkward after last night and addressing it first thing had been a good plan of attack. Teasing always broke the tension and got us both smiling and relaxed.

"I'll have to try harder next time then, huh?"

"Guess so."

She inched closer, and I felt the magnetic pull of her too sharply to resist. My eyes locked with hers, and I froze as her breath, minty and sweet, washed over me. And there was that damn strawberry scent again that had me thinking of her naked. Heart thumping, my eyes dropped to her lips. Damn, I wanted her.

"You two seem to be in a good mood this morning," Jamison announced as he swung through the bar door. Reese jumped and sidestepped to a more professional distance, and I snorted as I caught the dirty look she threw him. I stifled a grin. She'd wanted that kiss as much as I had. Damn Jamison and his bad timing.

"Good to see you smiling, mate. There hasn't been enough of that lately. After everything with Lijah yesterday..." Jamison's jovial tone was followed up with a smile, but there was an underlying seriousness. I knew he'd been worried about me well before everything had happened yesterday, but I couldn't find the right words to tell him about the HIV tests. Things might have been good with Reese and me now, but I still remembered her hand covering her mouth and the shock in her eyes when I'd first told her. I didn't want to see that from anyone else. If my tests were positive, I'd have to tell them, but until then, I didn't need to advertise what an irresponsible idiot I'd been.

"Yeah, sorry about that. I know I've been a downer. I've had a lot on my mind. But I'm okay."

Jamison clapped me on the back as the first of the day's customers rolled in. "All good, mate. I just hope you keep doing whatever has put you in a good mood." He looked at Reese pointedly. She rolled her eyes at him.

I pulled my shoulders back and stood straighter, unease curling through me. "It's not like that." I didn't want Jamison thinking Reese was just one of my casual hook-ups.

Reese placed a soft hand on my forearm as she laughed. "It's fine, Low. You don't have to defend my virtue."

"I'm not. I just don't want Jamison getting the wrong idea."

The smile slipped from her face and she didn't reply. She turned away to serve. *Fuck.* I'd upset her.

But the customers kept coming in a steady stream, keeping all of us busy pouring drinks, preventing me from smoothing things over. I couldn't help watching her from the corner of my eye, though. She was talking and smiling with her customers, but I knew better. When she was truly happy, it showed in her eyes. This was just fake bartender politeness.

The loudspeaker crackled with static before the caller announced the next race. The room emptied within a minute, everyone spilling out the doors to watch the race track-side. Reese had busied herself at the till, and I knew she'd deliberately found something to do that didn't require facing my direction. Hurting her was the last thing I wanted. I just didn't want anyone to think I was leading her on, especially Reese herself. But I needed to fix this. It hadn't been more than an hour since she'd smiled at me and I already missed it. I moved in close behind her, fighting the urge to wrap my arms around her.

"I upset you before, didn't I?" I asked softly to her back.

She tensed for a long moment before sighing. "Go out with me tonight, Low."

"What?" A spike of fear shot through me.

She spun around to face me, pinning me with a burning gaze.

"Go out with me tonight," she repeated, her body still while she waited for my response.

"I…uh…"

Her head dropped, and her shoulders slumped as she studied

the floor. My brain worked overtime, trying to process the conversation and what it meant.

"You don't want to?" She sounded small and hurt and that spike of fear turned into a spear of self-loathing. I was such an asshole. Despite my best efforts to keep things neutral with us, I'd led her on and I knew it. I should have stamped this out the minute I'd gotten that text message. I could have moved to a different area of the racetrack. I'd worked the bar plenty long enough, and I'd been due to move on for months, but hadn't because I liked my job at the bar and the perks that came with it. And then Reese had come along and I'd stayed for her.

"No! No, I don't mean *no*. I mean I do want to go out with you, but there are other things… I don't want to give you the wrong idea either." Going out alone, just the two of us, seemed like a very dangerous proposition. Every time we were alone, I spent the entire time fighting to keep my feelings for her in check. I didn't want to give her hope we could be a couple, even if that was what I'd wanted for weeks. I wanted her. And only her. I was done with casual. But I couldn't ask her for that. Plus, there was the problem that every time we were alone, and often when we weren't, that electric chemistry between us sparked to life and we ended up all over each other. How long before our restraint broke and we ended up in bed together? The thought of losing control with her, as magical as it would be to finally be together after weeks of denying ourselves, terrified me. I was toxic. And no good for her.

She looked as though I'd slapped her in the face. "If you don't want to go out with me, just say it. I thought after last night, things were different, but I guess I got the wrong idea."

Things ARE different! I wanted to yell. It wasn't just last night, they'd been different for weeks, at least for me. The flirting in the bar, the hours of talking down at the stables, the way she'd been the first over the fence to get to Lijah's side… She made everything different and made me want things I'd never given more than a fleeting thought to. I bit my tongue before I let that confession free. I couldn't tell her all of that, but I couldn't let her think she meant nothing to me either.

"Reese, I want to go out with you. I swear, you have no idea how much. But you know I can't get involved with anyone right now."

"Because of your medical stuff."

"Of course."

"I'm done with that excuse. What else you got?"

I blinked. Well, that was blunt. She'd been dancing around that idea ever since I'd told her, never voicing it in so many words, but I'd felt it coming. She'd been so patient with me. I knew I hadn't deserved it, and I guessed I'd reached the end of my grace time. Over Reese's head, I saw Jamison come out of the kitchen. He took one look at my face and hightailed it back.

Reese sighed, looking up at me with big, sincere eyes before she dropped her voice. "Look, I know your medical issues are huge, and they're scary. But don't use it as an excuse. Ask me out. Take me somewhere nice for dinner. It's you I want, Low. Whether you're positive or negative is irrelevant."

I blew out a tense breath, feeling some of the fight go out of me and sadness creep in. I wished I'd met her months earlier.

I ran my hands through my hair, frustrated with myself and the situation. A part of me wanted to run, but a much bigger part held me still. "This is so fucked up. I want nothing more than to strip you naked and have my way with you on the bar right now. But—"

"Stop trying to wrap me in cotton wool." She folded her arms across her chest. "I'm a big girl. I can make decisions like that for myself. You need to decide what you want. Either you want something with me or you don't. But you need to choose, without using your health as a factor. Because for me, it isn't."

She was putting herself on the line. Putting us on the line. I searched her face for any sign of doubt, any flicker of hesitation or an ounce of regret. But no matter how much I looked, there was nothing but steely determination shining in her eyes. "I'm not asking you to marry me, just stop thinking so far into the future. Give us a chance because I need this as much as you do. And I know you need it. Don't try telling me you don't. I see it in every look you give me. I feel it in every touch. Do you think I can't see the way you hold yourself back? You keep saying you can't do it, but you can't stay away either. So just stop. Stop trying to be so damn perfect, and just say what you really want."

Her words cut through me, pulling me in different directions. She was offering me everything I'd wanted back in the days of couch-surfing, with a junkie mother and no father in sight. I'd dreamt of having someone who actually gave a shit about me and didn't want to use me for a government pension or to steal money from to pay for her next fix. And I knew it was selfish, but I wanted to believe Reese needed me as much as I needed her. If she needed this, wouldn't I give it to her? Wouldn't I give her anything in the whole damn world just to see that smile on her face?

I wanted to be the man who made things better for her. I'd been trying to do that as her friend, but she wanted more, and was I really going to refuse her that? When I wanted her more than I'd ever wanted anything? She'd said to stop thinking so far into the future and maybe she was right. It was dinner; I wasn't asking her to go to bed with me.

I reached out and tucked a strand of hair behind her ear, tilting her face so she had no choice but to meet my eyes again. "You're crazy, you know that, right? Crazy beautiful too." The back of my hand trailed along her jaw.

"I'm not sure if I'm insulted or I can just admit the truth in that." Her shoulders relaxed, and a smile tugged at her lips.

"I like that you know what you want, Reese. And I like that you don't play games." I paused. My decision had been made. "Go out with me tonight."

My fingers snaked around the back of her neck, urging her closer, until my lips hovered above hers. Her dark eyes shone up at me.

"Actually, I'm not interested," she whispered around a grin.

"Smart-ass." My mouth crushed down onto hers, hungry and raw. Her fingers tucked around my belt buckle, pulling me closer until there was no space between us. All the pent-up frustration from not being with her last night coursed through me as I deepened the kiss and she moaned quietly. Her tongue flicked once more over mine before she pulled back. "We can't do this here. We're drawing a crowd," she murmured reluctantly.

Lost in our argument, I hadn't noticed that the race had finished, and a crowd was once more building up. Jamison had sneaked out from his banishment to the kitchen and was keeping them at bay at the other end of the bar.

"Tonight then," I whispered in her ear before releasing her. A thrill of anticipation shot through me. As fucking terrifying as getting this close to her was, I couldn't wait.

REESE

*A*fter work, Low disappeared without saying goodbye, but when I pulled out my handbag, I found a purple Post-it note stuck to it.

I'll pick you up at seven.

That was it.

God, he was such a guy. He hadn't told me where we were going, so who knew what to wear? But at least I'd managed to convince him the world wouldn't end if we went on one date.

I mentally searched through my wardrobe. Riding clothes I hadn't worn in over a year. Clothes fit for a nightclub that I'd bought with attracting attention in mind but didn't seem right when I was hoping to impress someone for more than one night. Or my work uniforms.

I groaned. I needed help. "Bianca!"

Fifteen minutes later, the two of us were back at my apartment. Bianca flopped across my bed, while I pulled clothes out of drawers and off hangers.

"How has it taken the two of you this long to get your act together? 'Bout time the hot date happened."

I held up a denim skirt and an off the shoulder top for her

approval. She wrinkled her nose and shook her head. The clothes built in a pile on the floor as I continued my wardrobe search. "I don't know if I'd call it a hot date. I had to guilt him into taking me. It's practically a pity date." All the hanging fabric muffled my voice.

"Yeah, right."

"It's true. He doesn't want to get involved with anyone while he…" My brain short-circuited for a moment, trying to come up with a lie. "While he has stuff going on."

Bianca waved her hand around, her armful of silver bracelets tinkling, but didn't seem to notice my slip-up. "They might be the words coming out of his mouth, but his body language says something different. And I've known Low a long time. You can't guilt him into doing something he doesn't want to do. If he didn't want to go out with you, he would have said no."

"You think?" I pulled out a little black dress and held it up in front of me.

"I think. Sometimes guys are dumb and just need a push before they realise what they want." She paused, as she caught my eye in the mirror. "I'll bet I know where he's taking you," she said in a sing-song voice.

"How? Where?"

"He has a favourite spot."

My heart sank. "Like a favourite spot he takes all his bar hook-ups?"

Her eyebrows shot up. "Oh my God, Reese, no. This is a restaurant. He doesn't take his hookups out to eat. Put that dress on."

"How do you know I'm not just one of his hookups?" Making out with him in an alley when we'd only known each other three days might have given him that idea.

"He's different. Haven't you noticed the complete lack of flirting with anyone other than you? He hasn't gone home with anyone in weeks. That's very un-Low like behaviour."

I had, but I figured that was more to do with the possible HIV than anything to do with me. I couldn't tell Bianca that, though.

"I've seen you two sneaking off after shift, and he introduced you to Lijah."

Tears pricked behind my eyes at the mention of Lijah's name and I swallowed hard. Turning away, I stripped out of my work uniform, shimmying into the clingy black dress.

"Lijah was his pride and joy. He doesn't take randoms back there."

I ran my hands down my sides, smoothing out the dress that flared around my hips, but hugged my cleavage. I did a little spin for Bianca and scored a wolf whistle for my efforts.

"Will this work, do you think? It's not too much for a first, proper date?"

Bianca jumped up and grabbed a pair of nude-coloured heels. "With these, it'll work."

"You sure?"

"You look amazing. Low will die."

Excitement trilled through me. I liked how I looked in the mirror. My long hair was glossy, falling down my back in a waterfall. My skin was blemish-free, which wasn't always the case since I didn't always feed myself that well, and my cheeks were flushed and pink.

With warmth creeping across my skin, I flicked the lock on the window and yanked it open, but I suspected my glowing face had more to do with the anticipation of seeing Low than the stuffiness of the room. I hadn't been on a date in such a long time, and despite the obstacles life had thrown in our way so far, I couldn't wait to have this night with him.

Bianca glanced down at her phone. "It's already six-thirty, so I'll take off before Low gets here and makes me the third wheel." She paused, her fingers moving rapidly over her phone. "Hey, your surname is spelt L-A-W-S-O-N, right? Why can't I find you on Facebook? I want to add you so I can stalk you and Low on your hot date tonight."

"I'm not on it. And even if I were, I wouldn't be broadcasting our date on social media."

"What? Everyone is on Facebook," Bianca stated without looking up. She peered at the phone screen. "Oh, hey, is this your sister? She looks just like you!"

I paused. "Can't be. My sister isn't on Facebook. She's not old enough."

Bianca scoffed and held the phone out to me. "Please, my niece is nine and she's had Facebook for a year. Is your sister's name Gemma?"

I stopped breathing, because Gemma's smiling face was right there on Bianca's phone screen.

I snatched it out of her hand and scanned every inch of the photo. It had to be recent. She'd cut her hair. I hadn't seen it that short since she was about five. The photo was only head and shoulders, but her beautiful face was lit up by a smile. She looked happy.

"It is your sister, right?" Bianca asked.

I nodded as I pressed on Gemma's profile and scrolled down. There was only one message. Well, only one that Gemma's privacy settings allowed me to see anyway. I had no way of knowing if there was anything else on her profile at all, but that one message was enough.

If anyone knows where my sister Reese is, please tell her to come home.

Hope rose in me like smoke from an ember on dry kindling. Maybe her injuries hadn't been as severe as the doctors had first thought. Maybe she was walking around right this minute, and I'd stayed away all this time for nothing. I let the flames of hope engulf me. Gemma wouldn't want to see me if she were still stuck in a wheelchair. Not when I'd been the one to put her in it.

I kissed Bianca on her on the cheek and handed her phone back. "You're the best. Thank you for tonight."

She looked confused but didn't question what I'd just been doing, as we resumed walking to the front door. I paused in front of it before I reached for the lock to let her out.

"Thanks again." I didn't elaborate and tell her she'd helped me in more than one way tonight.

She pulled me in for a hug. "You're welcome. I'm glad we got some girl time."

"Hey, that reminds me. Are you going to tell me what's going on with Riley?"

She shook her head quickly. "Honestly, it's long and complicated, and I'm sure he'll fill you guys in soon."

I still wanted to know what was happening, but I couldn't fault her. "Yeah, that's fair enough."

"Anyway, you need to go finish getting ready. Have a fantastic time and be sure to call me first thing in the morning. I want to know all about it. And I want specifics." She gave me an exaggerated wink.

"I'm not sleeping with him, B."

"Uh-huh, sure you're not. I've seen the way you two look at each other, you'll be ripping each other's clothes off before you even get to dinner."

That wouldn't be happening, but I couldn't tell her why or how much I wished it would.

When I swung the door open, Low was leaning on the wall opposite, engrossed in something on his phone.

Crap, what was he doing here already? I was dressed, but I was still wearing the same smudged makeup I'd worn to work.

"Uh, hi. Did you knock? I didn't hear anything."

"Nope."

Bianca glanced between the two of us. A knowing smile spread across her face and I gave her a swift elbow to the ribs.

"Be safe, you two!" she cried as she pushed past me and pranced off down the hall.

I cringed at her choice of words.

Low wore black tailored pants and a casual button-down shirt that stretched across his broad shoulders. His gaze ran down my body before coming back up to rest on my face.

"You're early." I had a zillion questions about Gemma's Facebook message running through my mind, but I pushed them aside for the moment. I wanted to concentrate on Low and give him my full attention. And I wanted to keep the news about my sister to myself for just a little longer. I needed time to work it all out in my head. And we had all night. I could tell him later.

He gave me a lazy smile. "I am. That's why I didn't knock. I didn't want to rush you."

I added thoughtful to the list of qualities I liked about him and motioned for him to come inside.

"That dress looks amazing," he whispered in my ear as he passed. "But I bet I'd like your camisole and boxer shorts more."

Goosebumps spread along the length of my neck. A fresh, clean aroma, with just a hint of cologne trailed him, and I fought to keep from following him, nose first. I needed to finish getting ready before I got sidetracked or we wouldn't end up leaving the apartment.

"Thank you," I murmured and closed the door behind him. "I just need to fix my makeup and we can go." I gestured to the lounge. "Take a seat. Remote's on the table. Watch whatever you like."

Leaving him in the living room, I scampered down the hallway to the bathroom. Not bothering to close the door, I splashed water on my face, welcoming the cooling sensation on my overheated cheeks, and wiped my face on a towel. Out of the corner of my eye, I saw Low appear in the doorway. I faltered for a split second before continuing my routine, smearing foundation over my cheeks. But it was hard not to feel self-conscious when he was watching me in the mirror.

"You don't need that stuff, you know." It didn't sound like a line. It fell from his mouth so naturally, it was as if he hadn't even thought about it. So instead of insisting I did, I accepted his compliment.

"Thanks. I like it, though. I feel a bit naked without it now."

"Now?"

"Yeah, I never used to wear much when I was riding a lot. Didn't seem to be much point. Not like the horses or the kids I taught cared. And I didn't like how it would run into my eyes when it was hot."

His reflection in the mirror was thoughtful as he nodded. Why did he have to look model-beautiful while I was half-dressed with only one eye ringed with liner?

"Are you really just going to stand there watching me put mascara on?"

"That was the plan. It's interesting."

I squinted at him in the mirror. "Interesting how?"

He folded his arms over his chest. "I don't know. All those little bottles in there, and you end up looking like a different person at the end." A tinge of pink appeared on his cheeks. "Sorry. That came out wrong. I don't mean it in a bad way. You're gorgeous with or without it."

Flashing him a smile, I pondered that statement for a moment before replying. "I'm not that sensitive. You don't need to apologise. I get what you meant." I wiped a stray fleck of mascara from the corner of my eye. "I think that's partly why I started wearing it. Sometimes I am a different person with it on."

His face fell. "Maybe I should start wearing some. It might be nice to be someone else."

My chest ached for him. I knew all about wanting to be someone else, even if only for a little while. It was easy, watching strangers on a bus, or in a bar, assuming their lives were perfect, and desperately wanting the same thing. I'd turned to alcohol and meaningless sex to combat that void within myself. But I didn't want to do that anymore, especially now that Gemma's condition might not be as permanent as I'd first thought. I didn't want Low to have to either. I just hoped we were on the same page about it. It was hard to know where we stood when he wouldn't ever talk about it.

"It only lasts for a night, though. Then you take it off and you're back to your same old self, your same old problems," I said as our eyes met in the mirror again.

"Like Cinderella."

"Pretty much."

I capped my lipstick and bent down to slip on the high heels Bianca had picked out for me. With his guard down and his vulnerable side on display, I was more attracted to him than ever. I wanted him to know that while alpha male Low with his flirting and banter was fun, this was the side of him I wanted more of. Had anyone ever bothered to look beyond the bravado? Had he ever let anyone in the way he let me? I made a vow to tell him before the night was out. I was sick of pussyfooting around with him. For my own sanity, I needed to lay it all on the line. I just hoped he was ready to hear it. I swallowed hard and forced a smile, trying to ignore how nervous the plan made me.

"I'm ready. Where are we off to?"

Low's face brightened. "You'll see."

18

LOW

*R*eese wolf-whistled long and loud. "That is not your car."

I flashed her what I hoped was a confident grin, but there was heat rising along the back of my neck. I almost hadn't driven the Aston Martin Vantage. Even though it was a good seven years old, the metallic grey body was sleek and flashy as hell. My taste in cars had changed over the years, which was why I never drove it, preferring the much more practical Ute I'd bought three years ago. But since this was a date, it seemed like a good time to bring it out of the garage where it had been sitting, gathering dust. I wanted to do this date right. Picking her up in my Ute with half a bale of hay in the back and mud sprayed up the side wouldn't be a great start.

I pulled the handle on the passenger door, holding it open while Reese climbed in, then I slid into the driver's seat.

Her gaze flitted around the interior of the car, her eyes growing wider as she took it in. "Are these seats heated? This car must have cost six figures."

"Probably. It was a gift from my grandparents when I turned eighteen. They overcompensated when I first came back to see them." My fingers dug into the leather-covered steering wheel. I didn't want to think about my mother tonight, or the way she'd kept me from my grandparents and the only real home I'd ever had. I glanced over at Reese, praying she didn't think I was a total tool. "For the record, this car isn't what I'd choose for myself."

"I'm not judging your car, Low."

"I know. But I don't want you to get the wrong idea about me. I have money. You know that. But I drive a very average-looking Ute most of the time."

She ran her hands over the smooth seat and met my eyes. Hers sparkled with mischief. "This car is pretty amazing, though."

A little of the apprehension in my chest eased, and a genuine smile crept across my face. "It goes fast too," I joked. Though it was the truth.

"Oh yeah?"

"Don't tell me that impresses you."

She laughed. "No, it doesn't. Sorry. I'm not much of a car girl. But I do like it. I like Utes too, though."

Of course she did. Because she was that sort of woman. Down to earth and low-maintenance. If I let myself think about, being with her would be so easy. We'd go riding together early in the mornings before work and double date with Riley and Bianca or Jamison and Bree on weekends. My grandparents would adore her. And waking up next to her every morning, touching her soft skin, kissing her most sensitive places—she was everything I wanted but couldn't have. But tonight, I could. Tonight, I could pretend we had a future. Tonight, there were no looming tests, no life-altering results. Just her and me and the illusion of all the time in the world.

I started the car before I voiced my thoughts and pulled out into the light evening traffic, heading towards the city. Reese gazed out the window and soon residential buildings gave way to shop fronts. The corners of her mouth turned up, her dark hair flowing over her bare shoulders. Happiness radiated from her, seeping into me like warmth from the sun.

"What are you thinking about?" I asked. She looked...free, tonight. I wanted to know why.

She turned, giving me a warm smile. "I had some good news today."

"Yeah?"

She nodded and opened her mouth as if to elaborate, but then a small frown dented the space between her eyebrows and she paused. "I'm not ready to talk about it yet, though. I need some time to think and process it before I talk about it. Is that okay?" Her expression was apologetic.

"Sure." I made sure the word sounded casual, but a tiny flicker of worry rose in me. Did she not trust me with her secrets anymore? Her answer confused me. I doubted there could be a bigger secret than the ones we'd already shared, but this night was supposed to be fun, and all about her, so if she wasn't ready to tell me everything, then that was her prerogative. I wouldn't push her, but the silence drawing out between us felt odd, and I wanted to fill it. "So. First date, huh?"

She studied me for a moment, not bothering to confirm the answer to my obvious question. "Have you gone on many of those?"

I swallowed hard, regretting that we were going down this path already. I knew how my answer would make me sound. But I wouldn't lie. Not to her. "None."

"None?" she squeaked.

"Dates aren't my thing."

I tried not to cringe.

"Not even in high school?"

I snorted. "Definitely not in high school. I took one friend home when I was in primary school and the next day he told everyone at school that my house was a drug den and my mum was smoking pot the whole time he was there. It was all true, but

I never heard the end of it. We moved right before I started high school, so none of the kids knew me. I wanted to make sure no one found out about her, so I never dated. Hooked up a few times at parties, but that was about the extent of my social life."

Reese listened in silence before reaching over the centre console and rubbing my shoulder. A flash of guilt churned my gut. My actions didn't deserve pity. Not by any stretch of the imagination. If I'd wanted to, I could have dated. There'd been plenty of opportunity after high school. I didn't know why I hadn't. I'd never given it much thought before. Casual sex was a habit I'd fallen into as a teenager and it had always just been the easier option. There'd never been a guy or woman who'd made me want more, and I'd never felt like I was missing out on anything. Until I'd met her.

We'd reached the main restaurant strip in the city and I wanted to change the subject before either of us could study my past actions in any more depth. "Restaurant's just up here."

Couples on dates and groups of friends walked along the paths. Others sat eating and drinking around outdoor tables or inside in cosy booths. The last of the day's sun was sinking somewhere beyond the high-rise buildings surrounding us, and a cool breeze blew in the open car windows as the streetlights flickered in deepening shadows.

I pulled around the back of the building and put the car into park.

"Thank God we got a decent parking spot. These heels aren't up to walking more than a few hundred metres," Reese said as we both pushed our doors open. We rounded the back of the car, meeting in the middle, and without thought, I held out my hand, pulling her close when her fingers entwined between mine.

Reese hadn't been exaggerating when she'd said her heels weren't made for walking. Even the short walk to the restaurant appeared difficult for her, but she didn't complain, just held my hand tighter when the tiniest slope put her off balance. We made it to the restaurant in comfortable silence and I tried to memorise how perfectly her hand fit in mine. How her skin was soft and smooth and the way she smelled faintly of strawberries.

I pulled her to a stop outside a busy Tapas bar. "You like Spanish food, yeah?"

"I've never been before, but I've always wanted to try it. There's nothing like this in Erraville." She bounced on the balls of her feet and peered through the large glass windows into the darkened restaurant within. She beamed up at me.

Something uncurled within me, something that felt an awful lot like a protective instinct. I loved that smile, and I loved when she was happy. I wanted to keep her that way. I wanted to make her smile and laugh. I wanted to see her get excited every damn day and all through every night. Reese and her happiness were worth more than the car we'd driven here. Her smile made me forget I was the junkie's son and the racecourse man-whore. Made me forget all about my stupid mistakes and the terrifying possibilities of the future.

Warmth flooded my chest, and I squeezed her hand. Unable to wait another moment to kiss her, I dropped my head and let the back of my fingers trace along her jaw before sliding into her hair. I smiled and tugged her closer. She came eagerly, lifting onto her toes to close the distance between us. I laid my lips softly on hers.

"Mmmmm," she murmured when she pulled away, her eyes still closed. "What was that for?"

"I didn't want to wait until the end of the date. I want to kiss you all night." My lips brushed along hers once more, her kiss making me reluctant to move even though we were blocking the path and forcing people to walk around us. It was too easy to forget where I was when I was with her. If I trusted myself alone with her, we wouldn't be out in public very often.

Her eyes glowed. "Me too."

"But we're late for our reservation. And my stomach is protesting."

She laughed and I pulled her toward the restaurant. A waitress dressed in a multi-coloured skirt smiled as we entered. She showed us to a little table on the far side of the busy room and winked at me. "Here, a cosy table for the lovebirds," she announced.

I smiled my thanks, glancing at Reese to see if she had any reaction to the waitress's comment. She didn't. She just gazed around the room, taking in the atmosphere. Spanish music played beneath the low drone of quiet conversations around us.

Reese settled into her seat and picked a menu from the table, flicking through it before she leant in and whispered, "It smells amazing in here."

"The food tastes even better."

"Can't wait. I'm starving."

Our waitress returned and took our drinks order. White wine for Reese, bourbon and coke for me.

"Would you like to order?" the waitress asked with her pen poised above her notebook.

Reese chose two plates. I chose five. Reese was right. The smells drifting from the kitchen were intoxicating. I wanted to order one of everything on the menu.

"So," she said after we'd both had a sip of our drinks, "since this is our first date, let's start with the basics. Is Low your real name?"

I laughed. "Do you think I'm using some sort of alias?"

"Maybe? It's a nickname, isn't it?"

I nodded and took another sip of my drink. "It's a nickname. Even my mother wasn't off her face enough to legally name me Low." I put the glass down and ran a finger through the condensation beading on the glass. "Truth, though? I wish she had. Because my real name is terrible."

"Couldn't be that bad. Tell me."

"I'm not even close to drunk enough to let that one slip, Reese."

She pouted, and it was adorable. I had to fight the urge to lean across the table and take that full bottom lip between my teeth.

"Well, we have something in common, because Reese isn't my real name either."

I frowned, picking up my glass again and taking a swallow. "Yes, it is. I've seen your paperwork."

"I changed it. Legally."

"No, you didn't. This is just a ploy to get me to spill my secrets, right?"

She quirked an eyebrow and I laughed.

"Well then, mystery woman. What name is on your birth certificate?"

"This is only our first date. I don't think I know you well enough to be divulging such sensitive information," she joked.

"I'll tell you if you tell me."

She pretended to consider that for a moment before winking. "Maybe when we know each other better, huh?"

She had a point. We'd covered a lot while sitting on hay bales cleaning tack and hanging out in Lijah's paddock, but I wanted to know everything. I knew how devastated she was over her sister's accident and how her estrangement from her family had led to her moving here. But what was her favourite colour? Did she like school? Did she want to travel? What was her biggest dream? We'd skipped most of the little, get-to-know-you things, instead focussing on the biggest problems, the ones neither of us could see past. But now, I wanted the chance to find out the rest.

"Deal."

I offered her my hand and we shook on it, but I didn't let go until our waitress returned with our first plates of food, forcing me to withdraw my hand from hers. I picked up a fork and speared a piece of chorizo from Reese's plate.

"So we're sharing then!" She swatted me away from her plate

with her fork and I grinned at her around the delicious meat in my mouth when she stole a prawn in a garlic sauce from my plate.

"Ohmigosh, it's so good," she mumbled, grabbing another.

The chorizo's spicy flavour danced over my taste buds. I finished chewing and swallowed, watching as she enjoyed her food. She grinned.

"Your mouth having another orgasm?"

She winked. "You know it."

I dragged my gaze away from her. I loved that she didn't get embarrassed by my teasing. Loved even more that she gave as good as she got.

We polished off our little plates in record time, our conversation slowing to comfortable silence as I inhaled my meal. Reese looked equally interested in the food, picking a little from each of the plates, making positive comments when she enjoyed something. The waitress was soon back over, ready to see if we wanted anything else. Reese shook her head, and I did the same. I was still hungry, but I was more interested in the woman sitting across from me than eating.

"I like this place. It has character." She ran her hand over the scuffed wooden table, well used, but still sturdy. The napkins were cloth, and the flowers scattered in vases around the tables were real. "I have something for you."

"Oh yeah?" I murmured, trying not to let on how affected I was by her. I was having trouble keeping my breathing steady. "What's that?"

She rifled through her handbag, then held out a blue Post-it note, giving me a cheeky wink as she passed it across the table. "I wrote this for you last night. After we, well…you know."

Her eyes locked with mine, and although I reached out and took the note from her fingers, I didn't look away. I couldn't. Her dark brown eyes sucked me in until I couldn't think of anything else. Heat rushed through me and I couldn't stop myself remembering the way she'd looked in the alley, her hair mussed up, aching and wanting for something only I could give her. My cock thickened as I heard her voice in my ear the night before, crying out my name in the midst of her orgasm.

Needing a break from the intensity between us, I scanned her neatly printed words, my eyes widening. The woman could write a note dirtier than most high school boys. I gave up trying to fight my erection and thanked God there was a tablecloth.

"My voice can do all that, huh?" I said, trying not to let on how affected I was by her.

She laughed. "I think I can actually see your ego inflating right now."

"Can you blame me?"

She shook her head with smiling eyes. Damn, I loved the way she looked at me. It would be so easy to get lost in her, for days, months, or years when she looked at me like that.

Her smile smoothed out and she bit her lip.

"Low?"

"Mmm?" I was still distracted by her teeth on her shiny pink lip.

"When is your next test?"

And just like that, my walls went up.

I dropped my eyes to my bourbon glass, picking it up and taking a long swallow. She cleared her throat before reaching out to wrap her fingers around mine.

"Come on, Low," she said in the voice she used when she spoke to the horses. Quiet and calm, designed not to scare them. "We've pretended this is our first date, we've done the meaningless chit chat, but it's not our first date. Not really. You aren't going to scare me off. You *can* talk about this stuff, you know?"

I sighed. "I know. It's just...I don't know if I want to."

She sat back in her chair and dropped my hand.

Shit.

I rushed to clarify. "It's not you, Reese. I just don't want to think about it! Especially not here, not now."

"Then when? You never want to talk about it. You want to stick your head in the sand and do this whole huge thing by yourself? There's never a good time for this, is there?" She'd gone from soft and understanding to irritated in about three seconds flat. "I know you want to protect me, but you can't. Not if whatever this is between us is real." She frowned at me. "Unless…"

"Unless what?"

"Unless this is still just some fling to you." Her face was so full of hurt and it punched me right in the gut, forcing me to sit back farther so I could breathe. The drone of voices in the crowded restaurant filled my ears, swirling and confusing my thoughts further. How had I given her the idea that this meant nothing?

I reached across the table and lifted her chin, forcing her to look at me. "This isn't some fling, Reese. I've spent the whole evening trying to stop myself from thinking of a future with you."

Her eyes widened, and her mouth dropped open for a fraction of a second before the most beautiful smile stole across her face. "But what does that mean? You want this? But…?"

"But I don't understand why you aren't running away screaming. I don't understand why you don't think us being together is a huge problem."

She sighed. "I'm not saying it, because it's an excuse. And it's not real. Trust me, I know all about burying your problems in excuses and lies and finding ways to forget, but at some point, it all just becomes bullshit."

I sighed. "It's not that simple, though."

"It is! If you like me, then let's do this. If you don't, we have to stop this. Let me go. I won't wait around for some fair-weather boyfriend. I'm in through this whole thing, or I'm out."

I scrubbed my hands over my face. My heart leapt into my throat, making the words harder to get out. "Don't you have any self-preservation instincts? I can't put you in danger like that! No matter what I want."

"Is sex all we are to you?" She gestured between us, her movements choppy.

Her words hit me straight in the gut. Maybe those first few days it had just been about sex, but then something had changed. I'd changed. And out in the stables we'd confided in each other, swapping stories, and my feelings had grown. For the first time in my life, I'd been able to open up to someone. It wasn't just about sex for me. Not at all.

"Because it's not for me. There's more than that between us, isn't there? I like you. I want to support you through this, but you won't even talk about it. You dodge the subject every time it comes up."

She slumped back in her chair, her posture matching mine.

"It's not just about sex, but the thought I could give this to you…"

"I never said we had to have sex. That, I can wait for. As long as you need. And anyway, I think we proved last night you don't even need to touch me to turn me on. But it's not the point. Let me in. If you like me, stop using the physical stuff as an excuse to push me away."

Her eyes held me like magnets, sharp and focussed. The urge to stand up, storm around the table, and pull her into my arms rose, deep and powerful in my gut. "I want this." My voice sounded strangled even to my own ears. "I want *you.*"

Her face softened and she smiled. "I don't need promises of forever. I just need you to stop putting obstacles in our way."

My nerves were raw, my muscles wound too tight. Brutal honesty was exhausting, but now that I'd started, I wasn't able to stop. "Everything in my life right now is terrifying. I don't want this thing between us to be like that."

"Then maybe you need to trust I have better judgement in this situation. You're blinded by your fear and you're ruining something I think we both need."

I frowned as her words hung in the air around us. I hadn't considered that she might need me as much as I needed her. But with that one sentence, a weight lifted off my heart, and one of my walls came crashing down. It reverberated through me as surely as the walls of the building around us would, and something shifted in my brain. "My appointment at the clinic is tomorrow. It's just a check-in. My actual test isn't for a few more weeks. But you could come, if you want to."

She studied me for so long, I wondered if she'd respond at all. But I refused to look away. She needed to know I'd meant what I said.

"Of course I'll come."

I nodded. "Okay."

We sat in silence for a few more minutes, both of us picking at the remainders of our plates. I was mentally drained and though we seemed to have come to some sort of truce, the atmosphere between us still felt off. I wanted to go back to the happy first date stuff. Not to forget the conversation we'd just had, but I didn't want to dwell on it either.

"Have you ever had a cronut?" I asked abruptly. I knew I was still avoiding the subject and trying to lighten the mood. It was a fall-back habit, but I prayed she'd let me get away with it. The doctor's appointment was a baby step; I knew that. But I was trying.

She seemed to get it. Her shoulders relaxed and she tossed her hair back from her face.

"A what, now? It sounds like it belongs on the wheel of a car."

"I'll take that as a no, then." I grinned at her devilishly as I stood up and held out my hand. "It's a croissant crossed with a doughnut. There's a place just down the road that does them. Prepare for your second mouth-orgasm of the night."

19

LOW

The waiting room reeked of antiseptic and floor cleaner, the toxic-smelling fumes strong enough to make me wrinkle my nose. I glanced around the space and wiped my sweaty palms on my jeans. Why wasn't anyone else bothered by the smell?

The receptionist bustled around behind a large desk, answering phones in a too-enthusiastic voice and typing so hard on her computer I was surprised she hadn't put a hole in her keyboard. A young guy to my right lounged in his chair, his thumb flicking over the screen of his phone. Neither seemed bothered by the complete lack of air in the small room, while all I could taste was the bitter tang on my tongue.

I didn't notice my leg twitching until Reese placed her hand on my thigh and squeezed. She didn't speak, but the calming weight of her hand made me want more. I wanted to pull her into my lap and bury my face in her neck. Or better yet, pick her up and get the hell out of this stuffy room. But since I couldn't do either of those things, I settled for letting my arm rest across her shoulders. I pulled her close and in one fluid movement the whole side of her body lined up with mine. She didn't move her hand, even when the spasm in my leg stopped.

This wasn't even testing day, just an appointment to meet the doctor and talk things out, but here I was, verging on a panic attack and planning escape routes. I didn't want to talk. I knew what I'd done and what my odds were. The HIV antibodies were probably circling in my blood right now, their numbers growing higher with each passing day. It was just a waiting game until they'd be high enough to show as a positive test.

Reese squeezed my thigh again, and when I glanced over at her, she smiled. That smile stopped everything. Stopped my shallow breaths and slowed my over-stressed brain. Her smile said she knew I was freaking out, but she was here. She was in this, and we were a team. How had I thought I could do this without her? Her touch grounded me in a way I hadn't expected. I breathed through my nose, and my chest inflated with air again, but this time, I almost didn't notice the obnoxious antiseptic smell. My nose filled with Reese's strawberry scent instead, and the familiar smell of her calmed the crushing pressure on my lungs. I couldn't keep running from this, not if I wanted her.

With my mind less overwhelmed, I noticed the patterns Reese was massaging on my leg with her thumb. Two hard presses into the muscle, followed by a gentler drag before she inched over and started the pattern again. Damn, it felt good, even through the thick fabric of my jeans. It'd been weeks since that night in the alley, so a pat on the head would feel good right now.

"Low Smith?" the receptionist called.

"Dammit," Reese whispered. "I thought you might have registered under your proper name."

I chuckled as we both stood. I'd forgotten all about our pact not to reveal our real names until we 'knew each other better.'

"Not knowing is killing you, isn't it?"

She grinned up at me and winked. "Maybe."

We followed the receptionist's directions, down a long hall with many doors, until we found the one we were looking for. A label on the door read Dr. M. Sloane.

"Oh my God, it's Mark Sloane!" Reese giggled.

"Who's Mark Sloane?" The giggling intrigued me. Reese wasn't a giggler. At all. But I liked it. I made a mental note to try to make her giggle on a regular basis. It was adorable.

Reese slapped me on the arm as her mouth dropped open. "Mark Sloane! You know, McSteamy?"

"Mc what?" I had no idea what she was talking about.

"Mc Steamy! *Grey's Anatomy?*"

"I don't watch it."

She shook her head sadly at me. "You poor, deprived little chicken. First *The Notebook*, now Grey's. Though you lied about *The Notebook*, didn't you? Does that make you a closet Grey's lover as well?"

This was the weirdest conversation to be having in the hallway outside a HIV testing office. I wondered if nerves had her babbling.

She seemed to come to the same conclusion as I had, a blush creeping up her cheeks. She shook her head. "Never mind. Come on, let's do this." She grabbed my hand, threading her fingers between mine, and rapped on the closed door with her other hand.

A female voice called us in and nerves churned in my gut again. The tiny office had open windows and fresh spring air slapped me in the face. I sucked in greedy lungfuls.

"Low?"

Dr. Sloane smiled as we moved toward her. She had fine lines around her mouth and eyes that made me think she had to be in her mid-forties. I hoped they were smile lines. If she was a friendly, smiley sort of doctor, maybe she wouldn't hold it against me when I puked all over her dark-stained desk. The nerves in my gut crawled up and strangled my throat, making it impossible to speak. I couldn't even open my mouth. So I nodded instead.

"I'm Reese." Reese introduced herself and offered a hand across the desk.

The doctor shook it firmly.

"Lovely to meet you, Reese. It's great you came along today to support Low."

We sat down in two straight-backed chairs that faced the desk. I kept my grip on Reese's hand as if I were a man drowning and she was my only way out of the waves pounding on my head.

"So, Low, what can I help you with today?"

Her question caught me by surprise. Wasn't it obvious why I was here? "I...um..." I coughed to clear my throat. "My GP thought I should come."

She smiled at me. I wished she'd take pity on me and help me out with some words. I felt like the Sahara Desert had blown in and my brain was short circuiting.

I must have looked at her blankly for long enough to make her uncomfortable because she opened my file and flipped through it.

"So you had unprotected sex on the twenty-third? And you were tested that week? You only had unprotected sex on that date?"

I nodded.

"No other time throughout your sexual history?"

I shook my head. "No, just the once."

She nodded, making notes with her pen. "Sounds like you don't need the safe sex lecture then. You knew what you needed to do. You just didn't do it." She didn't sound judgemental. She was just stating facts, but her words made me squirm as remorse mixed with guilt ate at me.

"I'm not sure why your GP bothered to have you tested at that point. HIV, even if you have it, wouldn't show up in a test that quickly. It takes a few weeks. That's why we do a repeat test. That should give us a definite answer one way or the other. Do you have your test booked in?"

I shook my head. "No, not yet."

She scooted her chair over a little and looked at her computer screen. "I can fit you in tomorrow if that suits you?"

My stomach clenched as panic made my heart thump. "Tomorrow? I thought it would still be a few more weeks? My doctor said three months."

"Eight weeks is normally enough, and you're close enough to that now. We'll do another test at six months if this one comes back negative, though. Just to be sure."

I knew the doctor was waiting for me to respond, but words wouldn't form. I'd prepared myself for a few more weeks of not knowing. I wasn't sure I was ready to let that go just yet. Cold, hard fear rushed in. It flooded my brain and took control of my actions, leaving me helpless. I froze. I wasn't ready for this.

But then Reese's soft voice broke through the fear wall. "Only the positive, remember, Low?" She tugged at my hand, drawing my gaze to her. "Better to get this over and done with, don't you think?" She sounded tentative, like I was a bomb that needed to be handled delicately.

Her eyes were big and full of hope. I couldn't keep stringing this along. It wasn't fair on her, and I was being a pussy. I needed to sort my shit out.

"Tomorrow is fine," I found myself agreeing. Reese and I both had to work, but I'd find someone to cover.

Dr. Sloane looked pleased. "Good decision. I can fit you in at four. You'll get the results almost straight away. It takes about an hour to process everything, but I'd prefer you to hang around if you can."

I nodded. Reese spoke to the doctor again, but their voices

faded. I heard nothing as I stared at a picture above the doctor's head. By 5:00 p.m. tomorrow, I'd know my fate. In twenty-four hours I'd either get to keep the woman I was falling for, or give up the best thing that had ever happened to me.

I wanted to vomit again.

20

REESE

*L*ow didn't say a word as we walked from the doctor's office back to the car. My mind was a jumbled mess of thoughts, and I didn't feel much like talking either. That hadn't gone how I'd expected it to. At all.

I hoisted myself into the passenger seat of his Ute and pulled the seatbelt across my chest as he slid into the driver's side. The keys jangled as he shoved them into the ignition, but he didn't turn them. I studied his profile as he stared through the windshield, his grip on the steering wheel so tight his knuckles turned white.

"Are you okay?" I rubbed at his stiff fingers, trying to loosen his death grip on the wheel, but he didn't let go. If anything, his grip only tightened. I hated that there wasn't anything I could do to fix this. My hand dropped back to my lap, and for a minute we sat in silence before his head abruptly snapped round to face me.

"Go out with me tonight."

It was more of a demand than a question, but I sagged back into the seat, relieved he was talking again. "What do you want to do?"

He shook his head. "I don't know. Something huge that will

make me forget about tomorrow. I'll be awake all night thinking about it if I don't have a distraction. Let's do something neither of us has done before."

A smile crept across my face. I couldn't deny that a distraction right now was a welcome idea. "I'm in. Ideas?"

He drummed his fingers on the steering wheel and stared out the windshield again, but this time a small smile lifted the corner of his mouth. Just when I thought I'd lost him to his thoughts, he turned the key, and the engine roared to life. He chuckled as we pulled into the city traffic, making me a bit afraid of whatever it was he'd decided to do. If it was skydiving, I'd kill him.

Our appointment had been a late one and the sun was just low enough to be eye-level blinding, so I dug through my handbag for my sunglasses as Low weaved his way through the maze of streets. We drove so long I was beginning to think he had no particular destination in mind, but then we pulled into a parking tower.

"The zoo? I thought we were doing something we'd never done before."

"We are." He pulled into a space and we both got out.

"Wouldn't it close soon?"

He set a cracking pace through the parking lot, his steps so bouncy I thought at any moment he might break into a jog in order to get there quicker. His excitement was so electric it practically sparked in the air around him.

I hadn't been to the zoo since I was a kid, but when we walked under the white stone archway that marked the entrance, I smiled up at it. At nine, I'd felt tiny in comparison, but it didn't seem so huge anymore.

On the other side, Low pulled me against the direction of the crowd, towards the ticket sellers. My gaze locked with a little girl as she passed us with her family. Her tired head rested on her father's shoulder as he carried her toward the exit. I smiled as she closed her eyes, her tiny bow mouth relaxed with sleep. Most of the crowd seemed to be leaving, but there was still a short queue when we reached the ticketing booths. We found a place in a line behind a middle-aged couple, holding hands. Two small suitcases on wheels rolled behind them as they took their tickets from the cashier and moved aside.

"Welcome!" the young girl behind the counter greeted us. "Just a regular night entry?"

"No, I'm interested in the Twilight Package. I don't have a booking, though."

The girl nodded and typed something into her computer, her neatly trimmed nails flying over the keyboard. She looked up with a smile. "That's no problem. We have plenty of vacancies tonight. A weeknight is a good time to come. Just the two of you?"

Low nodded and pushed his credit card towards her. I didn't protest him paying. I didn't want to argue about anything tonight. I was curious to find out what this Twilight Package was all about, though, and craned my neck, trying to see the papers the girl was printing.

When she was done, she passed Low our tickets and a handful of brochures and maps, and we made our way through the turn styles.

"What's the Twilight Package?" I asked once we were through the gates. We stood in a large courtyard that homed souvenir shops, food outlets, and the sky car station. Multiple paths led off from the large circle, with wooden arrows pointing out the way to various animal exhibits, shows, or facilities. The delicious aroma of fried food permeated the air, making my stomach rumble.

Low's eyes lit up as he took in our surroundings. "I saw something about it online ages ago and I thought it sounded awesome, like a bucket list kind of thing. We're sleeping here tonight. We get to feed the animals and talk to their keepers. It's like a behind-the-scenes night tour, with a bed at the end."

I stared at him, my mouth dropping open. "Seriously?" That would explain why our tickets had cost a small fortune.

"Seriously."

"I don't have any clothes with me! And where will we even sleep?" I looked over at the information booth, half expecting the young guy working there to hand us a sleeping bag and leave us to sleep on a garden path.

"There are cabins. But, shit. I didn't even think about clothes." His eyebrows pulled together and he squinted around the space. His gaze rested on the souvenir shop and his frown smoothed out. He laughed as he grabbed my hand again and pulled me through the door. "Look! Clothes! Grab whatever you need. We've got ten minutes until our guide picks us up, so choose quickly."

I pulled up short and nudged him with my shoulder. His excitement was infectious and was beginning to make me feel a little giddy. "You're acting a little crazy, you know that, right? This is insane." I took in the rows of T-shirts emblazoned with 'I heart Australia,' and hats with koalas on the brim. He was right. Whatever we needed for a night, we could get right here. We'd look like complete and utter tourists, but so did half the people who came to the zoo. We'd fit in perfectly.

He threw a pair of leggings covered in little Aussie flags at me. "Get these!"

I shook my head and laughed. He was like an overexcited puppy whose master had just come home from work. It was suddenly like everything at the doctor's hadn't happened, and we were just on a date, with nothing to worry about but having a good time. I hadn't noticed how tense I was, but my heart felt lighter, just being around him.

When he'd finished with the cashier, he pulled me back out to the information booth where a guide in a khaki uniform was waiting patiently for us.

"Let's go feed some animals their dinner!"

Hours later, when our guide dropped us back to the meeting spot, Low draped his arm across my shoulders and I tucked myself into his side. The zoo at night had been magical and a definite tick on the bucket list. We'd helped prepare food and fed seals, laughing as they'd propelled themselves out of the water and onto the concrete at our feet. After a quick walk through the wildlife hospital, we'd cuddled a young chimpanzee that had sat on my lap and played with my hair. I'd been reluctant to leave, but Low assured me I'd want to see our room.

Standing in the main courtyard now that it was dark and quiet was a different experience to when we'd been here earlier in the evening. Lights lit the paths that branched off from the space, but the shops had all closed, and only a handful of people milled around, mostly staff. Without the chatter of the earlier crowds, we could hear the occasional squawk or howl from the enclosures we'd just left.

"So, what now?" My voice came out sounding husky, and I tried to calm the ripple of excitement that ran through me. The anticipation of being alone with him was making my heart thump triple time.

Low dropped his arm from my shoulders and rifled through the paperwork. "This way." He pointed before picking up my hand again. The path became narrow, and the atmosphere grew peaceful. With lush gardens on either side and no one else around, I could pretend we were the only two people on earth, with only the birds and lizards for company. After a few minutes of walking, the path opened up.

"Low! Giraffes!" I squealed, rushing forward to the high, wooden fence. The smell of fresh, clean hay drifted on the slight breeze.

"I know, isn't it awes—holy shit, look at the cabin! It's practically a tree house!"

I'd been too busy admiring the animals to notice a small cabin off to our left. It sat high on stilts and would put us at giraffe head height once we climbed up there. Identical cabins stood on the other side of the circular giraffe enclosure, but they were at least a hundred metres away, and trees surrounded the sides, so the space still felt private.

"This is where all the giraffes come once the main park closes," Low read from a brochure, as one ambled along the fence line and stopped in front of us.

I nudged Low with my elbow. "This is the coolest thing ever," I whispered.

Low nodded, a satisfied smile crossing his face as he pointed to the balcony of our cabin. "The view is probably better from up there. Want to go look?"

We climbed the steep wooden stairs, each step lit by a dim, inset light and the moon above us. Someone had turned on lamps inside our room, but Low sat down on the top step and pulled me down next to him. "Wait, let's sit out here for a while before we go in."

With summer approaching, the air was warm despite the late hour. I got comfortable on the wooden steps, my arm tucked underneath Low's, our fingers still wound together. He hadn't let go of my hand for more than a few seconds since we'd arrived. And I didn't want him to. The touch of his warm, slightly roughened skin over mine was comfortable and reassuring. I felt safe with him. The night was dark and quiet around us, only the occasional snuffling and grunting of the giraffes as they congregated in their pen. I leant my head against Low's shoulder as he sat back to stare up at the heavens. I squeezed his hand.

"This is amazing. Thank you for bringing me here."

He didn't respond for a long time, but it was a comfortable silence that fell between us. This whole day had been one whirlwind after another, and it was nice to have a moment to just be.

"I'm scared, Reese," he murmured eventually.

I shuffled closer to him. "I know. Me too."

He looked down at me. "Only the positives, right?"

169

I smiled and strained up to kiss him softly. "Right."

He looked back up at the sky. "I don't want this to be the last night I spend with you." He said it so quietly, I thought I might have heard him wrong.

"Why would it be the last time? I'll still be here tomorrow night, and the night after that, no matter what happens."

He shook his head but said nothing. An uneasy feeling settled over me, but I didn't want to push him. So instead, I stood and pulled him up. "It's not tomorrow yet. We don't need to think about it until it is."

Something flickered in Low's eyes. "You're right. Tomorrow isn't what I want to be thinking about right now."

My stomach flipped at his tone. Smouldering Low was back, and though I knew this was far from the end of the conversation, I couldn't deny that look could make me forget my own name. I'd tried not to read too much into him choosing an overnight activity, but when he looked at me like that, I realised how much of a leap of faith tonight had been for him. He was trusting himself, trusting us, to be alone together. All night. I ran my hands up his arms, feeling the strength of his biceps underneath his T-shirt. His hands locked behind my back, and he dipped his head, brushing his mouth over mine.

My lips tingled as I trailed my fingers across his shoulders and into his hair. I pulled him down again, and his mouth covered mine. There was nothing rushed or urgent about the kiss. His lips parted, and he slicked his tongue into my mouth as I pulled him closer still, not wanting to let him go. He let out a low groan of pleasure that shot heat through me.

His hands ran up and down my back, holding me tight, and I melted into him. This was right. Everything about the way we fit together and the way my heart thumped triple time when I was in his arms... It felt right. I knew it in my gut. Any lingering fear over tomorrow's appointment evaporated until all that was left was him and me and the connection neither of us seemed able to deny.

Low walked me backwards to the door of our room, his lips only leaving mine long enough for him to find our key and open the door. As soon as we were inside, his lips found mine again and his hands skimmed my sides until they clutched my hips.

I moaned against his mouth and his fingers gripped me harder. He lifted me off the ground in one quick movement, and my legs wrapped around his waist without conscious thought. My brain had gone right out the window. I needed more of him. More of the man I was falling for. He blindly stumbled the few steps to the living area of the cabin and dropped to sit on the edge of the large white lounge. The thick bulge in his pants pressed against my core, increasing my frustrations rather than satisfying them.

His fingers brushed the skin of my lower back as he gathered my shirt and lifted it. He broke our kiss, pulling back just long enough for his eyes to seek my permission. Breathless and dizzy, I gave a tiny nod and he pulled the shirt over my head. His lips fused to mine the moment it was off, his kiss deep and demanding. I couldn't help myself from rocking on his lap, trying to find relief for the ache in my core, the pressure alone not enough.

I fisted the back of his shirt, and pulled it off him. I had to stop for a moment to admire the broadness of his shoulders and the cut of his abs. He was pure male perfection in my eyes. Lightly tanned skin over firm, strong muscle. When I looked back up, I'd expected to see his smirk, the one he always wore when he knew I was checking him out, but tonight there was no smirk. There was something in his expression that made me hesitate, and the need to ask what he was thinking rolled through me. But whatever the mix of emotions there, it didn't stop the way his gaze scorched me, making my breath hitch.

"Low?"

He didn't answer, just pulled my head back down, his lips crashing back into mine. But it only lasted a moment before he trailed kisses off the corner of my mouth, along my jaw, and down my throat. The lower he went, the hotter his kisses became, open-mouthed and wet as his tongue slid across my skin. My head fell backwards and I ground down on him. He groaned into the sensitive skin of my neck as his hands found the clasp of my bra. My heart fluttered. This was nothing like the time he'd had my clothes off in the alley. The alley had been hot, but it had purely been about getting off. This time when he unhooked my bra, I wanted him to really see me. I wanted him to know I was his.

I stilled as he pulled the straps down my arms, the cups falling away and exposing me to him. He dropped the bra on the floor, his eyes roving over my belly and across my breasts before he met my eyes. I loved the way he looked at me. Like he was unwrapping a present I'd picked just for him. "You're so beautiful," he whispered.

I grasped his hands, bringing them up to my breasts, and we both groaned as his hands cupped me, his fingers grazing over my already hard nipples.

My hands explored his chest, memorising the hardness of his pecs and the definition of his body. I gasped as his hot, wet mouth closed over my nipple.

"Is this okay, Reese? Tell me to stop if you want me to. I don't want to do anything you don't want." His voice was a muffled jumble of words, his breath hot against my skin.

I arched my back, my nipples standing erect and wanting. "Don't stop."

He smiled softly and sucked my nipple into his mouth again, making me moan. I wanted so much more. My breasts were well looked after, but my core ached as frustration and pleasure roared through me. I groaned, but he seemed to know what I needed, lifting me and laying me out on the lounge. I wrapped my legs around him again as his chest came down on top of mine. My skin erupted in tingles every place our bodies met, and I deepened our kiss, losing myself in him, in us.

We moved in unison, like we'd done this a million times together. His hips thrust into mine, his erection pressing on my core, eliciting spikes of pleasure over and over, but not nearly enough. We were too good together for this to stop here. His mouth never left mine, but the rest of his body pulled back just far enough to create a gap between us, and he fumbled with the button on my jeans. I grabbed at his pants as want and lust swirled through me, with a mix of something more. Something I knew would break him, so I kept it to myself, despite the way it rose through me and sat on my tongue burning, scalding. Instead, I concentrated on getting his fly undone.

The metallic noise of his zipper cut through our panting and groans, and he pulled back sharply, sitting back on his knees.

"Fuck." He looked down at me with unfocussed eyes, his breath coming in bursts.

I propped myself up on my elbow and reached a hand towards him. "We're fine. We're not doing anything wrong." I tried to force my words to sound casual, but part of me was worried he was going to pull the pin on the whole thing.

My fingers trailed along the lower half of his abs, and I watched in fascination as a shiver ran through him, his eyes dropping to my fingers in the waistband of his boxer briefs. A hiss escaped him, and his head dropped back as my hand dipped below the tight elastic, then lower to the erection straining behind it.

"Fuck, no. Stop, Reese. We can't." He placed a hand over the one I now had wrapped around his cock, and I froze, but for a long moment, he didn't move, trapping my hand. Then he groaned and I withdrew my hand slowly.

"Are you okay?"

He squeezed his eyes closed, his internal battle playing out all over his face.

"I need a shower." He kissed my temple and gently moved me off his lap before he pushed off the lounge. He walked in stiff strides across the space to the bathroom. He jerked the bathroom door open and hesitated for the briefest of moments before he seemed to steel himself and find his resolve. "A really bloody cold one."

21

LOW

*M*y cock wasn't getting the message that sexy times were over. None of my body was. Despite the cold shower pounding over my skin, every part of me wanted to go back out to the living room and finish what Reese and I had started. Just the memory of her, half-naked, with her fingers wrapped around my erection made me groan. Bringing her here tonight was both the smartest and dumbest thing I'd ever done. I dropped my chin to my chest and turned the cold water tap on harder.

"Low?"

My head snapped up, my eyes widening as Reese's dark head poked around the door. My gaze met hers through the clear glass of the shower screen, mischief written in the upward curve of her full lips. Shit. She'd be the death of me.

"Can I come in?"

"I think you already have."

"True." She pushed the door open wider and lifted a pile of fluffy white towels in her arms. "All the towels were out there. I figured you'd need one."

"You could have just passed one through the door, you know," I said dryly, my gaze following her as she crossed the room.

"You could have locked the door. But you didn't." She winked as she put the towels down on the sink and stood to face me. Fuck. She was still topless, the button on her jeans still undone. She was unashamed as her eyes roamed my body.

I sucked in a breath, loving the way her gaze lingered on my cock. "Why are you trying to kill me? I was just trying to get *that*"—I motioned to my junk—"under control. Blue balls are a real thing, you know."

She laughed. "No, it isn't." She opened the shower door and leant against the frame, crossing her arms underneath her breasts. She jumped and took a step back when some of the spray bounced back at her. "Shit, you weren't kidding about having a cold shower, were you? I'd planned on joining you, but that's freezing. I'll wait till you're done."

She turned to leave, but my hand shot out, circling her wrist, and with a quick yank, I pulled her into the chilly spray.

"Shit! Low!" she yelled, pulling back. "It's freezing!"

A laugh erupted from somewhere deep in my chest and I pulled her closer, shielding her from the water with my back as I cranked up the hot tap. As soon as the water turned warm, I stepped out of the way, letting the heat warm her chilled skin.

Water poured over her head, down her face and chest in rivers and lower to soak the jeans she was still wearing. I chuckled. "Better?" This shower had gotten a whole lot better for me as soon as she'd walked into the room.

She opened her eyes. "Always better when I'm with you."

My heart stuttered, and I brushed my lips across hers. "Me too."

Her answering smile was soft, but it got lost as I kissed her again, deep and slow as my fingers tangled in the back of her hair. I tugged on it, tipping her head backwards, giving me better access to her mouth and throat, our bodies pressed together in all the places that mattered most. The tension between us changed, and I didn't know if it was me or something I sensed in her, but the need for her intensified until I could barely breathe. Her hands dragged over my chest and down before she gripped my cock, stroking it once. Her eyes met mine and this time it was her asking permission. My hips jerked, my cock sliding in her wet grasp. *Shit.* Panic rose in me, but I stamped it down. I hadn't wanted things to go this far, but fuck, I couldn't stop her again. Not when I wanted it so bad. Not when tonight might be the only chance I had to be with her like this. I didn't know what tomorrow would bring, but if it brought bad news, I would still have this.

Her mouth turned up at the corner as she lathered soap in her palms, running it over my lower abs and letting it drip. Her soap slicked hand rolled over my shaft, and fuck me, it felt good. I'd come in about three seconds flat if I didn't distract myself.

My fingers found the waistband of her jeans and I tugged her closer, undoing the zip and pushing them down her thighs. She let go of me long enough to step out of the soaked material before finding me again.

Her underwear was a tiny scrap of black lace that barely covered her. Everything within me coiled tight—my muscles, my gut, my balls. That tiny triangle of material was all that stood between the two of us being completely bare. This was torture, having her here, naked and willing but unable to do anything about it.

But that wasn't entirely true. I may not have been able to lay her out and bury myself in her wet warmth the way I wanted to. But there were things I could do, things that would make her feel just as good as I felt right now.

"Reese."

"Mmm?" She'd been watching her fingers slide around my cock. My balls tightened again. Fuck. I had to stop watching her before I came all over her hand prematurely. We might not have been able to have sex, but I didn't want her thinking I couldn't last the distance.

"I want to touch you. That's okay? The doctor said, right?" I didn't want to kill the moment, but I needed her reassurance more.

"Show me your hands."

Without asking why, I held them out and she traced my fingers with the soap, one by one before she met my eyes. "See? You're fine. No open cuts. You can touch me all you want." I already knew it, but I needed her to say it. I needed her to agree this was okay.

"All I want, huh?" My hands slid up her arms and across her breasts, rubbing her nipples with my thumbs as I went. "Like here?" Her eyes closed as she nodded. If there was any good to come from this whole mess of a situation, it was that waiting this long to be together made touching her now all the sweeter.

My hands traced the swell of her hips and lingered at the elastic of her shower-soaked underwear. My fingers tucked beneath it, ready to pull it off, but something stopped me. As flimsy as that tiny scrap of lace was, it was still a barrier. Still a reminder that although we were taking this to a new place, the old rules still applied.

My cock twitched in readiness, but I ignored it, sliding my hand over the triangle of lace, then under the edge to touch her with my fingers. I paused for a moment, as nerves erupted within my gut, but I wouldn't put her at risk. Not in a million years would I get so carried away I'd do that to her. I couldn't. But I didn't need my cock to make her feel good.

My fingers slid through the wetness between her legs, eliciting a cry from her.

"Fuck, baby, you're wet."

Her eyes opened and she snorted. "We're in a shower, Low." She laughed, her eyes sparkling, her hair plastered to her face.

I ran my finger through her folds and circled her clit. She

stopped laughing, her eyes closing again. "Not the kind of wet I meant and you know it."

She nodded as her hand came back to my cock, and a groan escaped me. I ran my finger over her sensitive bunch of nerves, until her free hand clutched my arm, her nails digging into my skin. Then I slowly dipped one finger inside her. Her hand moved quicker over my length and I added another, my fingers sliding in and out of her, matching the pace she set. Her mouth dropped to my shoulder, her tongue licking water droplets from my skin.

A shudder ran through her, her walls clenching around my fingers as she cried out, the sound vibrating across my skin. Her legs went weak and she gripped me tighter as I ran my thumb over her clit, making her clench again. Having her here in my arms, watching her come undone, was the end of me.

"Fuck, Reese." My balls drew up, my lower abs contracting as pleasure roared through me. She pumped me harder.

"Just—" I don't know what I'd been about to say. Just be careful? Just don't get that stuff anywhere near you? But she cut me off, her mouth covering mine, our tongues tangling. I came into her hand, unable to hold on any longer. I broke away from her mouth, something between pleasure and panic coursing through me, and watched as hot spurts shot from my tip, only to harmlessly wash down the drain by the water falling from the shower head.

Her hand stilled and my fingers slipped from her body. Our eyes met.

"You okay?"

I didn't have to think about it.

"I'm fucking great." I dropped my mouth and kissed the grin right off her face.

22

LOW

I woke up in a tangle of limbs, Reese's shiny black hair draped across my chest. I picked up a strand, running my fingers along its length. It was soft as silk. The weak morning sun crept in beneath the blinds, but there was enough to light her face, peaceful and relaxed as she slept with her head on my arm.

I'd been so high when I'd pulled her into bed with me. Having those moments with her in the shower, watching her come undone under my hands, was a heady feeling. I wanted to do it a thousand times over, touch every part of her body and every inch of her skin. As I'd pulled her to my chest and tucked my knees in behind hers, I felt like a million bucks. She'd been practically purring as my fingers stroked her bare arm and fallen asleep within minutes, a small smile lingering on her face.

But sometime after midnight, a quiet darkness settled as Reese's breathing became deep and even, and the low beginnings of panic started up in my gut again. I'd managed to ignore it earlier, distracted by my libido, but with nowhere to run, it hit me square in the face. I'd lain awake for hours, memorising the way her body felt pressed against mine. I tried to lock in the rhythmic rise and fall of her chest and the soft sound of her breath as it blew across my skin.

My chest constricted, thinking about the test. I knew fear. Growing up with my mother, there'd been times where I'd had no idea where she was, or if she was even coming back. She'd left me in derelict motels or at strangers' houses for days on end, and I'd had to learn to fend for myself. One of her boyfriends over-dosed right in front of me and I'd watched the paramedics fail to revive him.

But nothing had terrified me the way this test did. With my mother, deep down, I always knew I'd land on my feet. I'd been taken from my grandparents, but they'd provided me a home and love, and in my heart, I knew I'd always have a place there if my mother never came back. But nobody could help me today. I'd made my bed and now I had to lie in it.

My arm beneath Reese's head was numb, and I pulled it from under her, watching as she stirred then settled back into sleep. I envied her. My muscles were tight, and my brain wouldn't stop. The anxious thoughts kept crowding in. I wanted to sleep, but the air was still, the room stuffy and hot. I needed to get out. I needed to run.

Not wanting to wake Reese, I slipped from the bed silently. I found the bag of clothes we'd bought the day before and slipped them on. My eyes raked around the room, searching for some-thing to write a note on, before I realised I knew exactly where I could find a pen and a piece of paper. I grabbed Reese's handbag, hoping she wouldn't mind, and of course, right there next to her wallet was a stack of Post-it notes and a pen. I dashed off a note telling her I'd be back soon and let myself out. The door closed with a soft click behind me.

I jogged along the path we'd walked last night, back to the zoo entrance and through the parking lot to my car. I pulled my phone out of my pocket and sent off a quick text message before starting the engine.

The city streets were still quiet this early, the sky still casting a pinky-orange glow along the horizon, so I made good time getting out of there. My breathing was still weird, shallow and too fast. I shook my head, trying to clear it. I just had to get there, then I could deal with this.

The car stopped with a jolt when I reached my destination. Jamison was already there.

"Hey, mate." He bounced on the balls of his feet, shifting from side to side, warming up. He wore running shorts and a T-shirt, his feet encased in expensive-looking joggers. He looked me up and down, his brow furrowing. "What the hell are you wearing? You look like you're going to an Australia day parade."

I looked down at my outfit—an I love Australia T-shirt, Australia flag shorts, and slip-on shoes with kangaroos on them. "Reese and I played tourist last night." I searched through the junk littering the back seats of my Ute and pulled out the running shoes that lived there permanently for times like this when I decided I just needed to run.

"I'm surprised you wanted to run this morning if you were with Reese last night," Jamison quipped, drawing my attention back to him.

"She's why I wanted to run this morning. I couldn't just lie there next to her anymore."

"You got something against snuggling? I got the impression you two were pretty into each other. Neither of you has said much, but I'm not blind to the flirting."

I sighed and stretched one leg up behind me. "I might have HIV."

Jamison dropped the arm he'd been stretching and looked at me. "You're serious?"

I NODDED. One thing I'd realised as I'd lain awake during the night was that I needed to tell someone else what was going on.

I'd been so secretive about this whole damn thing; letting Reese be my sole support. It wasn't fair.

Jamison let out a low whistle. "Shit, man."

"Yeah."

"You get tested?"

"This afternoon."

"So it could be all good still?"

I shrugged. "Could be."

Jamison stared at me for a second again. "You want to run?"

God, he was a good friend. I should have known he wouldn't freak out, but my stomach was still sick over even telling him.

"Yeah."

We set off at warm-up pace, but it wasn't long before I was pushing myself harder. Jamison kept up easily. We ran together often, and we were both fit, but he had more natural ability than I did, so I sometimes struggled to match his pace. I never minded; it was good for my fitness. But today I wanted to go out hard. I wanted the rush of endorphins and to be so out of breath that all I could think of was the burn in my chest and the ache in my thighs. If I pushed myself hard enough, my head would clear of thought. Running hard was good like that. All you concentrated on was putting one foot in front of the other and getting in enough oxygen. No time for thinking about life-changing tests.

I slowed to a stop at the far end of the park and leant over, resting my hands on my knees, trying to suck in more air. My lungs burned, but my body felt great. And my head felt clearer than it had in days.

"I need you to watch out for her."

Jamison turned his head from the spot on the grass where he'd collapsed at the end of our run. "Hey?"

"Reese. She's got personal shit going on. She needs a friend. If this test doesn't go well tonight, I can't be with her, man. I just can't." I wanted to be the one to help her reunite with her family. Or at least be the one to be there to pick up the pieces if they rejected her again. But I didn't know if I'd get the chance. And if I didn't, I wanted to make sure there was someone else who would.

Jamison pushed himself up onto his elbows, his shirt sticking to his chest with sweat. "Did you tell her that?"

I shook my head and tried not to look him in the eye. I felt cowardly. "Sort of. I don't know. No, not exactly."

"Let's just wait until you get your results, okay?"

I nodded. He was right. I was getting ahead of myself. "Yeah."

I stuck out my hand and pulled Jamison to his feet.

"She's a nice girl. You'd be stupid to let that go."

I didn't say anything. I knew he was right. But I'd put her first if it killed me.

23

LOW

*W*ith my thigh muscles aching, I staggered back to the Ute and fished my phone from the centre console. Three missed calls, all from Reese. I hit the return call button and cringed when it only rang once before Reese answered.

"Where are you?!"

Shit. Not even a hello. I was in trouble.

"Running with Jamison."

"Oh. Okay." She paused. "You suck at leaving notes, you know? A little more detail than your *I'll be back* note would have helped. Only Arnold Schwarzenegger can pull that off."

I snorted. She was cute as fuck when she was pissed. "I'm on my way back. Are you ready to leave? Want to meet out front?"

Reese was already waiting in her ridiculous Australia-themed outfit when I pulled up at the zoo entrance. I tried to judge how annoyed she was with me, but I couldn't help the laugh that escaped me. She gave me an exasperated smile, then punched me in the arm. Hard. It actually hurt. A tiny bit.

"I guess I deserved that, huh?"

"You deserve a kick to the balls, but since this is a weird day for you, I settled for your arm."

"My balls appreciate the slack. I'm sorry, though. I didn't mean to make you worry."

The corners of her mouth turned up and I leant across the gap and kissed her on the cheek. I'd been let off the hook easier than I deserved. Reese pulled her seatbelt across her chest, clicked it into place, then tucked one leg up beneath her. "What do you want to do today? Your appointment isn't until four, so we have time to kill."

"I was thinking about going out to my grandparents' house. If you want to? I've been meaning to get out there for weeks. There's a foal I want to see and I bet Gran will make us lunch if we ask nicely." My throat tightened every time I thought about the test this afternoon, but my grandparents' house had always been my safe place. Walking the fields of their property, breathing in the fresh air, and losing myself in the simple needs of the horses had always brought me a sense of calm and belonging I'd never felt anywhere else. I needed that today. I needed a hug from my gran and to see that look of pride in my grandfather's eye. I'd never been a screw-up to them.

She nodded. "Food and horses. I'm in." She looked down at her outfit. "Will your grandparents care I'm dressed like this?"

I slid my hand off the gear stick and down onto her thigh, giving it a gentle squeeze. "You're perfect." I meant it in more ways than just her outfit. She smiled and we sat in companionable silence for a while, as the landscape outside the car turned from urban concrete to rural green.

"Hey, is this a date?" Reese asked, turning her body so she faced me as much as her seatbelt would allow. When I glanced over, there was a glint of mischief in her expression.

"A date? Sure, I guess so." I had no idea where she was going with this.

"And we went out yesterday. So that was another date. That

means we're on our third official date. I think that means we know each other pretty well... I mean, you've had your fingers and tongue in some...uh...rather intimate places of mine..."

I raised an eyebrow at her and she laughed. "Are you asking me to do that again? Because I will."

"Right here in the car? While you're driving? Sounds dangerous."

"Don't tempt me."

She shook her head and laughed. "You're terrible. My point, before you tried to distract me, was we know each other better. You said when we knew each other better, you'd tell me your real name."

I groaned. "You really want to know?"

"It can't be that bad. What is it? Carlo?"

"Ha, no, but I'd prefer that."

"Ludlow?"

"No."

"Lowman?"

"Gag, no."

She paused for a moment, thinking.

"Longfellow?"

I choked on a laugh. "What the fuck, Reese? That's not even a name!"

"It is! I Googled it!"

I chuckled. "My name is not Longfellow, though that is an accurate description of me." I wiggled my eyebrows at her.

She rolled her eyes and gave me one of her almost painful punches to the arm.

"Come on then, Longfellow, tell me what your name is."

"It's Lowell."

She raised one of her perfect eyebrows. "What's wrong with Lowell?"

"What's right with it? It belongs on an eighty-year-old!"

"I kind of like it. I might start calling you Lowell all the time."

"Don't. Please."

She winked. "Don't worry, *Low*, I know all about having a name you hate."

"And you promised you'd tell me. So spill."

She groaned and shook her head. "I don't want to. It's never suited me. Only my mother calls me that name. And even then, it's only when I'm in trouble." She trailed off, her face becoming pained. I frowned. She couldn't even speak of her parents without that look of pure anguish invading her expression. This rift with her parents was eating her alive. I could see it clear as day, even if she couldn't.

She dropped her gaze to her lap. "It's Theresa, after Mother Theresa. My mother's choice. But Dad shortened it to Reese from the day I was born. He wanted a boy."

I scrunched my face in an over exaggerated look of disgust. "I can see why you'd change it. Theresa is terrible! How horrible to be named after someone who helped the sick and poor!"

I earned myself another punch to the arm for my sarcasm. I might even have a teeny tiny bruise if she kept that up.

She laughed. "Shut up."

I turned the blinker on and slowed down to accommodate the sharp corner and the gravel of the road we turned onto. "This is my grandparents' place."

Reese peered through the windshield and whistled. "This is all theirs? I can't even see the house yet! How much property do they own?"

I shrugged. "A couple hundred acres maybe? I'm not sure. Pop will tell you if you're really interested."

We rounded a bend in the driveway, and a sprawling, ranch style house with a wraparound porch came into view.

"Wow," Reese said quietly from the seat beside me. "It has a rocking chair and everything. This place is gorgeous. It puts my parents' little farm to shame."

Happiness settled over me. I wanted Reese to love this place as much as I did. I still remembered making this drive before I was even old enough to sit in the front seat of the beaten-up car my mother had driven me here in. This was the only real home I'd ever had. All the grandeur meant nothing, but the love and stability I knew waited for me inside was worth more than the property we stood on. I suddenly couldn't wait for Reese to meet my grandparents, and I kicked myself for doing it today of all days. But it had to be now, in case…well. Just in case. I didn't want to think about the alternatives too much.

My grandmother's slim figure appeared in the doorway as I pulled up the park brake. She wiped her hands on an apron tied around her tiny waist, then waved.

"She's like something out of a story book. Was she baking?"

I opened my door. "Probably. She loves to cook."

"I love her already."

We both got out, and I saw Gran do a double take when she noticed I wasn't alone. I ran up the steps and wrapped her tiny body in my arms.

"You turn up without warning and with a girl, Low? Well, blow me down with a feather, there's a first for everything," she whispered in my ear.

"Don't get too attached. It's new," I whispered back before I let her go. I frowned, not liking the way the words sounded. Why had I said that? It might have been new, but I was serious about Reese and I didn't like giving my grandmother the impression I wasn't. A voice in the back of my head whispered a warning to not get too attached myself, but I didn't want to give that idea any credit and snuffed it out before it could take hold.

Reese leant on the porch railing, smiling as she watched us. I held out my hand and she joined me, wrapping her arm around my lower back as I slung my arm over her shoulder.

"Reese, this is my grandma, Lucy. Gran, this is my friend Reese." Something flashed in Reese's eyes, making my stomach churn. I hated calling her my friend when what I felt was so much more than friendship. But to offer her more right now wasn't fair, even if it gnawed at my insides like a rat.

Reese offered her hand to my grandmother. "It's lovely to meet you, Lucy."

Gran accepted her hand and pulled her into her arms. "Sorry, sweetheart, but you're the first woman Low has brought home, so I need to give you a hug."

Reese raised an eyebrow at me over my grandmother's shoulder with a *you could have told me!* look. I shrugged.

"So, what are you two kids up to today?" Gran asked as she led the way into the kitchen, the sweet scent of freshly baked biscuits permeating the air.

"Nothing much. We have a few hours to kill, so I thought I'd bring Reese out to see your new foal."

"You mean your new foal."

Reese pulled my hand. "Hey? The foal is yours?"

I shook my head. "No."

"Yes, it is." Gran's voice was firm as she pinned me with a glare. "We talked about this." She turned to Reese, her tone softening. "He needs another horse, with Lijah gone. He can't keep working in that bar forever. Not if he wants to learn more about training."

"Gran—"

"Don't Gran me. You know I'm right."

I picked up a biscuit off the bench and shoved it in my mouth to avoid answering, turning to Reese instead.

"Have one," I mumbled between bites. "You have no idea how good these things are. You'll be mouth-orgasming all over the place."

Reese's eyes widened, and pink spots appeared on her cheeks. Oops, probably shouldn't have mentioned orgasms in front of my grandmother. But Gran took one look at Reese's shocked face and laughed.

"Don't worry, sweetheart. It takes more than that to ruffle my feathers."

Reese smiled politely but shot me another death look. I couldn't contain my laughter.

"Why don't you two go on out and see the baby, and I'll bring a picnic down." She looked over at Reese. "If you keep him out of the house, I might have biscuits left for dessert. They don't last long around this one."

The stables and a modest training yard were out beyond a manicured lawn and my grandmother's roses. I flicked my head at Reese, motioning for her to follow me.

"You'll find your pop out there somewhere. I think he was headed for the stables last I saw him," Gran called as she pulled cold meat and salads from the fridge.

Reese smiled as she closed the back door behind her. "She's great."

My chest swelled with pride. "Yeah, she is."

We strolled across the lawn in companionable silence, my arm around her shoulders, hers draped across my lower back, her fingertips tucked into the back pocket of my jeans.

"Sorry about the friend comment," I said, dropping my head so my lips brushed over the silkiness of her hair.

She shrugged. "It is what it is."

I frowned, emotions warring within me at her flippant comment. I didn't think she meant it. I'd seen the look in her eye when I'd downplayed our relationship. She was handling me with kid gloves, and I hated it. I wanted to tell her everything. I wanted to grab her by the shoulders, force her to look at me and listen as I recited the list of things I loved about her. Like how much I loved the happiness that radiated from her when she was on horseback. Or the way she was always quick to forgive and even quicker with a smart-ass comeback. And most of all I wanted to tell her I loved her for the way she cared for me, even when I didn't deserve something so pure and good. I loved the way she believed in me and believed in us, and I wanted her to know I felt the exact same way.

But how could I say anything with my future so uncertain?

My emotions raw, and a lump in my throat from suppressing my feelings, I stopped and took her jaw between my hands, dropping my lips to hers. I couldn't say the words, not yet, so instead I put everything I felt into kissing her. She responded immediately, as she always did, parting her lips and melting into me. My hands roamed down her neck and across her shoulders to her back as I revelled in the way we fit together. Everything I felt for her was a siren sounding through my body. It was in my head, my lungs, my gut, and my heart. She belonged here. With me. On my family's property, in my arms and by my side.

I lost track of how long we stood there, but I was unwilling to let her go. Our tongues stroked together, my heart racing as I locked my arms around her. For one of the first times in my life, I didn't need more. I didn't want her on her knees, sucking my cock. I didn't want to rip her clothes off and dive inside her. All I wanted was her. Her heart, her soul, and a future with the woman I loved. It was all within my grasp yet still so fucking far away.

I hugged her tighter and took a deep, calming breath that filled my lungs with her strawberry scent. Four hours to go. Four hours until I could tell her.

"Low! I didn't know you were coming around today! Did you run out of food at your place?" Pop's voice came from the stable doorway, and I led Reese over to him, wrapping him in a hug and slapping the old man on the back.

"I'm here partially for the food, partially for the company."

He turned to Reese. "He's talking about the horses, you know. Not me."

She grinned.

"Pop, this is Reese."

"Hello, sweetheart, it's wonderful to meet you. Low doesn't

bring friends home too often." Pop frowned. "Or ever, come to think of it."

I was getting embarrassed about the big deal they were making over this, but Reese laughed good-naturedly. "So I've heard. I'm honoured to be the first. This place is amazing."

"Thank you. We like it. Come see your foal, Low."

I shook my head but didn't bother correcting him. Once my grandparents got an idea in their heads it was impossible to talk them out of it.

Gran joined us in the foal's paddock, a picnic blanket tucked under one arm and a basket overfilled with food in the other. I took the basket from her, and she spread the blanket on the ground. The four of us watched as the little horse pranced around on his long, spindly legs, tripping over himself and falling into the patchy grass, only to right himself and take off at full speed again. He was a gorgeous little thing, and my heart felt a little lighter at the thought of training him.

"So how long have you two been together?" Gran questioned Reese when we'd all assembled sandwiches for ourselves, obviously ignoring my earlier comment about us being friends.

"We're not—" I jumped in before she could answer.

"I was asking Reese, Low, but thank you." Gran gave me one of her looks.

"Sorry."

Reese reached over and squeezed my hand. "Low's right. We haven't put a label on anything yet."

Her words stabbed at my heart. They might have been true, but that wasn't what I wanted to be telling my grandmother. I wanted to be yelling that Reese was my girl. I had real feelings for her and I was pretty sure she felt the same way. Why else would she be sticking around through all my crap?

"So you work at the racetrack then, Reese?"

"Sure do. I love it there."

"Reese is studying to be a vet," I piped up.

Grandma looked interested, but Reese shifted, suddenly looking uncomfortable. Pop shovelled food into his mouth, not paying attention to our conversation.

"Was," Reese said quietly.

"But she's going back to it."

"Maybe."

Gran's head turned from side to side, watching the back and forth between us as if she were at a tennis match. "Well, I hope you return to it. We could always use another vet on staff here and at the racetrack."

Reese lifted her eyes, and I saw the hope that flashed in them. "Really?"

Grandma nodded. "Absolutely. We have one full-time vet who travels between our properties, but we have more work than he can handle alone. And with the increased business over the last few years, we've been considering bringing on someone else full-time. You need to do a practical block at some point in your course, I assume?"

Reese nodded.

"Well, I hope you'll consider doing it with us."

"That would be amazing. I'll take you up on that if I go back."

"When you go back," I corrected.

She rolled her eyes. "When then."

I grinned triumphantly and she rewarded me with one of her killer smiles. Her happiness lifted a little of the weight off my shoulders.

Reese, Grandma, and I spent the rest of the meal chatting about trivial things, with Pop joining in on occasion. The conversation flowed, keeping my mind off the ticking clock. My grandmother liked Reese. I could see it in the way she listened to her every word and patted her hand. And Reese was in her element, relaxed and comfortable, talking about horses and the bar. My mind drifted to future meals we could have here as a couple, the Christmases and other holidays we would spend around the dining room table, the children we'd have one day running around, and Pop yelling at them to be quiet even though he'd instigated the game. Reese could teach our daughters to ride their ponies here.

Just like the night of our first real date, a future with Reese was all too easy to imagine.

Gran eventually stood up and brushed her hands on her pants. Reese jumped up to help her clean up the picnic mess, but Gran shooed her away. "Malcolm, why don't you take Reese out to see that colt you're training? Low can help me take this all back to the house, can't you, love?"

It wasn't a question and we all knew it. Gran wanted to talk to me alone. Reese didn't seem to mind, though, and Pop was already telling her about the colt and its bloodlines as she followed him obediently out of the paddock.

I gathered the plates and cups and placed them back in the empty picnic basket. Gran's eyes bored holes in my back, tension thickening the air between us, forcing me to face her. She examined me with her eyes narrowed and head cocked slightly to the side.

"What?"

I don't know why I bothered asking. I knew from experience she would only speak when she was ready, and I probably wasn't going to like what she said. But that was irrelevant. I was twenty-five years old, but I may as well have been ten to her.

"I've been watching you today, and you can tell me to mind my business if you like, but I have something I want to say."

I didn't respond. We both knew that despite her words, she would say whatever was on her mind, whether I liked it or not.

She grasped my hand and pressed her fingertips hard into my palm. "There's something eating at you, my boy, and I don't understand why you're holding that girl at arm's length when you're so obviously in love with her. Even as a little boy, you never thought you were good enough for anyone's love. I blame your damn mother for that. God knows, every time she'd dump you at our place, I'd try my best to give you all the love you deserved, but every time she came back to get you, I saw that same veil come down over your eyes. The one you have now, where you don't let nobody in for fear of getting hurt again. It kills me to see that her sins are still affecting you now, as a grown man."

I shook my head. "That's not it."

She raised an eyebrow. "It's not? You're sure about that?"

"My childhood sucked. So what? I'm not the only one who didn't come from a perfect nuclear family." I swatted at a fly that buzzed around us, watching as it disappeared towards the grove of eucalypt trees that bordered the property.

Gran sighed. "You might think that, Low. You might push your mother out of your mind, but she's always going to be a part of you. Her actions shaped who you are, and as much as I hate that, I also think you're a pretty damn fine young man. Not too many people could overcome the things you have and still end up a decent human being on the other side."

I let her words sink in. Gran wasn't one to lavish praise for no reason. She was warm and kind, but if you didn't earn her respect, you wouldn't get it at all.

"There's more going on, Gran, but it's stuff I don't want to talk about yet."

She stopped and eyed me warily. She wasn't happy I was keeping things from her. I could tell by the set of her shoulders. But then her eyes softened. "You don't have to tell me anything. I know I'm your grandma and you're entitled to your own private business. I just don't want you missing out on something that could be real good for you, just because you think you don't deserve it."

I couldn't tell her how right she was. That I didn't deserve Reese. Not because I thought I was gutter trash, like she feared, but because I couldn't offer her the future she deserved.

24

REESE

I would have been happy to stay on Low's grandparents' farm for the rest of the day, all week, or for the rest of my life, but all too soon, Low gave me a look and flicked his head toward the door.

I acknowledged him as tension built in my chest, threatening to cut off my throat, but I pushed the feeling away. He needed me to be strong, and I refused to let him down.

Lucy opened her arms and pulled me into a hug. I didn't hesitate, letting her tiny frame wrap around me. She squeezed me tight.

"Thank you for today."

Lucy was strangling me with the tightness of her hug, and my words came out sounding breathless.

"It was my pleasure." She pulled back and looked me in the eye before leaning closer. "Don't give up on him," she whispered into my ear. "He pushes people away, but he's worth it."

I hugged her again. "I know."

Low kissed his grandma on the cheek and engulfed his grandfather in a hug. Both Malcolm and Lucy looked at Low with such love and pride. Poor Low. If only his mother would have left him here for his grandparents to raise. He could have had a different childhood, one filled with love and security.

We climbed back in and Low steered the Ute back onto the dirt road, the roar of the engine the only sound around us. He drove faster than he had on the way in, and dust rose behind us in a cloud. His shoulders were hunched over the steering wheel, the easy relaxation he'd found at the farm seemingly lost already.

There was no point in asking if he was okay again. He wasn't. There was nothing I could say to make any of this better, so silence fell over us and I let the drone of the engine soothe my nerves. The tall buildings of the city loomed over us before he spoke again.

"Reese."

"Mmmm?"

"You need to ring your parents."

"What?" We were minutes away from the clinic, and a conversation about my family was the last thing on my mind.

"I think they'd want to see you, don't you? You'll never resolve this thing if you don't reach out."

"We're five minutes away from your appointment and this is what you want to talk about? This isn't important right now." I turned and looked out my window.

"It is important, and yes, we do need to talk about it now," he snapped, catching my attention immediately. I'd never heard him use that tone before. We stopped at a traffic light and when his gaze met mine, the intensity there shocked me. But his voice was softer when he spoke again. "Promise me you'll at least consider calling them. Family is everything, and it sounds like you once had a good one. I don't like you being so alone."

"I'm not alone. I have you and Bianca. And Jamison and Riley."

He flinched. It was small, but I saw it. My mouth dried, suddenly feeling like it was made from cotton wool.

"Promise me, Reese."

It wasn't that I didn't want to call my family. Ever since I'd seen Gemma's Facebook post, reconciling with them had been at the forefront of my mind, but I still hadn't found the nerve to do it. I had money put aside—money I wanted to use to buy Gemma a horse of her own. Maybe a beautiful palomino; she'd always loved the golden colour. But I didn't have enough saved yet. But by Christmas, I would. I'd daydreamed of showing up on my family's farm with a horse trailer in tow. Gemma would open the door and run across the grass, no sign of a limp, let alone a wheelchair. My parents would follow her out, their shock turning to joy when they saw me. We'd apologise and laugh and fall into each other's arms. Something stopped me from telling Low all of that, though. I knew it was a long shot, but I wanted it with every inch of my soul. I knew, deep down, it was a far-fetched dream, but I wasn't ready to have anyone take that tiny glimmer of hope from me. So instead, I told him what he wanted to hear.

"I promise."

He relaxed his grip on the wheel and sat back in his chair. "Good."

I wished he could see himself the way I saw him. He was about to go through a huge, life-changing event, but he was still thinking about me and my problems. If only he could see the good in himself and the kind heart he tried to tuck away. I wanted to tell him that when he'd walked into my life, he'd changed it for the better. He'd made me feel something again, and while I might not yet be whole, he'd been the one to begin healing the parts of me that were broken.

The minutes ticked by, both of us lost to our own private thoughts. My stomach sank to my shoes when Low pulled the car into the clinic parking lot. I had so much to tell him, but I couldn't utter a word. Once this was all done, and our nerves weren't frayed and raw, we'd have plenty of time to talk.

Low locked the car, passing me the keys to put in my handbag, and we walked to the clinic entrance together. The plain brick front and muted colours seemed more clinical than it had yesterday. I reached for Low's hand when he paused in the entrance. We stood that way for a moment, side by side, hand in hand, staring up at the building. I squeezed his fingers and looked up at him, waiting until he met my gaze. With sadness in his eyes, he stroked the back of his hand down the side of my face before he leant in and kissed me softly. I could feel his bleakness in that one simple brush of his lips.

"Only the positive," I murmured before he pulled away.

He nodded and led me towards the building.

My feet were as heavy as lead, but a chant started up in my head. "Be positive. It's negative. Be positive. It's negative." It distracted me enough that I barely noticed Low check in, and then I was following him down the hall.

I pulled up short at the doorway of the office we'd sat in yesterday. "I can wait outside if you want."

Without hesitation, he shook his head. "No, come with me. Please." He tugged on my hand. "I want you there."

"Okay."

I followed him into the office and sat down. Doctor Sloane's chair sat ominously on the other side, empty. I scratched at my arm. Low's leg bounced up and down next to me, and after a few moments, he stood up and walked around the tiny office. I said nothing, knowing he needed to burn off the nervous energy. Walking seemed like a better idea than the way I was scratching my arm raw anyway. I'd draw blood if I kept that up. I tucked my hands under my thighs, effectively sitting on my hands so I couldn't do it anymore.

The door opened behind us and Doctor Sloane moved around the desk to sit in front of us. Her relaxed demeanour was at complete odds with Low's nervous pacing. I almost expected her to kick off her shoes and put her feet up on her desk. But of course, she didn't.

"Hello, Low. Reese." She nodded to us both as she settled in and picked up a pen. "Sorry to keep you waiting." Her eyes followed Low as he moved restlessly around the office.

"Please, Low, have a seat. We'll get this done as quickly as possible." She gestured towards the seat next to me, and Low sat down obediently. She opened the paperwork on her desk and read through it before looking up at Low and smiling. She seemed like such a nice lady. Shame she had such a shitty job.

"Okay then. Now I know you would have already answered a lot of these questions with your GP, but for my records, I need to ask them again. Is that okay to do in front of Reese?" She shot me an apologetic look.

I stopped myself from offering to leave again, though the words burned on my tongue. He'd already told me he wanted me here. I didn't want him to think I was abandoning him.

He nodded. "It's fine."

I folded my hands in my lap and dropped my head to stare at them as the doctor's questions and Low's answers washed over me in dribs and drabs. How many sexual partners have you had? How often do you use protection? And on and on. The questions were so personal, and not wanting to make Low more uncomfortable, I sat as quietly as possible, trying to blend into the background.

When the barrage of questions was over, Low and the doctor stood up, and she walked him over to her treatment area. I watched from my chair as she snapped on gloves and prepared a needle.

It was over in less than a minute, and Low came back to where I was sitting.

"This won't take long. The rapid test results are available in less than half an hour. I'll just take these samples over to the lab and I'll be back as soon as I can with the results. You two can wait here if you like. You're my last patient of the day, so I won't need the office."

Low nodded and I reached out and rubbed his arm reassuringly.

"Thank you."

The doctor placed her hand on Low's shoulder as she passed by. He gave her a weak smile.

The door shut with a click and Low and I were alone again.

"She's good with a needle." Low examined his arm, a red puncture mark marring his skin. "I barely even felt that."

I nodded, scooting my chair closer to his and turning in my seat to face him.

"So now we wait." He lifted the wrist his watch was strapped to, then dropped his hand back to his lap with a sigh.

I felt the distance between us, both physically and in the sense we were both keeping secrets. Words seemed pointless. It had all been said before, except for the few little words I really wanted to say. The ones that might actually make a difference, but ones I knew he wasn't ready to hear. I couldn't talk, but I could do something about the physical distance.

I stood up and took two steps to stand in front of Low's chair. He watched me with shrewd eyes.

"What are you doing?"

I knelt on the floor in front of him and nestled myself in between his widespread legs. My hands rested on his denim covered thighs. "You were too far away."

He watched as my hand travelled up his thigh and over his abdomen, stopping at his chest. I lifted my eyes to meet his and he let out a slow, unsteady breath. "I like having you over here so much more." He smiled at me, a hint of his usual cheekiness breaking through.

My other hand followed the path of the first. Once I reached his chest I fisted my fingers in his shirt and tugged him forward to meet my mouth. He started out slow, but I quickly deepened it, my tongue tangling with his, my eyes closing. His hands snaked around my back, pulling me closer and shifting in his seat. He groaned into my mouth and I found myself reaching for his belt buckle without really thinking about the consequences of being in a public place. I could make this better for him. At least for a little while.

Low thrust a hand into my hair, fisting the strands as he pulled me even tighter. I frantically worked at his zipper, but he lifted me from my knees and pulled me up. I straddled his lap, pleased the chairs didn't have armrests to get in the way.

"Reese, what are we doing?" he said against my neck as I tipped my head back to allow him further access. His lips skated across my sensitive skin, his breath warm on the goosebumps that rose.

"I don't know," I mumbled. "Just want to be close to you." My breaths became erratic when he sucked my neck.

His hands found my own, stilling my frantic fumbling with his fly. "Not that I'm not enjoying it"—his hips rolled beneath me —"but this maybe isn't the best place for it. I'm sure the doc wouldn't approve of us getting down and dirty in her office."

I pulled back and grinned. "What she doesn't know won't hurt her."

He shook his head, laughing. "That turn you on, Reese? The thought of getting caught?"

I shrugged and went for his lips again, my hand sliding down underneath his boxer briefs.

"Shit," he gritted out as his cock kicked under my touch. "This is going to be so awkward when she busts us." But it didn't stop him from cupping my breast with his hand.

I shrugged again, trying to bite back my laughter. This was so incredibly inappropriate, but he was right, I was kind of getting off on it. It was a bit of fun, mixed in with all the serious. I needed it, he needed it. And the doctor wouldn't be back for half an hour. What else were we going to do? I'd rather go to third base with the incredibly sexy man in the room than scroll Twitter on my phone.

A weight lifted from my shoulders and a sudden conviction that this was all going to be okay fell down on me like a beam of sunshine. Hadn't we both been through the wringer already? Enough was enough. God or fate or whoever—they owed us one. They'd give us this one thing, I was suddenly sure of it. A bubble of laughter sprang from somewhere deep inside me. Bring on the test results. We'd slay them together, and then I'd take my man home, get naked with him, and tell him every damn thought I had about how amazing he was and how much I loved him.

Low pulled away sharply, snapping me out of my head.

"What?"

"Shhh." He held up a finger, motioning for me to wait.

The clip-clop of high heels on the tiled hallway floor echoed, right before the door handle turned.

"Shit," he hissed as I jumped off his lap. He yanked his shirt down over his open fly and leant forward, resting his elbows on his knees.

I gave him a wink as I slid back into my own chair, knowing he was covering up his erection. The doctor looked at us both strangely as she strode past on her way to her seat but said nothing.

I could barely keep my laughter concealed and when Low smiled at the doctor, this time, it was a real one. My heart skipped a beat and I slipped my hand into his. We had this.

Doctor Sloane folded her hands on the table and cleared her throat before looking Low square in the eye. "Your results were positive, Low. I'm sorry, but you have HIV."

LOW

$\mathcal{S}$ ilence ripped through the room as shrill and piercing as one long scream. Hell, maybe it wasn't the silence, maybe the screaming came from somewhere inside me, because suddenly, I couldn't hear anything else. *Positive. HIV Positive.*

I looked at Reese. Had she said anything? I didn't know.

Positive.

I swallowed thickly. The doctor asked me something, but I couldn't hear her over the noise in my head. God, it was loud. I nodded at her dumbly, having no idea what I was agreeing to, but knowing that I needed to give some sort of answer. I nodded again, for good measure, before I pushed to my feet and looked down at the two women still sitting on their chairs. The noise became a roar, like an angry sea, pounding on the rocks. I rubbed at my temples, but nothing I did made it any better.

Reese looked up at me with tears shining in her beautiful brown eyes. Why was she crying? I reached a hand out to her, and when my skin touched the silky smoothness of her face, she pressed her cheek into my hand. The roaring quieted.

Positive.

My hand dropped from her face and I spun on my heel,

aiming for the door, not entirely sure if my legs would make it that far. I heard Reese call out, heard the doctor say my name. I could hear again, but I didn't want to. I didn't want to hear, didn't want to be in that room. And I sure as hell didn't want to see that heartbroken look of pity on Reese's beautiful face. As much as I loved her, I didn't want that.

I let myself out into the hallway, the door slamming behind me. I took a sharp left turn then a right and another left, finding myself in an unfamiliar hallway. This wasn't where I'd come in. I was lost in the maze of clinical hallways, but it didn't matter, as long as I was putting distance between myself and that room. Between myself and the women inside it and their quiet pity that made my stomach churn. I'd done this to myself. I didn't deserve their pity.

The neon green exit sign filled me with relief. I'd lost count of how many random turns I'd made before I saw it, but an exit meant I could leave that room behind me. I pushed through the doors and sucked in gulps of the fresh air that slapped me on the other side. It wasn't quite dark yet, but the streetlights had come on, and the city street was bustling with peak hour traffic. All these people trying to get home, while I had no idea where I was headed.

I'd expected to see the car park, but I'd exited onto the other side of the clinic. It didn't matter. I didn't have my keys; they were still in Reese's bag. Not caring which way I went, I moved blindly down the road. Run. I needed to run. That would clear my head and take control of my pounding heart. But my feet wouldn't cooperate. I stumbled on the uneven footpath. A woman pulled her young son closer to her as they rushed past me. I didn't blame her. I wouldn't want my child anywhere near me either. Finally finding control of my feet, I broke into a run.

I don't know how long I ran for, aimlessly turning corners and cutting through parks. I puffed heavily when I eventually sank down into a bus shelter bench, unable to push my body any further. The wooden planks were rough and splintered under my hands, the shelter walls covered in graffiti.

I leant forward, my elbows resting on my knees, my head propped up with my hands while I tried to force air into my lungs. Jesus Christ. Positive? I was HIV positive. What the fuck was I supposed to do with that? I thought I'd prepared myself for this, thought I was ready for it, but damn if Reese's positivity hadn't rubbed off on me a little bit. She'd been so hopeful. And I'd gone and ruined everything.

"You getting on, buddy?" a male voice called, and I lifted my head wearily. I hadn't even heard the large bus pull in, but there it was with its doors open, and its driver and passengers staring at me. The driver gave me a curious glance. "You okay, mate?"

I nodded and pushed to my feet.

Climbing on board, I stopped in front of the driver, patting my back pocket and thankfully realising that my wallet was still tucked inside. I handed the driver my card.

"Which stop?" He took the card from my hands and hesitated over the card reader.

I looked at him blankly. "Anywhere." My voice sounded hollow, even to my own ears. "Anywhere but here."

He shrugged as I pushed past and sank down on the nearest seat. The bus pulled out into the evening peak hour traffic and I shifted uncomfortably as something in my pocket jabbed me in the thigh.

I pulled out my phone and stared at the number of missed calls. Had it been ringing this whole time and I hadn't even noticed? No, no, it was still on silent from when I'd switched it over at the clinic. But the thirteen missed calls from Reese were new. My finger hovered over the return call button, my heart longing to hear her voice. Instead, I hit the message icon and typed with uncoordinated fingers. I hit send before I could change my mind.

26

REESE

*T*he door slammed behind Low's back before I registered what was happening. I sprang out of my seat to follow him, but Doctor Sloane reached across the table and grabbed my arm.

"Let him have a minute, Reese. I'd like to speak to you alone anyway."

"With me?" Why would she want to speak with me? The urge to run after Low pulled me towards the door. I tugged at her grip.

"Low might not be in a place to listen and learn about his condition just yet. He needs time to come to terms with it. But there are things he needs to know, things you both need to know."

I glanced down as the doctor's slim fingers released my wrist and breathed as I sank back into my seat. She was right. He wouldn't be in any state of mind to listen right now. I could get the information and go through it with him later.

When I finally left the doctor's office, armed with brochures, phone numbers, and another appointment for in a few weeks' time, I was more confused and overwhelmed than ever. I moved through the empty hallway towards the waiting room, my footsteps echoing around me in the deserted space.

My pace increased as I neared the waiting room, expecting to see Low sitting there. But the room was empty except for the receptionist who tapped her fingers on the desk, looking annoyed. I peered around the bend of the hall to see if Low was on his way back from the bathroom or had gone in search of a water dispenser, but it was still empty. "Excuse me, the man I came in with? Low Smith? Did he come out this way?"

The receptionist shook her head, her large earrings swinging from side to side. "No, you two were the last appointment. I've been waiting for you to come out so I can close off for the night."

"Oh," I said quietly. "I'm sorry about that."

Her annoyance softened into a more tolerant expression. "There's another exit on the other side of the building. He must have left through that door if he isn't with you."

I nodded my agreement and thanked her. Maybe he was waiting for me at the car.

He wasn't. I could see his car from the clinic entrance, and he wasn't standing beside it or sitting on the hood. He wasn't inside it because the keys still jangled in my handbag. I pulled them out, unlocked the doors, and slid into the driver's seat. My hands rested on the steering wheel before my head followed a moment later. Breathing in and out as deeply as I could, I tried to fight off tears. I wouldn't do this. I wouldn't allow myself to cry right now.

Not knowing what else to do, I fumbled through my bag for my phone and rang Low's number. I wasn't surprised when it rang out, but I hit redial anyway. Again and again, I hit redial. Again and again, it went straight to his voice mail.

"Shit!" I threw my phone onto the passenger seat hard enough for it to bounce off and onto the floor. What was I supposed to do now? Wait here until he came back? Drive around looking for him?

The repetitive beeps of my message tone cut through the

silence in the cab and I dove across the gear-stick, scrambling to retrieve my phone from the floor mats.

I can't do this anymore. I'm sorry.

I stared at the text message for what felt like hours before I registered the words. And when I finally did, it was with a mixture of anger and determination. Goddammit, he wasn't going to do this. No way was he breaking up with me, just because his tests were positive. I hit redial again.

It was dark around me and the parking lot was empty when I gave up dialling, slamming my hand onto the steering wheel in frustration. Where the fuck was he? And how the hell was I supposed to find him when he had all of Sydney to hide in?

I searched through the glove box, coming up triumphant with registration papers. His address was neatly printed in bold on the left-hand side.

It was a ten-minute drive to Low's apartment, but it was ten minutes too long. It gave me too much time to stew on the last few hours and my confusing mess of emotions. Sadness coursed through me. The test hadn't gone the way we'd been hoping, and that was bitterly disappointing, but somewhere within me there was also a sense of relief. This wasn't the eighties; it wouldn't kill him. Or me. Not that he believed that right now, obviously, but it was fact. This didn't need to change anything between us. Not in the ways that mattered. I hadn't been lying when I'd said I wanted him no matter what. If I could just find him, just see him for a few moments…

After I parked his car on the street outside his building, I ran up the stairs and banged my fist against his apartment door. His keys sat in the top of my handbag, and I debated just letting myself in. It didn't feel right, though, invading his personal space like that when he'd never even invited me over before. Plus, what if he had an alarm?

I let my head drop back and roll across the back of my shoulders, trying to ease the tension in my neck while I waited for him to open the door. When he didn't appear after a few moments, I thumped on the painted black wood again, this time pressing my ear to the door to listen for sounds of life. I couldn't hear anything from the other side. No TV, no radio. No voices. Crouching down, I craned my head to the side so I could see the gap at the bottom of the door—no light spilled from underneath. I groaned. He wasn't here.

He wouldn't be at work now. The track would be closed for the night, and even if he was, I wouldn't be able to get in there without a management-level swipe card. I paced the length of the hallway before pulling out my phone again. I hit dial on Jamison's phone number and raked my fingers through my messy hair while I waited for him to pick up.

"Reese!" he yelled when he picked up the phone on what felt like the hundredth ring. I pulled the phone away from my ear. Distorted sounding music and a crowd of people nearly drowned him out. "Hang on! I'm just going somewhere quieter."

I drummed my fingers on my leg, until the noise on his end quieted.

"Is that better?"

I didn't bother answering. "Is Low with you?"

I could almost hear Jamison frowning. "No? Should he be?"

I shook my head, not that he could see. "No."

"What's going on?"

"Nothing, nothing, I just…I lost track of Low and he isn't answering his phone. If he calls you, can you tell him to call me? It's really important."

"Yeah, of course. Is he okay, though?" The worry was clear in Jamison's voice. "Are you okay?"

I sighed. "I don't know the answer to either of those questions. Look, I've got to go. If he calls you, though, please, Jam, call me back."

I could hear Jamison's protests even as I hung up the phone.

I wracked my brain. I doubted Low would go to his grandparents' place. He hadn't wanted to tell them about the tests this afternoon, so I didn't think he'd go straight there to spill his secrets. And if I called and he wasn't there, I'd only worry them.

Damn it. If he wasn't with his grandparents, at home, or with Jamison, he had to be at work. A light suddenly lit up in my brain and I could have smacked myself in the forehead for being so dense. I absolutely could get into work without a swipe card! I had my gap in the fence; the one I used to sneak in and see Mabel. I'd probably get stopped by security before I could even make it to the stables from the outer paddocks, but I had to try.

I ran down to the car and gunned the engine as soon as it kicked over. I swerved between other cars on the road, earning myself an angry honk from one driver, but it was only minutes later that I pulled up alongside the high fence of the racecourse. The sky was dark and overcast with clouds so thick that even the moon was barely visible. Floodlights spaced evenly around the perimeter of the property gave me enough light to see clearly, though, and for now, there wasn't a security guard in sight.

I slipped between the gap, barely registering Mabel's nickers of welcome as I sped past her paddock. I ran flat out for the stables, my lungs burning, knowing I was probably being watched on CCTV. I slid to a stop in front of the stable doors and yanked them hard.

The darkness was so complete inside the barn I had to stop and fish my phone out of my pocket. I flicked up the menu to turn the flashlight on, the beam of brightness cutting through the barn like a search light. I followed the pathways through the huge building, the scent of fresh hay and horse filling my nose, but every turn I made found only more darkness. I shined my light into every corner and peered over each stall door, but every time I just found myself staring into the eyes of confused horses.

"Hey! Stop!" a voice yelled from somewhere behind me, and I sighed. *Busted*. Low wasn't here anyway, and now I was probably about to be arrested. *Great*. The horses moved restlessly in their stalls, one letting out a nervous whiny. I turned around slowly and raised my hands, though it was just security, not the cops.

"My name is Reese. I work here," I called to them, not wanting to yell and scare the horses any more than they already were.

The two security guards wore matching Lavender field uniforms, walkie talkies sitting on their belts. The shorter of the two shined his flashlight directly into my face, making me squint.

"I'm just looking for Low Smith. That's it."

The guard lowered his flashlight, as the taller one leant in closer. I held my breath, as a sense of dread pooled in my stomach. This hadn't been my smartest idea.

"I know you," he declared, moving back a step. "You were there when the horse died on track."

I nodded, recognising him as the guard who'd tried to stop Low and me from getting to Lijah's side when she'd gone down.

"You can't be here."

"I know. I'm sorry. I was just leaving. Honest. I don't want to cause any trouble."

"We'll escort you out."

I thanked them and they followed me back to the gates near Mabel's paddock.

"How did you even get in here?"

I gave the tall guard an embarrassed smile. "There's a hole in the fence just down there a bit." I paused. "Am I pushing the friendship if I ask you to just unlock the gates for me?"

He huffed but held his swipe key up to the little black box. It beeped, flashed green, then slowly the gate swung open. I breathed a sigh of relief that I'd avoided police custody for breaking and entering and strode over to Low's Ute that sat waiting on the side of the road. The static of the guard's walkie talkies crackled, and I heard the tall one report that there was a hole in the fence that needed fixing. I guessed I wouldn't be making any early morning stops to Mabel's paddock anymore. That sucked.

I turned the key in the ignition but sat there with the engine idling, trying to work out what to do next. When I still had no plan after several long minutes, I pulled out onto the road and began to drive aimlessly. It was better than sitting at home. He certainly wasn't going to turn up there.

The headlights of other cars shone in my eyes and glinted off the raindrops that began falling on my windscreen. I peered through the windows anytime I saw people out on the streets, but none of them were ever Low.

I drove past the Marx Club, its sign lit up in neon and a short queue of people waiting to get in. I pulled over sharply. Jamison's words that first night we'd all gone out together rang through my head. *It's our local.* Meaning they went there regularly. It was a long shot, but at least it was a shot. And at least there was alcohol there. My stomach flipped at the thought of getting a drink.

I hadn't deliberately cut back on drinking, but with my thoughts occupied by Low, I hadn't needed the oblivion I used to find there. I'd lost myself in him and his problems instead. Probably not healthy, but neither was the way I'd been drinking and partying. I was surprised to realise I hadn't missed it. Until now. But I had a mission. I'd get him and drag him home where we could hash this out. We'd work through his fears and mine. We'd work through it all. Together. He just had to be there first.

REESE

$\mathcal{T}$he pounding bass and bodies writhing on the dance floor didn't give me any of the usual thrill I felt when I walked into a club. I nodded distractedly to Riley's brother, Mark, when he waved to me from behind the bar, but my focus was on the booth we'd sat at the last time we were here. A group of women crowded around it. They all wore sashes over their dresses that declared them bridesmaids. They had a row of shots lined up in front of them, and their big smiles and glassy eyes told me this wasn't their first round.

My gaze drifted to the spot where I'd danced, knowing Low was watching. It took nothing to remember how his gaze had burned through me, and I wished I could go back. But looking at things through rose-coloured glasses wasn't going to get me anywhere, was it? Low and his misguided need to protect me from himself had always been a major barrier between us. But at least back then there'd been hope. Right now, I felt pretty hopeless.

I pulled myself out of the memory and scanned the bar. If he was here, that's where he'd be, not reminiscing like I was. I couldn't see the far end of the room with the amount of people in the way, so I pushed through, my heart thumping quicker every time I noticed a tall, dark-haired guy who even remotely resembled Low. I pulled up short when I hit the opposite wall. No Low.

"Reese?" The familiar voice came from behind me and when I turned around, Jamison was sitting by himself at the end of the bar, nursing a tumbler full of dark liquid.

"Oh, hey, Jam."

His eyes were as glassy as the bridesmaids' had been.

"Come sit?" He patted the empty barstool beside him.

I scanned the room once more, but nothing had changed. Low wasn't here. A wave of exhaustion rolled through me and combined with the stress and anger of the last few hours, an empty seat and a glass of wine suddenly seemed like a great idea.

I slid onto the barstool and asked the bartender for a drink before I turned to Jamison. I wanted to ask him what he was doing here, but he beat me to it with questions of his own.

"So you didn't find him, then?"

I shook my head. "I've checked his place, and I just broke into the stables at work because I thought he'd be there for sure. But nope."

Jamison shook his head and let out a low whistle. "Shit. He got bad news at the doctors today, didn't he?"

I froze. "He told you about that?"

Jamison nodded, and I let out a long breath. Not having the sole responsibility of knowledge made all of this a little easier to bear.

"Any other ideas where he might be?"

Jamison brought his glass to his lips and swallowed before he answered. "He runs when he's stressed. But I don't know that he'd go any place in particular."

My shoulders slumped, and I twisted the stem on my wine glass, watching as the pale yellow liquid sloshed around. "I'm all out of ideas. This was my last resort." I sighed. "What are you doing here tonight, anyway? Did you come alone?"

He nodded. "I had a really shitty day."

"Bet you can't top mine. Low broke up with me via text message."

"I walked in on Bree and some guy having sex in her apartment."

My eyes grew wide. "Holy shit. What did you do?"

"Turned around, walked out, and came here."

I tucked my arm beneath his and hugged it to me briefly, since I couldn't give him a proper hug while we were sitting next to each other. "You're so calm. I probably would have punched the guy in the face." I didn't voice that I'd also like to punch Bree. That callous bitch. Jamison was one of the sweetest guys I'd ever met. He didn't deserve this.

He laughed and held his drink up a little. "These help."

My heart went out to him. The pain in his eyes made me wince and even though I could tell he was putting on a brave front, he'd obviously had his heart smashed to pieces.

The bartender came back and we both ordered another drink, pushing cash across the bar into his waiting hands.

"Well, we're quite the pair tonight, aren't we? Low broke up with you in a text message? I think you win the shitty day contest."

I shook my head. "No way, you're being generous. You walked in on your Mrs. cheating. That's worse than a text message breakup, no doubt. Plus, we've only been together a few weeks…" I shrugged, but tears pricked at my eyes and I blinked furiously for a moment to keep them in check.

"Doesn't hurt any less, though, huh?"

Tears under control, I glanced up at him. "No, it doesn't. I thought… I know it sounds lame, but I thought this was something special."

"Then fight for it."

"Oh, I intend to. But that's easier said than done when I can't find him and he won't answer his phone."

"So you're stuck here drinking with me, huh?"

"I'd rather drink with you than drink alone."

"Cheers to that." Jamison held up his glass and I clinked mine together with his. "Here's to shitty days and drinking to forget about them."

"I'll drink to that," I murmured before downing the rest of my glass.

28

REESE

*T*he first thought I had when my mind switched out from the darkness of alcohol induced slumber was, *where's my phone?* I cracked an eye open but closed it when pain sliced through the swirling fog in my head.

I reached an arm across the bed and breathed a sigh of relief when my hand made contact with another warm body instead of the little piece of technology I'd been searching for. He was back. I hadn't heard him come in, but he was here. I opened my eyes, as everything within me calmed and relaxed. If he was here, that meant he wanted to sort this out, he wanted to make this work.

My vision cleared and I snatched my hand back in horror as I realised the sleeping body next to me wasn't Low's. I clapped a hand over my mouth before I could scream. Memories from the night before washed over me. Searching for Low. The club. Jamison. Alcohol. So much alcohol.

Guilt flooded me like an ice-cold tsunami and I stifled a sob full of self-loathing. One night without Low and I was back to this? Back to getting drunk and sleeping with random men just so I could forget for a few hours? But it wasn't the accident, or my father's cruel words I'd been blocking out last night. It was Low's rejection.

I was going to vomit, and I probably couldn't even blame it on the alcohol. Disgusted with myself, I ran for the bathroom and emptied the contents of my stomach into the toilet. I knelt on the cold tiles, retching, and let the tears fall. Once they started, I couldn't stop them. Falling tears and dry heaving turned to sobs and I grabbed a towel, stuffing my face into it to muffle the sounds of my misery. How had I gone from the amazing day out at Low's grandparents' place, with the horses, and the love that permeated the air there, to this? Vomiting on the bathroom floor with a man who certainly wasn't Low in my bed. I'd regressed weeks' worth of progress in the space of a few hours. The hate I felt for myself right now overwhelmed me, and a fresh batch of tears poured not just from my eyes, but from my heart.

"Hey, kid." Jamison stood in the bathroom doorway, and I groaned, burying my head further into the towel. Why was he still here? Didn't he know one-night-stand etiquette was to just leave quietly? Maybe if I stayed here on the floor crying for long enough, he'd get scared off. Guys hated tears.

"Reese."

I looked up at him, positive I had yesterday's mascara smeared down my cheeks and the stench of vomit on my breath. "What?" My voice was tired and flat.

He held out a glass of water and some ibuprofen. "Thought this might help."

Despite wishing the ground would open up and swallow one of us whole, I took the drink and tablets gratefully, eyeing him as I swallowed them down. He was wearing the same clothes he'd had on last night. Jeans and a short-sleeved button-down shirt. The jeans were rumpled this morning, though, and the shirt wasn't buttoned correctly. I sighed.

"You okay? I heard you get up. I wanted to come in while you were vomiting to see if you were okay, but you know…" He looked at me sheepishly. "I wasn't sure you'd appreciate it."

"I don't blame you, but thanks anyway. You've gone well and above one-night-stand etiquette."

Jamison's mouth dropped open and he shook his head, slowly at first as if he were trying to grasp what I'd meant. Then a smile spread across his face, and he laughed.

"Why are you laughing? Low is your best friend. We are awful people." I scrubbed my hands over my face, wiping away a fresh batch of tears.

"Oh my God…you think? No, no, no. Reese. No. We didn't have sex. Just look at yourself." His eyes dropped down my body and for the first time, I realised that I was still wearing the clothes I'd had on last night. I was as rumpled as he was but, yes, still fully dressed.

"We didn't?" I frowned as I tried to sort through my black hole of a brain. But I had very little beyond drinking at the club. A spark of hope ignited within me.

He laughed. "Wow, I'm sorry. I didn't realise you were that drunk. No. We didn't. We shared an Uber back here. You said I could crash because we drank all my cash and I didn't have my cards with me. But we just slept. I swear it."

"So, nothing happened. At all?"

Jamison crouched down to my level. "Nothing. We're friends, Reese. And Low is my best friend."

"No, I know that. But it's just…" So unlike me, I finished in my head. I heaved a sigh of relief and let the last of the tears I'd been holding in slide down my face. Jamison sat down next to me on the cold tiles and put an arm around my shoulders.

"I know you, Reese. You wouldn't cheat on Low."

I sighed. "Thank you." He was right. I wouldn't. I should have known, even intoxicated, I wouldn't ruin this thing between us. It was too important. Every bone in my body screamed it and I was an idiot for doubting myself. Old habits died hard, though.

"In fact, the more drunk you got, the more I had to listen to you talk about him. And some of that was way more detail than I ever wanted to know about my best friend. You know, you might have an unhealthy obsession with his abs." He pulled a face and I laughed, but my smile fell quickly.

"Has he called you?" I could hear the desperation in my voice, but I didn't care.

Jamison shook his head, then sighed. His gaze became determined, locking mine in place, and I stilled under the intensity.

"I don't know exactly what's going on with you two, but you're good for him. I hope you know that."

I shrugged. "His grandparents said much the same thing. But I don't know about that. He keeps pushing me away. There's this connection between us I can't deny, and I know he feels it too. But maybe that isn't enough."

Jamison settled back against the bathroom wall. "Don't say that. You didn't know him before. He always had people around him, but he was lonely. The different hook-ups every night—it was just something to fill his time. It didn't make him happy. He was always the life of the party, but something inside him was broken. He could never let himself feel anything for anyone. He had walls so firmly up around him that even Bianca, Riley, and I had to fight tooth and nail to get a real friendship out of him. But you're different. You get him. Something about you heals that broken bit within him."

Jamison broke off and I stood there gawking at him with my mouth hanging open. Jesus. Who knew Jamison was all poetical and deep? Or that observant even? I smiled as his words sank in.

"But what you don't know, Jam, is that he did the same thing for me. Everything inside me that's broken doesn't feel so bad when he's around either."

Jamison nodded, then gave me a wry grin. "Guess we better put you two broken halves back together, huh?"

I groaned and punched him in the arm. "And here I was

thinking you could be a poet with your deep and meaningful observations. But then you come out with a line so corny it belongs on a fortune cookie." But my smile faded as quickly as it had appeared. "Seriously, though, we need to find him. I'm worried."

"I know. Don't worry, we will."

29

LOW

$\mathcal{T}$he bottle of tequila clenched in my fist and the empty bottle of Jack on the coffee table announced I was drunk. And if exhibit A and exhibit B hadn't been enough proof, the way the room spun was the clincher.

There was a clock on the shelf, I knew that much for sure, but no matter how much I squinted at the glowing green numbers, they refused to come into focus. My eyes strained until my brain ached. Something would bust open if I kept that up.

I slumped against the lounge room wall, the wooden floor-boards hard under my ass, but I was so numb I barely noticed. I must have been sitting here for hours. Days maybe? If I could just work out what time it was, maybe I'd know.

I'd made it home from the clinic well after dark, then Rob, my neighbour had wanted to chat when I'd gone over there to get my spare keys. Why did he always want to chat? It was better here, with my Jack and my tequila and nobody talking.

My body coursed with alcohol-induced warmth, my head fuzzy enough I could almost forget why I was drinking. Almost. More tequila would take care of that.

I lifted the bottle in my hand and took a long swig. Didn't I have a glass? I was sure I'd started this not so little drinking session with a glass. My gaze moved around the living room, to the front door and to the tiny stretch of hallway I could see. Nope. No glass. No idea where that went. I should get up and get another one, but fuck it. Who cared? I was a grown up, I could swig straight out of the bottle if I wanted to.

Yeah, being a grown up and doing whatever I wanted was working out well for me, wasn't it? Be a grown up, sleep around, catch a sexually transmitted disease that would ruin my life. Yep. Being an adult was awesome. Fuck, I was an idiot.

My ringtone pierced the silence and self-loathing around me. The phone vibrated on the floorboards, the screen flashing up Reese's name and a photo of her smiling face. It was one I'd taken of her at the zoo. Was that really only a few days ago? It felt like a lifetime. I swallowed the lump in my throat as I watched it ring. The call diverted to my voice mail eventually, just like the other thirty or forty times she'd called since I'd left her.

Guilt swamped me. What an asshole I was, just getting up and leaving her there like that. She was probably still willing to forgive me, because she was *that* woman. The one who always saw the best in people but let them walk all over her because of it. And now I'd done it to her.

I picked my phone up and flicked through the photos of us at the zoo. Reese, sticking her tongue out as I'd snapped a pic of her in front of the chimpanzee enclosure. A selfie of the two of us, with a koala asleep in a tree behind us. And one where she hadn't noticed me, too busy staring up at a giraffe as she fed it. She was so incredibly beautiful. I didn't deserve her, but, God, I wanted her. My whole body cried out to touch her, to have her near me. I just wanted to hold her and bury my face in her sweet smelling hair. But that was why I couldn't have her. Not anymore. Not after this. She deserved better after all the shit I'd put her through, and all the shit to come in my future. She deserved someone who could give her everything. Someone who could give her a proper, stable life.

A timid knock on the door snapped my head up. My breath got stuck in my lungs, and I held it there, frozen in spot with the bottle of tequila halfway to my lips.

"Low?"

My heart squeezed painfully at the sound of Reese's voice. I let the breath I was holding out in a whoosh and hoped like hell she couldn't hear it through the door.

"Low? Please. If you're in there, let me in."

I didn't dare move for fear she'd hear me. Fuck. Not only was I an idiot and an asshole I was also a coward now. Yet another reason to add to the growing list of reasons I needed to leave her alone.

But damn. Her voice was like honey. Sweet and pure and I wanted to drown in it. I wanted to wrap myself around her, feel her silky hair and let her talk in that honey-covered voice until everything felt right again. The ache inside me widened and I took another slug from the bottle as silently as possible in an attempt to fill the void. God, how much longer until I'd pass out? It couldn't be much longer.

Reese went silent and I tried to imagine what she looked like on the other side of the door. Just knowing she was only a few feet away and not being able to touch her...I dropped my head into my hands as that pain hit me like a punch to the face.

Idiot. Asshole. Coward.

Something jingled in her handbag. What was she doing out there? Then it dawned on me with horror—she still had my keys. She could walk in here at any moment and I'd have to face her. My stomach took another nose dive at the thought of confronting her.

The jingling stopped, and there was a minute of silence. I was just beginning to think she'd left when there were more muffled sounds from outside, and a thin stack of papers slid under the door. A pink square stuck on the front stood out sharply against the more subdued colours of the papers beneath.

A tapping noise came from the door and I lifted my eyes as her soft voice, resigned this time, came again.

"Read it, Low. I mean it, even if you don't want to hear it. Maybe you'll believe me if it's right there in front of your face."

Her soft footsteps on the floorboards of the hallway dimmed as she walked away, and still, I sat there staring at that bright pink Post-it note. Because of course it was a Post-it note. It was exactly the same as the other eleven billion of them she had at her place.

I let the tequila bottle slip from my fingers, not caring where it landed, and dragged myself up, using the wall for support. I held still, waiting for the spinning room to stop. *Don't pass out yet, jerk. Get to the paper first.*

Fuck, I was drunk.

I tried to pull myself together as I stumbled across the living room to the front door, smashing my shin into the coffee table as I went. The pain barely registered, though I was sure it would in the morning. I knelt down and picked up the papers.

It took me a minute to focus on the words, my eyes taking even longer to focus than when I'd tried to read the time. *Goddammit, brain, just work for one more minute!*

When my eyes finally adjusted, small, neat writing had trailed off the square and onto the papers beneath.

Only the positives, right, Low? Here are three I know for absolute sure. I'm positive you're my best friend. I'm positive I'm in love with you. And I'm positive I want this. I want us. Always.

Her words knocked the breath out of me and I slumped back on the solid wood, as if I'd been kicked in the gut. I wanted to throw the door open, run down the hallway, and keep going until I found her. I wanted to wrap my arms around her, kiss her amazing mouth, and tell her I loved her. Tell her I should have said it before now, at my grandparents' place or at the zoo or the restaurant or in the car. I could have told her at any of those times that I was falling in love with her. That I *was* in love with her.

My fingers curled into a fist and I thumped the door behind me. I couldn't do that. So instead I stared down at the papers in my hands, leafing through them for so long the words blurred together again.

I couldn't stay here. It wouldn't do either of us any good to be this close to each other. I couldn't go back to working with her, day in and day out. It wouldn't work. Not for me and not for her.

On unsteady but determined feet, I made my way to my bedroom and pulled a suitcase out from under the bed. My stomach lurched at the movement, but my determination was stronger.

I leant on the wardrobe door for a long moment, willing myself to stay conscious, but the bed called me. God, it would be so much easier to just go lie down and pass out. But if I didn't leave now, would I have the same resolve in the morning?

I got the wardrobe door open just enough to pull a backpack down from the top shelf and cursed as an old baseball mitt, a belt, and a pile of old tax returns came crashing down around me.

Propping the bags open on my bed, I threw socks and under-wear into them. Next went a pile of T-shirts and shorts, and I shoved a few jumpers on top, not knowing how long I'd be gone.

That would have to do. I'd just leave the rest. I wouldn't need it.

I shouldered my backpack and dragged my suitcase back to the lounge room. I stared at the glossy sheets of paper Reese had left me before grabbing them off the table and stuffing them into the side of my case. I eyed my phone as I added my wallet and spare keys to a pocket of the backpack, grabbing it at the last second. I should leave it, so I wouldn't give in to the urge to call her. But I wasn't that strong. I vowed to turn it off instead and let the battery die. That way there'd be plenty of time to talk myself out of any late-night phone calls while it charged up.

I leant on the door for a minute, surveying my comfortable apartment before I let another wave of determination carry me through the doorway. The door closed behind me with a solid thunk, the locks sliding into place automatically. And for the first time in twenty-four hours, I felt the air in my lungs. I felt like I could breathe. With a plan in mind, I could breathe again.

30

REESE - TWO MONTHS LATER

"Can we go back to Lotti Boutique? I think I need that belt we saw there earlier." Bianca bounced on the balls of her feet, chirping like a happy little bird as we waited for the escalator to deliver us to the third floor of the shopping complex. Bianca's enthusiasm for shopping knew no bounds, and I enjoyed her overly positive presence. "And you need to buy that dress you tried on."

I shrugged. "Maybe. I'm still tossing up between that one and the green one at Lisette's."

"Both are hot. Wear the black one tonight when we go out and we'll dance and drink and find you a man." She wriggled her eyebrows at me suggestively, but her face fell when her gaze met mine, and concern furrowed her forehead.

I laughed, hoping it didn't sound as forced as it felt. "It's fine, B. I'm over it." My tongue felt thick as I forced out the lie. I was still as in love with him as the day I'd written it on a Post-it note and pushed it under his door. Feelings like that didn't just go away.

"Are you, though?" she asked quietly.

"Of course!" I said, trying to sound breezy and carefree. I'd been trying to put on a brave face in front of my friends for months. I didn't want to be a downer, and pretending to be okay even when I wasn't helped keep me going. I'd lived with the pain of losing my family for over a year, and now I felt Low's absence just as keenly. I couldn't let myself think about any of it too much or it would consume me whole.

Bianca narrowed her eyes and I wished the damn escalator would hurry up so I could get out from under her eagle eye gaze.

"You never talk about him or what happened. It would eat me alive if I were you. Wondering where he is and why he left."

I shrugged. "It's no big deal. I've told you this before. We weren't even officially together."

"Yeah, and I already called bullshit on that. You might not have been calling him your boyfriend, but that was only a matter of time. For him to just up and leave without a word..." She shook her head.

"He left a message at work, letting us know he wasn't coming back, so it wasn't exactly without a word." Except it was. It was without a word to me.

"Oh, come on. He left without saying goodbye to any of us. I'm still annoyed about it and I wasn't the one sleeping with him."

"I wasn't sleeping with him." At least that part of the story was true.

Bianca waved her hand around the air dismissively. "Details, details, whatever. You two were totally digging on each other."

I sighed as we finally stepped off the elevator and headed towards the boutique we'd already spent an hour in that morning. "Can we please drop it? I don't want to do this again."

She reached out and squeezed my arm. "Yeah, of course, I'm sorry. The whole situation just pisses me off. The way he... Reese?" Bianca's blond head flipped back to where I'd stopped in the middle of the Saturday afternoon crowd.

My hands clutched at my stomach, the sudden ache within as surprising as the abrupt stabbing pain in my heart. Bianca rushed back to my side as a guy behind me mumbled something under his breath and detoured around us. "Reese! What's wrong? Are you sick?"

I tried to form words, but I couldn't speak, couldn't move. My vision narrowed and focused on a family across the walkway. The woman wore a long, flowered dress that brushed her ankles and a pair of brown leather sandals. A man with dark denim jeans, a flannel shirt, and a Stetson perched on his head. But the cause of the sudden pain inside me was the dark-haired girl looking up at the man from her wheelchair. He smiled fondly at whatever she had said and ruffled her hair. The woman said something before pointing to a sign, and the three of them headed to the food court.

They were out of sight before my feet unfroze and moved me in the same direction. Bianca asked me something, but I didn't answer, her voice just a drone in the background. I picked up the pace, breaking into a jog before I lost the family in the crowd. *My family.*

My heart thumped and a tiny cry escaped my lips. Was it really them? Why would they be here in Sydney? Our property was a twelve-hour drive from here, and my father hated the city. I could count on one hand how many times he'd brought me here as a kid. I slowed as I entered the food court and watched them find a table.

A sudden pain bloomed in my arm and I snapped my head to see Bianca pinching me hard.

"Ow! What was that for?"

"Oh, hallelujah! You're back! You were off in fairy land and I had no idea where you were taking me. I thought I was going to have to call a medic for a moment there."

I shook my head. "Sorry, I just…"

Bianca followed my line of sight to my family sitting around the table. My mum and sister had their heads close together, discussing something. Maybe the menu of the burger place? I edged closer, as if taking two steps farther would allow me to hear their conversation above the din of the food hall.

Bianca went quiet for a minute. Her voice was quiet when she spoke again. "Reese, that little girl in the wheelchair could be your twin. Is she…?"

I nodded. "My sister. With my parents."

Gemma was eleven now, I realised. Her birthday was in October. I'd been too scared to call her. Too scared to hear them say Gemma was still in a wheelchair. I'd nurtured the glimmer of hope until I'd almost convinced myself that Gemma's injuries were non-existent. I'd planned to show up there at Christmas with a new horse and everything would go back to normal. But the truth was right here in front of me. Even though I'd tried to hide from it, it had found me anyway. There was no denying the serious nature of Gemma's injuries when they were staring me in the face.

"Are you going over?" Bianca asked.

I shook my head. "I can't." The words were heavy in my throat like lead.

"Why not?"

"We don't talk. We're…estranged."

Bianca nodded. "But you look like you really want to go over there…"

I glanced over at her, silently pleading for her to understand without explanation. "I can't, B. They hate me," I whispered.

Bianca rubbed a soothing hand in circles on my back while I tried to blink back tears.

"I'm sure that's not true."

"I put Gemma in that chair, B, and I thought by now things might be different. My dad…he…I just can't. I don't want to make a scene."

With one last glance at my little sister, I dragged Bianca away.

She followed me reluctantly, shooting me concerned glances every few steps. "Okay, well, if you're sure."

I didn't answer as I tried to control the vicious trembling in my hands. I tucked them into the pockets of my cut-off shorts before Bianca noticed. "I'm sure. Can we just go, please?"

Bianca gave up her search for the perfect dress immediately and led me out to the car park where we'd left her little red Suzuki. She slid behind the steering wheel as I slumped into the passenger side, dropping my chin to my chest and letting my hair form a protective wall around me.

Gemma was still in the chair. The knowledge hit me like a sledgehammer over and over, again and again, taking chunks out of the hope I'd been secretly harbouring for months. What a fool I'd been to even think she might just magically get up and walk again. Had I really thought she'd have some physical therapy and then walk and run around like other kids her age? A tear dripped from my eye and landed on my jeans. It had been over a year. If Gemma was still in that chair after a year, then she wasn't getting better.

"She looked happy," Bianca said, breaking the silence.

"Who?" I looked at her blankly.

"Your sister. She was smiling and laughing. She looked happy."

"She's in a wheelchair because of my stupidity. I ruined her whole damn life."

"She didn't look as though her life was ruined. She looked like a happy kid on a shopping trip with her family."

She didn't get it. She hadn't been there when my father had kicked me out of the hospital and told everyone within shouting distance that I'd ruined our family. She hadn't seen the venom in his eyes or heard the rage in his voice. She hadn't seen my mother's tears as she stood silently behind him. Bianca hadn't felt the way my soul had torn in two at the sight of my little sister crumpled on the ground, a mess of arms and legs, or the way her tiny body had been rushed through the corridors on her way to surgery.

"I don't want to talk about it."

Bianca shook her head. "It seems there are a lot of things you don't want to talk about."

3 1

LOW

*P*lastic chairs formed a circle in the middle of the room, and the sunlight streaming through the large windows bounced off the pale yellow walls. Large ceramic pots sat in the corners of the room, their green plants fake, but effective in brightening the space. When I'd first come here, it had felt like an institution, but things had changed. Now the circle felt like a safe place, and the people I'd met here had become family. I sat down next to Will, who had his long, jean-covered legs spread in front of him. He offered me a lazy smile and raised his fist in greeting.

"Hey, mate."

I bumped my fist against his. God, he was a baby. His freckled face and red hair made him look even younger than his nineteen years.

"What's doing?"

People trickled into the room and took their seats. Most were young males, but there were two women, plus Frank, who had to be nearing fifty. Not that you'd know it with the way he acted. He pulled more pranks than any of the young guys did.

I was always early to things, so I knew we still had a few

minutes to kill before whoever was leading the group today would begin. "Nothin'. You?"

"Just enjoying the view." He grinned and I laughed, following his gaze to a dark-haired guy across the room.

"You still hoping Tim will dump his boyfriend for you?"

"Nah, that'd be a dog act, to hook up with someone else's partner in here. But that don't mean I can't take in the sights while I still can. Only a few days left, then we're out."

I nodded, shifting in my seat, trying to get comfortable.

"You looking forward to going home?" he asked, diverting his attention back to Tim. Tim continued to scroll through his phone on the other side of the circle, unaware of Will's infatuation.

"Yeah, I really am. I appreciate everything I've learnt and all, but I left my life in pieces. Who knows what I'm going home to, but I've got to go sort it out. I've done all I can here."

He nodded, finally giving me his full attention. "You're a different guy from when you came in here, you know. Remember how that first week or two you wouldn't speak to no one and wouldn't even look at us in group times? I bet you didn't even hear a word for the first month."

"I might have been in denial for a while." I chuckled.

"A while? You took that shit to extremes, brother. You were the absolute worst out of all of us. Doc kept tryin' to tell you that this thing wasn't a life sentence, but you were hell-bent on beating yourself up over it. Pessimistic son of a bitch."

I punched him in the arm. "Fuck off. I wasn't that bad."

He gave me a look that clearly said I had been. "It's all right. We all knew you'd only just gotten your diagnosis. We were all in the same boat."

The night I'd left my apartment, I'd stumbled into the nearest taxi and given the driver the brochure I'd grabbed off the coffee table. It was one of the papers Reese had shoved under my door, along with the Post-it note, laying her heart on the line. The HIV

Association of Australia ran a live-in clinic for newly diagnosed patients. You could stay for as long as you needed to, and they taught you how to manage your HIV and offered counselling and support. I was still drunk when the driver had pulled up in front of the big white, hospital-looking building and I was shocked when they'd even agreed to give me a room. Shocked, but so bloody grateful. If they hadn't let my drunk ass in, I probably would have turned around and gone home and never looked back. In hindsight, it was only liquid courage that got me that far. But once I was in, I'd known I'd done the right thing. Well, at least I had once I'd recovered from the world's worst hangover.

"It's been weird, hasn't it? Good weird, though."

Will nodded. "Yeah, but I'm keen to start living again. Being in here is like being in limbo. I miss my friends. I miss going out."

"You miss hooking up." I laughed.

Will blew out a long breath. "You know it."

"So no settling down in your near future then?"

He shook his head. "No way. I'll be responsible, of course. I'll take my meds and I'll have 'the conversation' before things get heated, but I'm not about to turn into some nun." He eyed me shrewdly. "And you're going home to your Mrs. Right?"

"I hope so, though I doubt she'll even speak to me."

Will grinned. "Then you get down on your hands and knees, confess to being a dickhead, and beg for her forgiveness."

"That easy, huh?"

"It could be. You won't know until you try."

"It's a lot for someone to take on. And she's already gone through a lot of shit. I don't want to add to that."

Will's ginger eyebrows pulled together in the middle. "Maybe you should let her be the one to decide whether you're a burden or not? You're way too pretty to be sitting at home alone on Saturday nights for the rest of your life, Low. And you know we've learnt that's likely to be a really long time. Ain't neither of us about to die from AIDS at thirty no more."

He was right of course. Not so much about me being pretty, but about letting Reese decide for herself. I was past all the self-loathing I'd been carrying around. I'd done a lot of work on myself while I'd been here—therapy groups, meditation, even some yoga, though that had been a bit of a disaster at first. I'd felt like a dickhead and had spent an entire class paranoid one of my balls would pop out the leg of my shorts. I'd realised quickly that running shorts were not suitable yoga attire and was better prepared for my second class.

I'd run hundreds of kilometres, using the time to search my soul and pushing my body until I found that state of bliss where my mind felt clear again. The counsellor I'd been assigned to had helped me realise I pushed people away, to avoid them leaving me. He'd explained it was a way of keeping control, after a life-time of abandonment. My father when I was a baby. My mother. School friends who'd turned their backs on me when they'd found out how we lived.

And I'd talked about Reese. I'd talked about her so much Will had actually banned me from saying her name for an entire twenty-four hours once. But she was one of the few who'd never left me, and who I could trust when they said they loved me. She'd stood by me, time after time. No matter how hard I'd tried to push her away, she'd pulled me right back. And if she gave me another chance, I'd be damned if I'd ever let her go again.

I nudged Will with my shoulder. "You're pretty smart, you know that?"

"Handsome too, right?"

"You're definitely not modest, that's for sure."

He shoved me with the palm of his hand as the door opened. The nurse who ran the clinic came in and sat down, crossing her legs at her ankles.

"All right, you lot. Who's got something they want to talk about today?" She looked around the circle, meeting the gaze of each patient.

239

I raised my hand, and when the nurse nodded to me, I stood up and cleared my throat. "I don't have any fears or questions. I'm fresh out of those after two months in here."

There was a sprinkling of quiet laughs from the now familiar faces around the circle, but the nurse smiled proudly, as if my words had just made her day. I grinned back at her.

"I don't have fears, but there is something I want to talk about."

Will sat back in his chair and folded his arms across his chest like the cat that ate the canary.

"I met this amazing woman a few months ago. And I finally feel like I deserve her."

32

LOW

*A*fter therapy, I wandered back to my room. It was small but cleaned daily, with a single bed underneath a window that overlooked a tidy courtyard. There was a small writing desk and a TV on the wall. We weren't required to stay on grounds, but I'd only left a handful of times in the past few weeks, just to grab myself a pizza or more toothpaste. I'd enjoyed the solitude here, the time to think and reflect on how I'd gotten to this point in my life. All I'd thought about for months were the choices I'd made and the choices I needed to make in the future. Part of me was scared to leave the safety of the clinic, but the real world hadn't stopped while I'd been gone. I knew that. It was time to re-join it. And it was time to claim back the love of my life.

I sat on the bed, the springs beneath me protesting. I might not have had my shit together completely, but I'd done all I could here. It was time to move on and get my life together outside the safety of the clinic.

A yellow slip of paper on my desk caught my eye and my heart skipped a beat. I stood and crossed the room to pull the little square of paper off the desk, its sticky backing providing little resistance. I skimmed the words, my breath leaving my body in a whoosh. For a second I'd thought she'd been here. Which was stupid because she had no idea where I was, and I hadn't turned my phone on since I'd called my grandparents and the racetrack the morning after I'd arrived. The nurses wouldn't have allowed her into my room while I'd been at a session anyway. But for a second, I'd hoped...

The note was just a message from reception. *Please return your grandmother's call. Urgent.* A flicker of worry shot through me as the words sank in. Gran wouldn't have called me here if it wasn't important. I'd explained everything to her over the last few weeks. I'd taken to slipping down to reception after hours, when it was quiet and dark, to keep her updated on what was going on. It was enough to keep her worry at bay, and there was no reason for her to call and check up on me. I'd only just spoken to her last night.

I dropped the note and jogged down the hall to the reception desk. "Can I use a phone, please?"

The receptionist nodded and pointed to the other end of the desk where a phone sat in its cradle.

The phone rang once before Gran answered. "Low?" She didn't even say hello. My heart sank and nerves churned in my gut. She had to have been waiting with the phone in her hand to answer so quickly.

"It's me." My voice cracked and I coughed to clear it. "What's wrong? Is Pop okay?"

"He's fine. Your friend Jamison called."

Jamison? Why would he be calling my grandparents? He knew of them, but as far as I knew they'd never met.

"I didn't tell him where you were. I didn't know if he knew and that's not my business. But he asked if I could get a message to you, and I agreed. Only because he sounded so worried," she added in a rush.

"It's fine, Gran. What's wrong?"

"He said you need to come home. Reese..." Her voice trailed off and in the silence my mind raced.

"Reese what? Is she okay?" Panic shot through me. It had to be bad if Jamison had tracked my grandparents down just to get a message to me. I ran my free hand through my hair, every muscle tensing, ready to grab a set of keys and fly down the highway to Reese's place. Fuck! I didn't even have a car here, and I wasn't going anywhere with this damn landline keeping me tethered.

"I don't know. Jamison just said she wasn't in good shape and he thought you should know."

I paced around in tiny circles, which was as far as the short cord on the phone would allow. The linoleum squeaked under the soles of my shoes. "What does that mean? Have you seen her?"

I imagined my grandmother, sitting on the edge of her flowered lounge, shaking her head.

"No, love, I was waiting for you to call me back to see what you wanted to do. Maybe you should call her? Or I could go over there and check on her for you."

"No, it's fine. I need to see her and make sure she's okay. Thank you for calling. I love you."

I hung up before she could argue and sprinted out of the office, down the hall, and skidded to a stop in the doorway of a room identical to my own. I didn't waste time knocking, taking the liberty of opening the door myself.

"Will!" I yelled as I barged in. Will and Tim, who were sitting on the single bed, jumped apart looking guilty. I raised an eyebrow at Will but didn't bother questioning them over what they were doing in here alone together. It wasn't my place to judge.

"I need your car."

"What?"

"Your car keys, where are they?" I asked, scanning his bare desk and the bedside table that looked much the same way.

He stood up and opened the drawer on the bedside table, and pulled them out. "Where are you going in such a rush?"

"Reese."

Will gave me a grin and dropped the keys into my outstretched hand. "'Bout time, brother. Go get your woman."

I frowned. "You're an idiot. Who talks like that?" Then I punched him in the arm to let him know I was joking. "Thanks, man. I'll bring it back as soon as I can."

I ran back down the hall to my own room, snatched my wallet and my useless dead phone, and sprinted out to the parking lot. Will drove a Ford that had seen better days, but all I cared about in that moment was if it had a phone charger and enough petrol to get us back to Sydney. Sliding into the driver's seat, I leant across to rifle through the glove box and almost cheered when I came up victorious, phone charger in hand.

Impatient, I started the car with one hand while shoving the charger into the cigarette lighter with the other. Connecting my phone proved more difficult, with me jabbing at it uselessly, before I took a deep breath and calmly plugged it in.

The way I drove out of the car park was anything but calm, though. I navigated my way through the back streets on my way to the highway, continually glancing over at my phone, willing it to have enough charge to make a damn phone call. I drummed my fingers on the steering wheel and told myself to calm down and take a breath. I didn't even know what was wrong with her, and I wasn't going to be of any help to anyone if I got myself killed on my way home. Plus, Will would kill me if I wrote off his car. Trees and buildings whizzed by in my peripheral vision, but I concentrated on keeping the car moving down the highway without breaking the speed limit too much.

The ding from my phone, signalling it had finally turned itself back on, broke the tense silence that seemed to crackle in the air around me. And then the messages came flooding in. Message tone after message tone. Goddammit, turning your phone off for two months created quite the backlog. Though I supposed that could have been avoided if I hadn't just up and left and had maybe told someone where I was going. Guilt washed over me. I couldn't believe I'd just left Reese without a word. And not even just Reese, messages were pouring in from Jamison and the rest of the crew as well. I'd make it up to all of them. I just had to get to Reese first.

"Siri, call Reese," I commanded when the message tone fell silent and hoped like hell my phone would understand me for once. "You fuck this up and I swear I'm switching to Samsung," I muttered under my breath.

"Calling Reese," Siri said in her overly polite voice.

"You live to see another day, iPhone."

Reese's phone went straight to voice mail. "Fuck!" I yelled and slammed my finger on the cancel button.

Jamison was next, and unlike Reese, he answered right away. Like Gran earlier, he didn't say hello either. He wasn't quite as nice as she had been, though.

"Fuck you, asshole. I'm not even going to ask where the hell you've disappeared to. Are you coming back?"

I cringed internally at the seething anger in his voice. I was going to have to do some major apologising to him later.

"I'm on my way. What's wrong with Reese? She's not answering her phone."

"I know. I've been calling her for a week now. She hasn't been at work either. B said something about her family. But she's not talking and she won't let any of us in. You're a last resort. We thought she might hate you enough to at least open the door and punch you."

Her family. Shit, something must have happened. "Is she at her place?"

"I don't know, probably. B, Riley, and I have all gone over there multiple times and she won't let any of us in. We're pretty sure she's in there, though. We didn't know who else to call."

"Okay. Thanks, Jam. And I'm sorry. I'll explain later, but I need to sort this shit with Reese out first."

Jamison's voice softened. "I'm still pissed as hell, and I'm probably going to throat-punch you when I see you. Just so you know, because you fucking deserve it."

"Fair enough. I'll take it graciously."

Jamison snorted. "Just go see if you can get Reese to talk to you, will you?"

"I'm on it. I'm halfway back to Sydney already."

33

LOW

I made it back to Sydney in under two hours. I had no idea how I hadn't picked up a speeding ticket along the way.

The stairs to Reese's apartment creaked as I thundered up them two at a time. Hesitation slowed me when I reached her door, though, and I stared at it for a long moment, catching my breath. My heart felt like it had travelled north and lodged in my throat. I forced my fingers into a fist and knocked on the door, giving her a few minutes, then knocking again harder when nothing happened. I pressed my ear to the door, resting my hands and chest against the scratched wood surface. Nothing. It was possible she wasn't home, but something told me she was.

"Reese!" I yelled, then strained my ears for even the slightest noise coming from inside the apartment. "It's me. Low."

Nothing.

"I know I'm the last person you want to see, but I just need to know you're okay." My voice cracked. "As soon as I see you are, I'll go. I swear."

More silence from the other side. I slumped against the door and turned my forehead into the wood. The tiniest of noises came from the other side and my heart leapt into my throat. What was that? A hiccup?

"Reese! Open the damn door. I'm not leaving until you do!" I thumped the door again, in earnest this time. "I swear I'll break this damn thing down if I have to." Now that I knew she was inside, there was no way I was leaving until we hashed this out. It had been too long coming.

I pressed my ear to the door again and immediately wished I hadn't. Her muffled sobs ripped my chest open as physically as if I'd been stabbed with a knife, my insides spilling out right there on her doorstep.

The lock clicked next to my ear and I stepped back as the door cracked open. One beautiful brown eye appeared in the gap, the whites shot through with red. Her skin was bare of makeup, and her dark hair tousled in a messy halo. She looked like hell. And yet she was still the most beautiful woman I'd ever seen.

"Go away, Low. I'm not interested in anything you have to say." Yet she'd opened the door. Not for Bianca. Not for Jamison.

For me.

It had to mean something. She went to shut the door, but I grabbed it before she could. She pushed against me for a second before she walked away and let it swing open behind her. Her feet were bare, a pair of sleep shorts sitting low on her waist revealing long tan legs and a hint of smooth skin where her shirt rode up. I stayed in the doorway, studying every inch of her while trying to give her space. She turned as she reached the lounge; the circles under her eyes were so dark that from a distance they could have been mistaken for bruises. Exhaustion weighed heavy in her voice.

My hands balled in an attempt to stop myself from striding across the room and reaching out for her. I wanted to touch every inch of her skin until I was certain she was really right here in front of me after so long. If I could just pull her into my arms, I could start to make this better, and maybe I'd get some relief from the constant ache I'd carried around since the day I'd left. Fuck, I'd missed her.

"Well, come in if you're going to. No point standing there after you've made such a big show about letting you in in the first place."

It wasn't really an invitation. Beneath the exhaustion, I heard the underlying anger. Anger that was warranted and well-deserved. I stayed still, unable to let myself get close to her until she honestly wanted me in her space.

She sat down on the floor, between the lounge and the coffee table and flashbacks of sitting in the same position in my own apartment pounded through my skull. It felt like a lifetime ago. She tucked her legs up tight to her chest, wrapping her arms around them as the silence between us drew out. It was a long time before she looked up, and when she did, her eyes were full of pain and unshed tears.

That one look smashed whatever willpower I'd mustered, her pain consuming me as surely as if it were my own. I slammed the door shut and took three long strides into the room. I fell to my knees beside her, the soft carpet cushioning the blow. "Talk to me? Please?"

She pulled her legs tighter to her chest and laid her cheek on her knees. Her eyes were huge when they met mine. "What do you want from me, Low? You up and left without a word, and now you're here, out of the blue, wanting to talk? Don't you think it's a bit late for that?"

"Maybe." I edged closer, ignoring the way my skin hummed as my arm brushed hers. "But I'm going to try anyway. I'll try every damn day if I have to. If that's what it takes. And even if you hate me, I'm not going anywhere until you're okay."

She snorted. "You might be waiting awhile then."

This couldn't just be about me leaving. Not solely, and not after this long. She wouldn't quit showing up at work and lock herself in her apartment over me. I knew her better than that.

She was stronger than that. Whatever had happened was bigger than just me and my bullshit.

A tear rolled down her cheek and I brushed it away without thinking. She blinked, her eyes closing as she leant into my touch. A flicker of hope lit up within me, and my heart began to beat again. Needing more, I tucked a strand of her dark hair behind her ear, fingers trailing over her skin. Our gazes locked as my palms found the back of her neck and I paused before I pulled her closer. My brain shut down and before I could analyse what was happening, my lips crashed down onto hers. Her mouth melded to mine as if we'd kissed this way a thousand times, and I wondered how I'd gone two months without this. Without her.

She let out a tiny noise that sounded an awful lot like a cry, and my heart stopped. I pulled back an inch to investigate, but her mouth chased mine, claiming me again, and so instead I pulled her closer, feeling a shudder run through her as she relaxed into my arms.

There was no time to analyse or dwell on everything we still needed to sort out. Nothing had changed between us. I knew that. The heat and connection between us burned so brightly, I thought it would engulf me. Her lips sent a shot of molten lava right to my heart, every emotion, every feeling I'd suppressed about her for months exploding free. And I kissed her as if it were the last time, because it was already more than I'd dared to hope for.

It took a long time for my head to clear and to find the willpower to pull away. And when I did, my lips hovered only centimetres from hers, our breaths mingling in the tiny gap between us.

"Reese," I breathed, my gaze flicking over her as I tried to read her expression. "I'm sorry. I wasn't thinking." Being this close to her was torture. All I wanted was to pull her into my arms and do that again and again, for the rest of our lives.

Reese's gaze lifted from my lips and she stared at me with

those sad, glassy eyes. Neither of us moved for a silent moment that seemed to drag on for an hour.

"Do it again," she finally whispered.

"Do what?"

"Kiss me." She said it so quietly, I could barely hear her, despite being only inches apart.

I inched forward, bypassing her mouth, and placed a kiss to her temple. My lips lingered over her warm skin, and I fought the urge to trail more kisses along the side of her exposed neck. I couldn't tell what she was thinking when I wasn't looking into her eyes. And I needed to know how she felt more than I needed to kiss her.

It was Reese who moved next. In one fluid movement, she lifted herself from the floor, straddling herself across my thighs. Her hands locked around my neck and she pulled my head down, the same way she had the last time she'd kissed me, just moments before the doctor had told us I was HIV positive. She kissed me hard, her mouth unrelenting on mine. I pulled away again.

"Reese?" I tried to regain the eye contact we'd had a moment earlier, but she avoided my gaze.

"Shut up, Low." Her voice was husky as she silenced my questions with her mouth. My brain warred with my body. This wasn't right. I'd started the kissing, but fuck, we were avoiding the problem in the same way we always did. We couldn't keep doing this. We needed to talk. But dammit if my body would listen. My lips responded, opening and allowing her access as my hips ground up to meet hers. My cock hadn't seen any action in months, and my hands itched to grab her by the hips, lay her out on the carpet next to us, and take her hard. I groaned into her mouth, as her hands frantically grasped at my shirt, tugging it over my head, before our lips crashed together again. She had one hand down my pants and wrapped around my aching cock before I came to my senses.

"Jesus, stop, Reese!" I grabbed her hand and jerked away from her all too tempting lips.

She pulled away, panting. "What?"

"This isn't what I'm here for."

Her eyes narrowed. "Isn't it? Then why the hell are you here? Because unless you're here to fuck, I'm not interested." She stood up, anger radiating from her in waves, and moved to the kitchen, grabbing an unopened bottle of bourbon from the table on her way. My gaze followed her.

"Don't do that. Don't pretend all we are is physical. I'm not going to sleep with you just so you don't have to think. Whatever it is, you're going to have to talk about it first."

She cracked the cap on the bottle of bourbon. "You know, I've been thinking about drinking this for days. But I haven't. I didn't want to go back to that. But what's the point? I don't want to feel like this! I just want it to stop. Just for a while, and since you don't want me..."

She shrugged and poured a shot, but her fingers trembled, and she made no move to lift it to her mouth. I scrambled to my feet and crossed the small living room, placing my hand over hers. She glared up at me, those brown eyes blazing, all sass and defiant, daring me to stop her.

And then her entire facade broke. Her face crumpled, her chin dropped to her chest, and a sob burst from her mouth.

I gathered her in my arms, tucking her head to my chest and cradling it with my hand as her misery poured from her. "Sshh-hh," I soothed, running my hand up and down her back over and over. Nothing I did helped, but she made no move to leave my arms, so I just kept doing what I was doing and pressed kisses to the top of her head.

Her slight frame shook with grief, and I lost track of how long we stood there like that, her tears soaking my chest. It could have been minutes; it could have been hours. But all I knew was there was nowhere else I wanted to be. No one else I wanted to be holding. This felt right. For the first time since I'd walked away from her, I was complete again.

The sobs became hiccups and not long after that, she became still and quiet, her breathing evening out. Her head became heavier on my chest, her knees buckling. I scooped her up in my arms, frowning when she weighed less than nothing. Had she lost weight? Her arms came around my neck and I carried her down the hall to her bedroom.

I laid her down, pulling the ruffled grey blanket from the end of the bed over her shoulders. She watched every move I made, her dark eyes following me around the room as I laid down facing her.

"Gemma's still in the wheelchair," she whispered softly.

"Your sister? How do you know?"

"I saw her. Bianca and I. When we were shopping last week-end." She bit her lip and swallowed hard as her eyes filled with tears again. "If she was going to make a recovery, she would've done it by now. Her injuries must be permanent." For a second, I thought she was going to burst into tears again. But she sucked in a deep breath and let it out slowly.

"Why her? It was me not paying attention. It's my fault." She took another shaky breath. "I've ruined her life."

I sneaked a hand across the gap between us, and one by one entwined my fingers between hers. I squeezed them gently. "It was an accident; you know that. And how do you know you've ruined her life? Even in a wheelchair, people still have good lives."

"It's hardly the same as being able to walk."

"No, it's not. But I have some experience with long-term conditions that change your life forever. You can choose to be happy with the hand you've been dealt."

I smiled at her softly, as her face paled.

"Shit, I didn't mean…"

I pulled her blanket up around her shoulders, tucking it

around her. "Sssssshhhh, I know. But my life isn't over, and neither is hers. It was an accident. People make mistakes."

I shifted on the bed and sighed. "Me especially. I made a huge mistake. I'm so sorry about the text message and for taking off. And everything else I put you through. I just had to be alone and work out what this all meant."

She played with the fringe on the blanket. "Did you do that? Work it out, I mean? Where have you been?" The anger from earlier had evaporated, replaced by honest interest.

"At the clinic. The one in the brochure you left me."

"Oh." She looked down at our fingers still joined together. "I hoped that's where you were. But then you were gone so long, I thought... Did it help?"

I reached out, tucking one finger beneath her chin and tilting her face so she had no choice but to look at me.

"I've done more counselling than any one person should ever have to do in a lifetime. But it helped. I learned. I talked."

"So you're good?"

I smiled for what felt like the first time in months. Maybe it was. "I'm good. But you aren't and that breaks me."

She looked away again, as if the truth of the situation hurt her further, and the smile fell from my face.

"I've lost them. I saw this Facebook post Gemma wrote, and I was stupid, but I thought that maybe it meant she was okay. I convinced myself that something had changed—that she'd had a successful surgery, or maybe the injury hadn't been as serious as the doctors first thought. I read all these articles about injuries that looked serious early on but after a few weeks the patient regained feeling. And I let myself think I'd be able to go home. I was saving up to buy her a new horse, and then I was going to show up with it, and everything would just go back to the way it was. I'm such an idiot."

"Don't say that. You let yourself hope for the best outcome. There's nothing wrong with that. What did your dad say when you saw him last week?" An inkling of anger began to rise in me. Her dad was a jackass for the way he'd treated her. He was no better than my mother. You didn't treat your child that way, no matter what they'd done. I didn't need to be a parent to figure that one out.

Reese shook her head. "I didn't speak to them. I couldn't. My feet were made of cement and I just stood there watching them, hiding behind some stupid pot plant."

I frowned, taking a moment to think that through rationally. Maybe she couldn't see the other side of this. Fuck. I didn't have any right to waltz back into her life and start handing out advice like I was some sort of expert. But if I didn't say it, who would? Reconciling with her family was the most important thing. Even if it meant the gap between us widened.

"Reese, look at me. If you didn't talk to them, then you really don't know how they feel. It's been a long time. Things might be different now that everyone has had time to calm down and get used to the situation. You've been gone a whole year without a word. Maybe they're worried about you. This is what I was trying to tell you months ago. You need to resolve this. Even if your father disowns you for good, don't you want to at least find out for sure? Don't you want the chance to talk to your sister? To your mother? This can't have been easy for them either."

She was quiet.

"Stop living in limbo. Positives only, right? Let's go there. Right now. Let's just leave and see what happens. You could have your family back by the end of the day."

"Or I could have no one."

"You won't know unless you face it. And you'll never have no one. You'll have me. If you want me." The words fell from my lips effortlessly, because it was nothing but pure honest truth. But those words terrified me. I was terrified she wouldn't care I was trying to ask her for a future together.

"I don't have you, Low. I don't even know what this thing between us is."

"You've always had me. And I know I fucked this up a hundred times over, but I'm here, trying again. And I'm going to keep on trying until you believe I'm in this for real this time. All you have to do is let me."

A tear dropped from her eye, but the tiniest of smiles pulled at the corner of her mouth.

"You really want this?"

"I was always planning to come back to you, Reese. I had to fix myself first, but I was always going to fight for us. I want this. I'm willing to beg for it."

"I don't think that will be necessary." She smiled softly and everything within me exploded—lust, love, regret, fear, happiness, hope. And relief. A tidal wave of emotion.

"Fuck, I've missed you," I growled as I pounced on her, fusing my mouth to hers and pushing her onto her back.

"I hated that you weren't here. I've wanted to talk to you every day, and not being able to sucked," she mumbled between kisses.

I dropped my lips to her again. "I know. I want you to choose me. The HIV will make even simple things harder for us, but I want to be selfish. The thought of you being with someone else fucking eats me inside. I'll keep you safe, I swear it. I know I don't deserve your trust yet, after the way I left, but I'm asking you for it anyway."

Her warm breath misted over my lips. "I never doubted your ability to keep me safe. It was you who doubted yourself."

I buried my face in her neck, loving the way I could feel every inch of her beneath me. I lifted my head and waited until her eyes met mine. And everything I loved about her was right there, staring back at me.

"I love you, Reese. I have for a long time, and I should have told you before this all happened, but I was an idiot and I was scared. I know you said it once, but you need time and—"

She pressed a finger to my lips. "I hoped every day that you were at that clinic, and that you'd come back when you were ready. I'm not saying a phone call wouldn't have been nice." She rolled her eyes. "But I get it. I did the same thing, so I can't fault you for running when your back was against a wall. But my feelings for you didn't just stop when you left. If anything, they only increased."

"Yeah?" My spark of hope ignited into fireworks.

"Yeah."

34

REESE

*L*ow rolled over, putting space between us, lips swollen and eyes unfocussed from hours of kissing. Hours of kissing that easily could have led to more, but neither of us had pushed the boundaries. He'd seemed content to just hold me, and kiss, and whisper how much he loved me. It was enough for now. He'd said he wouldn't leave again, but words were just words after all, and it would be a while before I fully trusted him again. He knew my feelings hadn't changed in his absence, but something had stopped me from actually saying those three little words back to him. I felt them in my heart, but the words had never reached my lips.

"Let's go now," he said quietly.

I lifted my head to see if he was serious. "What? To my parents' place? We can't. You only just got back. It's a twelve-hour drive."

His lips brushed mine again, eliciting tingles that spread farther than just my mouth. "Don't care. As much as I'm enjoying this, we can't just lie here making out all day. You need this."

"It doesn't need to be today."

He jumped off the bed and yanked the blanket off me. "Yeah, I think it does."

"Hey!"

"Come on, I'll drive. What do you need?" He opened my wardrobe door and rifled through it, looking for God only knew what.

I got up and shoved him aside, laughing. "Anyone ever tell you you're bossy?"

He dropped a kiss on my cheek. "No more than you are. Pack some stuff. I'll run home and get mine and meet you back here in an hour."

My breath caught at the thought of him leaving again. It must have showed on my face, because he immediately pulled me into his arms again, hugging me close to him. When he pulled back, he ducked his head and cupped my chin, his ice blue gaze burning into mine.

"I'm coming back, baby. Every time. No more running, I promise. I know what I have here. What *we* have here. From now on, we only run *to* each other."

I nodded, a bubble of happiness rising within me. I'd never heard him speak so surely and it made my heart swell.

He was back before I was even half ready. I'd procrastinated by wandering around my apartment, tidying up and delaying the inevitable. Twelve hours suddenly seemed like a quick trip around the block. I wasn't ready for it. Just the thought of confronting my parents made me physically sick. My stomach was queasy and a fine sheen of sweat had broken out on my forehead. I wiped it away with the back of my hand.

And I stalled. "I still need to have a shower."

Low nodded, settling himself down on the lounge. "Okay. I'll still be here when you get back."

A smile tugged at my lips. I loved seeing him there on my lounge again, like he'd never left. Every nerve in my body had come alive when I'd heard his voice through the door. He'd been pale with panic the last time I'd seen him, but now he looked tan and healthy, and...happy even. It made my heart full. He loved me. That part of me that was still upset with him buried itself a little deeper beneath my contentment and excitement over his return.

I dragged myself away from Low and into the bathroom, glancing in the mirror as I turned the taps on in the shower. Jesus. I looked like shit. Hours of crying over the last week had made my skin red and blotchy, and my cheeks looked hollow, thanks to the crash diet misery had forced on me. I was sure I didn't smell that great either. And there was Low, out on my lounge, looking like a sex god. Damn him.

I let the water pound over me and waited until it turned cold before I stepped out and wrapped myself in a towel. When I looked in the mirror again I was marginally happier with the reflection staring back at me. At least I was clean and smelled good, even if I still looked like I'd been on a bender. I pulled on yoga pants and a long flowy top, aiming for cute but comfy, and when I left the bathroom, I looked almost like my regular self.

"I thought you'd gotten lost in there," Low called when I stepped out of the bathroom, his eyes slowly travelling up and down my body. "You ready to go?" He stood and shouldered the bag I'd packed and left on the lounge.

"If I say no, can we just stay here and make out instead?"

He stepped closer and tilted my chin up. A chuckle rumbled through him, making my knees go weak. Happy, smiling Low was sexy.

"As tempting as that sounds, we're going." He leant down so his lips brushed my ear. "But don't think I'm done kissing you. I don't care who's around, I've waited so long to be with you, I'm going to kiss you whenever and wherever I want. Including at your parents' place."

"No arguments here."

His warm breath brushed over the sensitive skin of my neck.

"There are other things I have planned too. Just so you know." He stepped back and winked, seemingly oblivious to the shiver of anticipation that ran through me. My stomach flipped deliciously. I'd missed him.

The sun was low in the summer sky by the time we made it down to Low's Ute, the interior of the cab still warm from the heat of the day. A wave of exhaustion hit me like a sledgehammer, and I laid my head on the window as Low pulled onto the road. It wasn't late, barely 8:00 p.m., but I couldn't remember the last time I'd had a full-night's rest. I closed my eyes, letting the drone of the engine and Low's warm hand covering mine lull me to sleep.

I woke up with a start, my head cracking painfully on the window before I realised where I was. Still in the car with Low. Driving to my parents' place. Right. I rubbed my head.

"Shit, did that hurt?" Low handed me a bottle of water and I took a few sips as I peered out through the windscreen. "Good morning, by the way."

The sun was just coming up over the horizon, and dirt roads lined with trees replaced the city streets we'd been on when I'd fallen asleep. "How long have I been asleep for? We're only about twenty minutes from parents' place!"

He looked over at the GPS, nestled in a phone cradle. "Twenty-three minutes according to this."

"I'm surprised you even have phone reception out here."

"Me too. I kept thinking I'd wake you when it cut out, but so far, so good. And it looks like your parents' place is at the end of this road anyway."

I gazed out through the dusty glass and nodded at the familiar stretch of road. I'd driven down this road a million times. "Yeah, it is." I bit my lip and the water in my hand trembled. Low took it from me and I glanced at him gratefully.

"Nervous?"

"That obvious?"

"You just nearly spilt that water all over yourself, so yeah. Kind of."

I shook my head. "I can't believe you drove all night. You should have woken me."

"You looked like you needed the sleep."

"How tired are you right now, though?" I reached across the centre console and let my hand rest on the back of his neck, running my fingertips through the ends of his hair.

"A bit." He tried to stifle a yawn and failed miserably.

More like a lot. I could tell just from looking at the dark circles under his eyes. He must have been awake for at least twenty-four hours now.

I raised a hand and pointed. "The turn off is just there."

Low indicated and turned into the road that led to my parents' place. It would have been funny if I hadn't been so nervous. No one indicated out here; there was no need. It's not like we had traffic lining up behind us. He'd been hanging out in the city too long.

We passed a few farmhouses before my childhood home came into view. It was about fifteen acres. Not a huge property but enough for my dad's horse riding business and a few large plots of vegetables that never yielded anything much because we were all hopeless gardeners. There was no wraparound veranda like Low's grandparents' house. It was a simple, three-bedroom clad cottage, desperately in need of painting. But the flaking paint was one of the only things that still looked the same. A ramp replaced the front steps, and at the door sat a tiny wheelchair. I coughed, but it didn't ease the tightness in my chest. Low pulled up next to a large white van that was also new. I wondered where my father's four-wheel drive was. Maybe he wasn't home.

Low turned the car off, but neither of us made a move to get out. We just sat in the early morning silence. The rising sun backlit the house, forcing us to squint.

"It's early, maybe we should have stopped and waited for a more decent hour."

"They're farm people. They don't get up by dawn?" Low questioned.

I sighed. "Yes. They'll be up."

"Time to rip the Band-Aid off then, Reese." He opened his door and slid out, taking a moment to stretch before he walked around the hood to my door. He held his hand out to help me down, and I accepted it because my legs suddenly felt like they wouldn't hold my weight. Low's hand slid to the small of my back, and I tried to ignore the way my skin tingled under his touch. Even through the fabric of my shirt, my body reacted to him.

"I'll be right beside you the whole time."

He threaded his fingers through mine and we walked side by side to the front door. My fingers trailed over the back of the child-sized wheelchair, and my eyes misted with tears. I blinked them back. I couldn't cry before we'd even begun.

My knocks on the door were feeble at best. But Low squeezed my hand and I mustered the courage to knock again, louder this time. My breath caught in my throat as the lock on the door turned. The door swung open, and my sister's dark eyes and hair, tousled with sleep, appeared in front of me. She looked even tinier than she had from across the shopping centre food court, her small frame tucked into her wheelchair. Her eyes grew big as she took me in.

"Reese?"

Then she squealed in excitement. "Reese!" She gave her wheels one hard push, which sent her careening straight into my legs. Her thin arms wrapped around my waist tightly. "Oh my God! I can't believe you're here!" Her face was pressed to my belly, muffling her voice. The mist I'd been trying to keep out of my eyes overcame me, and this time, it wasn't just mist. My eyes filled with tears and I let them spill down my cheeks as I cradled her head. I wove my fingers into her dark strands and held her tight. I hadn't expected her to open the door, but I was so grateful she had. I knew she wouldn't blame me for the accident. She was a kid. They were forgiving by nature. Especially Gemma. But if my parents, my dad in particular, wouldn't let me see her again, well, at least I had this. At least I'd had a few stolen moments with her. And that was worth driving to the ends of the earth for.

"Gemma, who is it, sweetheart?" My mother's voice called from the back end of the house, shaking me into action.

I pulled out of Gemma's embrace and knelt down in front of her, so our faces were at the same level. I wrapped my arms around her, in a proper hug, and when I let go, I took her face in my hands and stared at her million-dollar grin.

"You're back," she said simply.

I nodded, and over her shoulder I saw my mother walk into the room. She dropped the dish towel she'd been holding when she saw me. She didn't say anything, though, and I chose to ignore her for the moment and focus on Gemma.

"Gemma, listen, I don't know how much time I'll get, so I need to say this quickly. I'm so sorry. I'm sorry for the accident and for not being here ever since. I hate myself for all of it, and I completely understand if you hate me too. But I really hope you don't. Because I love you and I miss you like crazy."

Gemma's brow furrowed. "I don't hate you. Why would I?" She glanced over her shoulder at our mother before looking back up at me. "I don't understand."

I looked over at my mother and she shook her head slightly as she came forward. Hadn't my parents told her what had happened? She paused behind Gemma's wheelchair as I stared at her, not knowing what to say. Why hadn't they told her what happened? The planes of my mother's face were so familiar. She didn't look any different from the last time I'd been in this house. She was a stunning woman, only a few strands of grey hair giving away she was approaching fifty. My sister and I got our dark colouring from her.

"Reese," she said, still hovering behind Gemma. "I...your father..."

My heart sank. And suddenly her face changed, a look of determination crossing her features. She grabbed the handle of Gemma's chair and yanked her away from me.

The oxygen in my lungs went with her. This had been a mistake. She didn't want Gemma touching me and I was seconds away from having the door slam in my face, leaving me standing out on the step like a salesman who'd tried to sell her something unwanted. She pushed Gemma and her protests behind her, blocking her from my view. I closed my eyes, not wanting to watch my mother shut me out yet again and waited for the slam.

When it didn't come, I opened my eyes. We were almost identical heights and builds, so there was nowhere to look but into her eyes. I racked my brain for the right thing to say, something that would make her understand how sorry I was and how much I missed her. But the truth was, I'd said it all before. I'd said it the day of the accident when I'd sat sobbing on the hospital floor. I was saying it again, by standing here on her doorstep. The ball was in her court. Even Gemma had gone quiet in the midst of the stand-off between us.

But then my mother took a step forward and her soft arms wrapped around me, engulfing me in her embrace. And I let her, because in that moment I felt the pain within her, a mirror of my own. The familiar smell of the perfume she'd worn every day for as long as I could remember wafted over me. A noise came from her throat that was something between a gasp and sob, and a tremor that rocked her whole body followed. She buried her face in my shoulder as the sobs overcame her, and I found myself rubbing her back unconsciously as she cried on my shoulder, my own tears dripping down my face.

"Shhh, Mum. It's okay," I murmured over and over as her

shoulders shook and she clutched me in a vice like grip, as if she were afraid I might disappear again. Gemma looked on quietly from her chair but didn't say anything as my mother pulled me tighter. I'd missed her hugs and her touch. I'd missed this house and the fresh air. I'd missed the love I'd gotten here.

"I'm so sorry," I mumbled, not knowing what else to say. What I'd done was so huge, words couldn't fix it. All I could do was ask for forgiveness. The tears coursed down my cheeks as my hand continued to rub circles on her back.

Eventually she pulled back and looked at me with her tear-stained face. She held me tightly by the shoulders and shook me a little to get my full attention. "You have nothing to apologise for, Reese. It's me who made a huge mistake. It's me who needs to apologise."

I shook my head. "No, Mum, I—"

"Stop. I should have never let you walk out of that hospital. Not the way you did. That wasn't right. You were a child. I was the parent. All I can say in my defence is that I was in shock and not thinking straight. I couldn't think of anyone but Gemma until I knew whether she was going to live or die. But it's not a good excuse."

"It is. It's fine. It wasn't your fault—"

"You're right, Reese. It wasn't her fault. It was mine," a deep voice said behind me.

I whipped around. My dad stood behind Low, his broad shoulders in a khaki work shirt, his ever-present Stetson perched on his head. His eyes bore through me, as if Low wasn't even there, and Low discreetly moved to the side. Dad ignored him as he inched closer to me, occupying the space Low had just vacated.

"We've been worried sick about you. I tried to ring you, over and over until we found your phone in a drawer in your bedroom and realised you hadn't taken it with you. We tried all your friends, but no one had heard from you. And then I got a phone call a few months back, and I thought it was you, but you would never answer when I called, and you never called again. We just hired a private investigator in the city to look for you." He took a deep breath, the lines around his eyes and mouth deep crevices. Unlike my mother, up close, I realised he'd aged since I'd last seen him. Was it the stress I'd caused? Or his own guilt over why I'd left?

Words stuck in my throat. I'd come here expecting to fight. Fight to see my sister and to fight for their trust again. I hadn't expected apologies, and I had no idea what to do with them.

"I...I behaved terribly. The things I said to you..." He coughed and looked down at the scuffed wood of the landing. "Well, I'm ashamed of what I said. Gemma's accident was just that. An accident. What I said was just in the heat of the moment. I never meant it. It took me a few days to realise that, and I'm so sorry, sweetheart. There's been a hole in this family ever since you left. I never wanted that. I never wanted you to go..."

I'd heard enough. I closed the gap between us in a quick movement and stepped close into him. His arms wrapped around me and he squeezed me so tight I thought I'd pass out from lack of oxygen. "Thank you," I whispered in his ear.

He pulled back enough to look at me. "For what?"

"For all of it. I know that couldn't have been easy for you to say. And for what it's worth, I'm sorry too."

He shook his head. "What's harder was living the last year without seeing you. Without knowing if you were even okay. I know you're an adult, but you're still our baby. You always will be, no matter what you do."

I buried my face in his broad chest and let another round of tears fall from my eyes. His shirt smelled of straw and dirt, but I didn't mind at all. He smelled of comfort. Of home. Of love.

From behind me, Low sneezed. Loudly. All four of us turned to look at him.

He shrugged. "Sorry, I've been trying to hold that in, to let you all have your moment. I'm Low."

Gemma snorted with laughter as Low offered my father his hand to shake. I stepped out of my dad's arms and into Low's, wrapping my arm around his waist.

"Thank you, too," I said quietly.

He nodded. He knew what I was thanking him for without me saying it. I would have come back eventually, without his prodding. Or maybe they would have found me. But he'd made it happen sooner, and after wasting a year, wasting any more time would have been heartbreaking.

"Have you two eaten? Gemma and I were just making breakfast if you're interested."

"I'm interested," Low said cheerfully.

I smiled up at him happily. "So am I."

REESE

*L*ow was dead on his feet by the time I showed him up the stairs and into my old bedroom. He sank into the mattress without even bothering to take his shoes off and was asleep before I'd shut the door behind me.

I wasn't tired after sleeping all night in the car. I walked around the quiet house, running my fingers over familiar objects and staring at the old family photos on the walls of the hallway. I called Bianca and filled her in on everything that had happened and asked her to let the guys know Low was back.

My father's students arrived for their lessons and made their way to the stable to saddle up their horses. They made me smile. My father had gotten busy while I'd been away. He would have never been able to run a class on a Tuesday morning a few years ago, and it made me happy. He deserved the success.

In the afternoon, Mum drove the van to the top of the driveway to wait for Gemma's school bus and when they returned, the three of us crowded into the little kitchen and got busy preparing dinner. For an hour, I could pretend nothing had happened between us. We'd made dinner together like this a million times before, and the conversation and laughter flowed.

A little more of the black cloud that had been hovering around me since the accident lifted, relief settling in its place. Bianca had been right about Gemma. She was happy. She was a pro with her wheelchair, manoeuvring herself around easily and chopping veggies behind the kitchen table, which was an easier height for her to manage. She laughed and smiled and chattered happily about school, and her friends and catching the bus home with the Ryker brothers that lived on the next property.

We had potatoes and a roast in the oven when Low appeared at the top of the stairs, rubbing his eyes and looking adorably sleep-tousled. My mouth dried watching him stretch, his shirt riding up and revealing the lower planes of his hard stomach. My mother gave me a knowing look and I rolled my eyes. But I couldn't help grinning.

"Is there anything I can help with?" Low asked as he came and sat at the table with Gemma. She gave him a grin, passing him a knife and some of her assigned vegetables to chop. He pulled them across the table and picked up the knife with an air of expertise. He smiled when he caught me watching him, his knife moving rapidly across the chopping board. "I did a few months in the racetrack kitchens before I started in the bar," he said by way of explaining the stack of perfectly julienned carrots in front of him.

"I'm impressed."

My dad walked in just after six, while the four of us were playing cards around the kitchen table, the delicious smell of roast meat wafting around us. He leant on the doorjamb and paused for a moment before he stood behind Gemma and dropped a kiss on her head. He did the same with my mother, and then on mine.

"So, is Low your boyfriend, Reese?" Gemma asked as we placed plates of food on the table.

I glanced over at Low, unable to help the grin that spread across my face. "Yep, he is."

"And is Low a real name?"

I laughed and my mother shushed her. My father looked like he was interested in the answer, but he had better manners.

"How's uni?" Dad asked instead, his forkful of beef hovering in front of his mouth. "You should be nearly finished, right?"

I shook my head. "No, I dropped out when everything happened. I've only just re-enrolled, so I'm a year behind."

Dad frowned, but Low stopped eating and grinned. "You have?"

I nodded.

He kissed me on the cheek. "You're amazing."

"Not really. But I figured I couldn't work at your bar for the rest of my life."

"You own a bar, Low?" my mother asked.

"His family owns a racetrack," I answered for him.

My father raised an eyebrow. "Which one?"

"Lavender Fields."

Dad whistled long and low. "I know that place. That's an impressive family business you have there."

"Thank you. My grandparents have worked very hard for it."

"I'll bet. And what do you do there?"

"Dad, can you stop with the third degree, please?" I groaned. He seemed to have forgotten I hadn't lived with him for over a year now and was quite capable of vetting my own men. "Low does a bit of everything. He's working his way around each department at the racetrack, getting to know the business from the ground up."

Dad nodded. "That's admirable."

I breathed a little easier. I didn't want Dad getting the idea that Low was some spoilt rich brat, when the truth was he'd had to fight tooth and nail since he was a kid, just to survive.

Low squeezed my knee under the table and let his hand linger there, his thumb tracing patterns on my leg, until his touch was all I could concentrate on.

When I looked back up from my Low induced haze, Mum was watching us, a small smile lifting the corners of her mouth. The room had grown dim while we'd been eating and she glanced at the clock before announcing it was time for Gemma to do her homework and get ready for bed. She stood, resting her hands on the back of Gemma's wheelchair, and threw my father a look. He hastily stood up and excused himself, stating he had paperwork to do. Gemma protested, but my mother wheeled her to her bedroom on the ground floor anyway, leaving Low and me in the quiet kitchen.

"Want to come for a walk?"

He brushed his lips across mine. "First chance all day to be alone with you...what do you think?"

I laughed and stood, pulling him up by his hand, our chairs scraping on the tiled floor. His hand rested on the small of my back. The cool night air drifted over me as I descended the newly installed ramp and stepped onto the grass. I paused, waiting for him at the bottom, and when he caught up, I slid my fingers between his.

The inky black sky above us was lit with thousands of visible stars, and I tilted my head back, taking it in. "I've missed this."

"Mmm. So different from the city sky."

I nodded, enjoying the silence, only interrupted by the slight wind in the trees and the buzzing drone of cicadas. It was dark beyond the pool of light spilling from the house, but the moon did its job and my steps were sure as I led Low through the night. The barn was a few hundred metres from the house, but I'd walked the path thousands of times over the years.

We stopped just outside and watched the dark silhouettes of horses moving in the paddock. Low fitted himself to my back, locking his arms beneath my breasts and dropping his mouth to the side of my neck. He kissed me gently.

"I think I'm going to take the foal."

"The one your grandparents wanted you to have?" I smiled into the darkness. "That's fantastic. He's a beauty."

"So are you."

I closed my eyes, letting the back of my head rest against his chest, enjoying the way being in his presence made me feel.

"Are we okay?" he murmured, his mouth moving up my neck, trailing kisses to the sensitive spot behind my ear. His lips sent shivers down my spine, and my heart rate thumped double time as I considered his question.

I turned so we were face-to-face and slid my hands behind his back, tucking my fingers into the back pocket of his jeans. I breathed in his scent and tried not to remember how bleak the weeks without him had been. I'd gone through the motions of work and kept myself busy researching my uni options. But it had all been with a Low-shaped hole in my heart. I'd willed my phone to ring, but every time it had, it wasn't him. My throat felt thick, as if the words were stuck. "I just wish we hadn't lost all this time." I sniffed. "God, I missed you."

He tightened his arms around me. "I'm so sorry, baby. But the things that were going through my head...it was just so full of HIV and what that meant for me and for the future. And then there was you." He pulled back, ducking his head a little so he was closer to my eye level. "I couldn't stop thinking about you."

"Yeah?"

"I couldn't stay and hurt you. You could be stuck with this thing for life if I fuck up, even one time. That was all it took for me. One time."

I pressed a finger to his lips. "Stop. We've been through this. You won't ever do that. And if you'd just stuck around long enough to talk to Dr. Sloane, you would have known HIV isn't what it once was."

"I know. But I wasn't ready to hear it then. I couldn't sort anything out with you before I'd sorted it out in my head."

"And now?"

"I know better now. I'm on medication to control it and to make it safer for you. There's medication you could take too…" He looked at me impishly. "I know it's a lot to ask, but it's the safest way…"

"I'm already taking it."

His head jerked back. "You are?"

I nodded. "I hung around and listened to the doctor the day you ran off. She gave me a crash course in HIV and how to protect myself. I started the tablets the next day."

"And you've taken them this whole time?"

I nodded. "I wasn't sure if you'd come back, but if you did, I didn't want to waste any more time waiting around. This disease has already stolen so much time from us, I didn't want to give it more."

Low took my face between his palms. His fingers cupped my cheeks and tipped my chin until his eyes stared into mine. Black replaced the icy blue in the darkness, but the love I saw there burned brighter than the sun.

"You deserve a life, you know. You're a good man who made a mistake. This doesn't have to define you. And it doesn't change how I feel about you." I reached beneath the back of his shirt, trailing my fingers over the ridges of bone and muscle. "I was angry you left without talking to me, but I understood. We're the same. We run. And you learnt early that only relying on yourself is the safest way to avoid being hurt. I get it."

He swallowed hard, the bob of his Adam's apple visible even in the darkness, and his voice was husky when he spoke again.

"You're amazing." His lips hovered over mine, only centimetres apart but frustratingly far away. I moved to close the gap between us, but he held my face tighter, stilling me until he'd said his piece. "You're amazing and beautiful and I don't deserve you. But fuck. I want you, Reese. More than I've ever wanted anything in my life." His lips crashed down on mine, stealing my breath and my thoughts. I couldn't touch him enough. My palms roamed his back as I pressed myself to his chest. Heat pooled low in my belly as he deepened the kiss, controlling it and making me melt further into his arms. A fog of desire invaded my brain where the world faded and it was just me and him.

"So we're good?" he asked again, when he finally pulled away. Through my erratic breathing and hazy head, I saw the corners of his mouth turn up, making me want him to just shut up and kiss me more than ever. But with the break from his lips came a tiny amount of clarity and there was something else that needed to be said before I lost myself in him again.

"We're good. But we're doing this, right? For real? You can't wrap me in cotton wool and treat me like some breakable valuable your grandmother handed down to you. You have to kiss me and touch me. You have to sleep with me and next to me. I want you to tell me you love me and stop leaving me when times get tough, because you know this won't be the worst thing we ever have to go through. Just…stop holding me at arm's length because you think you'll hurt me. You won't. We'll be careful. Every time. We can go slow—"

He pulled me to him, my breasts crushing against his chest, his lips brushing my ear. "Fuck. That. I don't want to go slow. I want to go back to that afternoon before my diagnosis. I had so many plans for that night…all the things I wanted to do to you… do with you…"

The ache in my core increased as he kissed me hard.

"I was hoping you'd say that." I pulled a foil wrapped condom from my back pocket and waved it in front of him.

His eyes widened. "Seriously? Here?" He shot a worried look back towards the house as if my dad might be watching us through the window while he polished his shotgun.

I raised an eyebrow. "Well, we could just wait until we get back to Sydney, I guess…"

Low warred with his indecision for exactly three seconds before a grin spread across his face. "Fuck it." He grabbed me by the hips, lifting me high and slinging me over his shoulder. A startled laugh escaped me as I dangled down his back and he slapped my ass for good measure. He yanked the barn door open, the horses looking up at us curiously as he strode between their stalls. The familiar smell of horses and hay filled my nose as Low's strong arm tightened over the back of my thighs.

Low hit the far end of the barn and stopped, looking left and right. "Fuck. Where?"

"Shearers quarters. Through there." I pointed to the door on our right. My father had never run sheep, so the shearers quarters hadn't been used in years. But since our cottage was small, my mother always kept the beds made up for any overnight guests. It wasn't fancy, but it was more appealing than getting it on with hay poking you in the ass.

The door swung hard into the wall as Low charged through it and stopped abruptly. There was a window in the little room but it was dark outside and I couldn't see a thing. "Light's over there." I nudged him towards the wall on our right. Low groped around until he found it, flicking the switch that turned on the single naked bulb in the ceiling. The weak yellow light did little, but it was enough to illuminate the two single beds pushed up against the wood walls of the room.

Low dropped me onto the nearest bed, covering my body with his own, and excitement shot through me as every delicious inch of him pressed me hard into the mattress. My hands bunched in the back of his shirt and pulled it over his head. He loomed over me again, hovering on his arms before kissing me, and my stomach flipped as my libido skyrocketed. He was pure male. Broad shoulders, smooth, tanned skin, and hard muscle. His gaze locked with mine, and he paused.

"Are you nervous?" I whispered as I scratched my nails along his bare back. I wriggled beneath him, wanting more, but I needed to know he was okay first.

"Honestly? Yeah. I think I am."

I studied him, noting the slight tremble in his arms and the indents deepening between his eyebrows. "We're both taking tablets. And we have protection." I reached up and smoothed his frown lines with my finger. "You know you've seen me naked already, right? You do remember that? And it's not like you're a virgin. So what else is there?"

He shook his head. "It's not that. I'm a one-night-stand guy. I always have been. In and out, thank you, goodbye. I've never been with someone I love..." He looked embarrassed all of a sudden. "I want this to be good for you."

My insides liquefied until I was a puddle on the floor and he huffed out an ironic laugh.

"Plus, don't forget, I haven't had sex in months. This might all be over before it even begins. So yeah. Forgive me if I'm a bit nervous."

"Stop thinking so much and just kiss me."

He kissed me softly this time. His lips brushed over mine, once, twice, three times, before he opened his mouth and deepened the kiss with his tongue. My fingers reached up to tangle in the hair at the base of his neck, while tingles spread out from my lips. I wriggled until my legs wrapped around his waist and moaned as his cock pressed against my core, ramping up the heat already building there.

"I love that sound," he groaned as he rolled his hips against mine. "I want to hear it all day and all night." He dropped his mouth to the sensitive skin of my neck, kissing a hot trail from the soft place behind my ear and down my neck, across my collarbones. "But louder."

The V-neck of my shirt left a hint of cleavage bare and he kissed every square inch of exposed skin before sitting me up off the mattress and tugged the shirt over my head. His blue eyes bored deep into mine, and I stilled under his gaze. The heat in his eyes burned through me, stopping between my legs, and I ground up into him, desperate to ease the ache there. His mouth landed on my lacy white bra, sucking the nipple through the sheer fabric, and I moaned again as my nipple hardened under the wet heat of his mouth.

"Not loud enough." He moved to the other nipple and repeated the action.

God, I wanted more. I pushed him back and sat up again, so I could unhook my bra at the back. His hands were quick to slide the straps down my arms, the bra landing somewhere on the floor before I lay back down. He placed open-mouthed kisses over my exposed skin, his tongue flicking over my nipples, making my back arch trying to get closer to him. He sucked one nipple into his mouth, rolling the other between expert fingers. I pressed up into his mouth, my eyes falling closed as his fingers flicked open the button on my jeans. His attention moved from my breasts to pull my jeans down my thighs. Toeing off my shoes, I shoved my jeans down the last few inches with my feet, the need to be naked in front of him and have our bare skin touching overwhelming.

Low ran his fingers beneath the elastic of my underwear and slipped them down my legs, lifting each foot before replacing it on the mattress. His gaze burned over my skin, making my toes curl, but I forced myself to lie still. I wanted him to see me. I'd wanted it from the night we met. And he'd seen me naked before, but this felt different. This felt special. This was our reward for waiting so long. Wetness pooled between my legs and I ached for him to touch me there, my clit throbbing for attention. I squeezed my legs together, trying to relieve the tension.

He sat back on his knees and undid the button on his own jeans, drawing my eyes to the delicious V muscle that ran down either side of his hips and under his jeans. His cock sprang free, hard and proud when he undid his jeans.

I raised an eyebrow. "Commando, huh?"

He grinned and placed a kiss on my belly button before he looked back up at me. "That's just how I roll."

I grinned. "Lucky me then, hey?" I let my hand trail along his hard length before wrapping my fingers around the base. He hissed through his teeth and I looked up at him.

"Be careful with that. I have a serious case of blue balls."

I stroked him again, and this time I cupped him with my other hand, squeezing his balls gently. "They don't look blue."

Low's head dropped back, pleasure and pain both evident on his handsome face. "You'll pay for that," he said and moved himself out of my grasp.

"Oh yeah?" I couldn't help teasing him.

He slid off the bed, kneeling on the wooden floorboards. Wrapping his arms around my thighs, he tugged me down the bed so my ass was on the edge of the mattress, my legs spread around him. He looked down at me, bared and on display for him, and ran a finger through my wetness, making pleasure shoot through my most sensitive nerve endings.

"You know, I dreamt of tasting you the entire time I was gone. I can't wait any longer. Be loud this time, Reese. Be real loud."

His mouth lowered to my pussy and my back arched, legs opening farther as he ran his tongue through my already wet folds. I moaned, not because he wanted me to, but because I couldn't help it.

"Not loud enough." His tongue flicked over the sensitive bundle of nerves and back through my folds, dipping inside me and repeating the action over and over until I was writhing and biting my tongue but determined not to give him the satisfaction of moaning again. But then he slipped a finger inside me, and I lost the battle as a moan ripped from somewhere deep within me. I opened my eyes to see his smug grin.

"Ssshhh now, you'll scare the horses." He moved his fingers again, pressing up against my G-spot while his tongue slid over my clit.

"Screw the horses. They're old and half deaf anyway," I groaned.

Low's chuckle vibrated over my pussy, only heightening the sensation. His tongue was relentless, rhythmically working my clit while his fingers slid in and out, until I saw stars. My moans echoed off the walls as I came, clenching around his fingers.

He kissed his way back up my torso, my skin ultra-sensitive and covered with goosebumps, my breaths coming in pants. I curled in on myself, savouring the orgasm high. I opened one eye and smiled at his satisfied face. "Happy with yourself?"

He chuckled. "I'm just glad we're so far from the house. Too bad if someone decided to take an evening stroll, though."

I pulled him back up on the bed next to me and he kissed me slowly. I tasted myself on his lips and his erection pressed into my upper thigh. I looked down in surprise. "When did you put a condom on?"

"While you were blissing out. I meant it when I said I'd look after you. I'm not going anywhere near you unless it's gloved."

"You can't infect my leg," I joked.

His gaze turned broody, his voice dropping to a dark whisper. "I know. But I don't plan on leaving my dick resting on your leg any longer either." He rolled me to my back, nudging my legs apart, and pressed against my entrance. The tiniest flicker of worry rolled through me but evaporated when I looked into his eyes and saw nothing but love there. The protective way he held me dispelled any fear I might have been harbouring. His gaze dropped to my lips before his mouth covered mine, and he pushed inside me with one long, slow thrust.

"Ohhh." My head kicked back and my back arched. Already sensitive from his earlier attentions, my body ached for him, and he filled me, stretching me deliciously.

I'd expected him to be cautious, but he'd obviously put his nerves behind him as he worked himself in and out, confident and rhythmic. He braced himself on his arms, and as much as I loved watching his biceps bulge and his abs flex, I wanted him closer. I pulled him down on top of me, wrapping my legs around his waist and pressing my fingers into the muscle of his back, before they slid down to his ass. My hips rose to meet his, urging him to go faster. He groaned into my mouth and kissed me hotly, his tongue tangling with mine. "I'm going to come if you keep moving your hips like that," he gritted out.

"I want you to," I whispered back and thrust my hips at his again. He increased the pace as I pressed him closer.

A tremble coursed through him. "I love you," he murmured.

"I know. I love you too."

He stilled and kissed me, slow and sweet, before rolling his hips into mine again. I gasped at the sudden movement. He reached between us, finding my clit, and I dug my nails into his back as sensation exploded through me again. After a few more thrusts, his body jerked, signalling his release.

His pace slowed, until he pulled out. He sat up and pulled the condom off his still mostly hard penis and tied a knot in the end. He examined it quickly.

"What are you doing?" I asked, lifting my head from where I lay sinking into the mattress, as boneless as a jellyfish. "Come back here, it's cold without you on top of me."

"Just making sure there are no breaks in the condom." He looked at me, relief fuelling his expression. "We're good."

I leant across and kissed his chest. "We're great."

Low pushed to his feet and pulled on his jeans. I gave him an exaggerated pout as his cock disappeared beneath the denim, but snuggled up onto his chest when he lay back down next to me. I pressed my nose into the side of his neck and breathed deep, even breaths as my fingers trailed across his skin, content and happy to stay in his arms for as long as he'd let me. The silence drew out between us, our breathing evening out, and it was sweet and peaceful. For the first time in a long time, everything felt right. Neither of us had anything left to run from, nothing left to hide. We were finally on the same track, running together.

"Were you worried?" Low asked eventually, his voice muffled from his lips resting on my forehead.

"About what? Sex?"

"Yeah, I guess. Having sex with someone who has HIV. Was it playing on your mind the whole time?"

His body tensed as he waited for my reply. I shook my head without thinking, but then stopped, wanting to be honest. "I thought about it. For a minute, and then your tongue was all over me and it was hard to think of anything else."

I laughed, but his face was still serious. Concern burst my happy little after sex bubble and I pressed up on my elbows to look at him. "Were *you* worried about it the whole time?"

He shook his head and relief filled me. "No, I wasn't. Which worries me a bit."

"Why?"

"I don't want us to ever get complacent. I know we're both taking the tablets, but it doesn't guarantee I can't transfer this thing to you. We can't ever slip up, Reese. We can't."

I hugged him, hoping I could hold him tight enough to reassure him that everything was fine. I wasn't worried about him running again, and I recognised his words for what they were. He needed time to process a fear, so I simply held him, while he held me. We lay there for a long time before I whispered, "You're safe with me. Everything we do together is on me as much as it's on you. You won't let me get careless, and I won't let you get carried away in the moment. We'll work these things out together."

His eyes went glossy. "I really do love you."

"And so you should, because I'm awesome," I said with a laugh, but I had to blink back the wetness welling in my eyes.

He brushed my hair back off my face and kissed me softly on the lips. "Always a smart-ass."

My heart swelled at the sound of his laugh and the tender way he looked at me, and we lay back down together, a tangle of legs and arms. I sighed as a quiet contentment flooded through me.

He might not have been perfect, but neither was I. And the one thing I was positive of—the only one that really mattered—I was positive he was perfect for me.

THE END

Thank you for reading Only the Positive! I hope you enjoyed it! Would you mind leaving a review wherever you bought this book? (or any other platform you talk reading!) Reviews mean everything to new authors, and I'd love you forever.

ARE you a member of the Drama Llama Romance Family? Be sure to sign up for my mailing list at www.ellethorpe.com/news-letter so I can get to know you! Plus! There's a super secret, newsletter only, novella freebie coming in early 2019 so make sure you're signed up and ready for that one!

ACKNOWLEDGMENTS

Oh wow. I have a confession. I've dreamed about writing the acknowledgements on a book since I was fourteen. Because writing the acknowledgements means you finished. You sat, and slaved and poured your heart and soul into a book, day after day, possibly for years. (I started Only the Positive in October 2016, so it's pretty close to two years for me!) But I finished. And that is the sweetest feeling in the world.

Firstly, thank you to you, the reader. Thank you for taking a chance on a new author. There's so much more to come from me, and I hope you'll stick around to see it.

To my beautiful critique partners, Jolie Vines and Zoe Ashwood - We may have never met in person, but that doesn't mean I don't love you both to pieces! Thank you for your advice, your creativity, and for the way you both inspire me to be better. Thank you for the daily chats, and for picking me up off the floor when it all felt too hard. This book would never have made it out into the world without you, I know that for certain. Team Rabbit forever!

To my beta readers - Michela Hannigan, Kirsty Dyball, Tamara McCall, Shannan Fecht, Tracey Savill, Telina James, R.I

Griffin and Jen Martin. Thank you for your time, your enthusiasm and your advice.

Thank you to my editor, Emily Lawrence at Lawrence Editing and my cover designer Kassi Snyder at KassiJean Formatting and Design. Thank you to the bloggers, reviewers and bookstagrammers that have helped me promote Only the Positive.

And last, but never least, to my beautiful family. To my husband Jira who will always be my biggest fan, despite never reading a word I've ever written. Your unending support and blind faith in me made this possible. Thank you for picking up my slack around the house and never once complaining when you haven't seen me in days because I'm lost in my writing cave. I love you.

To my tiny humans, Thomas, Felicity and Heidi. Always chase your dreams. This book is proof that if you work hard, they come true.

ABOUT THE AUTHOR

Elle Thorpe lives on the sunny east coast of Australia. When she's not writing stories full of kissing, she's a wife and mummy to three tiny humans. She's also official ball thrower to one slobbery dog named Rollo. Yes, she named a female dog after a dirty hot character on Vikings. Don't judge her. Elle is a complete and utter fangirl at heart, obsessing over The Walking Dead and Outlander to an unhealthy degree. But she wouldn't change a thing.

You can find her on Facebook, Twitter and Instagram (@ellethorpebooks or hit the links below!) or at her website www.ellethorpe.com

facebook.com/ellethorpebooks

twitter.com/ellethorpebooks

instagram.com/ellethorpebooks

goodreads.com/ellethorpe

pinterest.com/ellethorpebooks

ALSO BY ELLE THORPE

*Only the Positive (Only You, #1)

*Only the Perfect- Novella (Only You, #2)

Jamison's story is coming November 2018!

*Only the Negatives (Only You, #3)

Gemma's (all grown up) story is coming in 2019!

…and more to come!

Printed in Great Britain
by Amazon